EVERFONT

Everfont

Alexander Rob

E. L. Marker
Salt Lake City

E. L. Marker
an imprint of WiDo Publishing
Salt Lake City, Utah
widopublishing.com

Cover design by Steven Novak
Book design by Marny K. Parkin

ISBN 978-1-947966-57-4

IN MEMORY OF JAMES DYAL,
One of my first mentors,
and one of the greatest men I've had the privilege to know.
You have had a profound impact on my life. I will always
remember how you believed in me and the lessons you
taught me.

Prologue

THE TWIN MOONS HUNG HIGH IN THE SKY, SUR-
rounded by a blanket of stars. The heavenly lights looked
down on the city of Everfont, with an eye particular to the palace, the largest building in Gritt, and pale light illuminated a
lone figure seated within.

He sat on his throne and rubbed his weary eyes. It had been
a long day and he was at his limit. The morning would come all
too soon, and he would have to rise early to meet it. More and
more there was little time for him to rest during the nights. It
was the cost of being King. Progress never slept and thus, rarely
did he.

Two men entered the audience room. One, draped in black,
with a black mask and hood covering his face. The other, dressed
in dingy street clothes as though he were from the slums. They
both knelt before him, a formality the King wished could be
done away with. There was so much time wasted with people
rising and falling before him.

He had done the math once. If he did away with the foolish
tradition, it would save him nearly an hour each day.

"Rise," he said, waving his hand wearily. "What news have
you brought me?"

The man in black spoke first. "Good news, my King. There are only three Imperials left in the city."

The King frowned. "You're sure?"

"I have been thorough in my work."

"Why are they not already dealt with?"

"They use their powers in short bursts," the man in black, known only as the Seeker, replied. "It is hard for me to track them. Two of them are in the Post. I can faintly feel their powers coursing through the ground. The third pulses infrequently, sometimes in the slums and other times in the Water Gardens. He may be a member of the guard."

The King thought for a moment. Clever, hiding amongst the ranks of his own soldiers. It would give an Imperial unfiltered access to the city as well as a consistent stipend. He was surprised no other Imperials had thought of that arrangement earlier. Perhaps some had, and they had merely been taken by the Seeker. He often killed his prey without formal notice. Not that the King minded. The less he heard about it, the better.

It pained him. Some nights, he wept for the loss of innocent life, his soul cracked from the weight of the choices he had made. However, the price was worth the cost. They stood between him and the future of Gritt. He would do anything to save his people, even if it meant sacrificing some of them so others could live.

"I give you leave to interrogate the guard," the King said, some of his weariness fading, strengthened by his resolve. "Find the man and kill him."

"It will be done, my King," the Seeker said with a bow.

The other man, the one dressed in clothes from the slums, spoke. "The other two Imperials are from the Post. This I can confirm."

The King turned his eyes upon him. This knowledge was not new, though the Seeker would have no way of knowing—he rarely involved anyone else in his hunts. "You've found a way to lure them out?"

The Post presented a particular conundrum for hunting Imperials. It was a space beneath the city, protected by ancient Imperial magic. It prevented anyone unwanted or uninvited from entering. If it wasn't so, these two nuisances would have been dealt with long ago.

The man shook his head. "Not yet. They will be wary of the upcoming treaty. I fear they may flee before I have the chance to lure them away."

Escape. No, that could not be an option for them. If they ran, it could undermine everything the King worked for. A chance to get at them was the only reason the King was signing the criving treaty. He leaned forward, eyes narrowing. "You're not going to let that happen, are you?"

The man wilted as the King continued. "It's been a year. Still, you have been unable to bring them to me. Still, they have slipped through the nets of my guards and the traps you lay for them. I thought you would have had the pair of them captured by now."

"They are wary," the man said, his voice quavering as he spoke, "and cunning."

"All the cunning in the world will not save them from the combined might of the King's Hand," the King said. "I have allowed this treaty to happen as a contingency, should you fail in your mission. If they are not brought to me before the treaty is signed, I will strike." He leaned forward. "If my guards find them before you do, you have no bargain. You will be given to the Seeker so he can have his fun with you."

The King did his best to keep the disgust, as well as the fear, from his voice. The Seeker was a necessary evil, but that did not make his habits any less distasteful. The King looked forward to the day the Imperials were all gone. Once they were exterminated, the Seeker's usefulness would be expended, and he would quietly dispose of the man in the shifting sands of the Aredine Desert.

That day was close. So close. . . . All he needed was to get rid of these last three. Three lives before he could put Everfont on a path to peace—and what were three lives, compared to what he had already taken?

"I will not fail you," the man said.

"Good," the King said. "Then you are dismissed."

He waved them away with a flourish of his hand. They left as quickly as they came, disappearing into the shadows. The weariness the King felt weighed heavier on him than before, the gravity of his orders resting squarely upon his shoulders. Gods forgive him for what was required. He knew his actions would send him to the depths of white-fire, should death ever take him. But they were necessary.

He would save the city of Everfont.

And he would save the world of Gritt.

Chapter One

BREATHE IN.

"I swear I saw her run this way," a guard shouted. A group of them had followed her into the alley. Despite the fact there was only one of her and several of them, they entered the alley warily, hands clutched tightly on their spears and swords.

"Did she scale the wall?" another asked.

"Not enough time. The wall watchers would have seen her. Search the alley!"

Breathe out. Slowly, so they didn't hear. It was difficult because she was curled up so small. She was hiding behind the old beggar who sat here, her insides all crunched up. She had twisted herself into an awkward angle, trying to keep any part of her body from poking out from behind him, with her chest pressing tightly against her knees.

"You there. Did you see a girl run through here?"

"Don't bother with him. That's old Cackler. He's blind and deaf and has no tongue. Won't have anything useful to say about the girl."

"Crives, man. The poor sand-licker won't have anything to say about anyone! How does he even get by?"

Breathe in and hold. Their footsteps echoed on the cobble-stones, growing closer. If she exhaled now, they would hear her, and she would lose the most important tool left to her. Surprise.

"Eh, some of the local stalls feed him. It's hard not to take pity. Man was a hero before he was this."

Ryan rolled her eyes. If only they knew who he really was and what he had really done. They wouldn't speak quite so highly of him.

"Really? This pile of filth?"

"Careful what you say. He can't hear you but the rest of us can. He saved the King's life. Show him his due respect."

"Huh. Well, here, Cackler, take some drops."

Go.

Ryan burst out from her crouch behind old Cackler as he wheezed a laugh. The guards cried out in surprise. One of them dropped the small leather pouch he had been extending and Cackler snatched it up with a snakelike arm, tripping the man in the process. The guard tumbled to the ground in a heap while Cackler and Ryan's eyes briefly met. He gave a small nod as she sailed past.

The guards—there were five—folded their arms over their heads and some reached for their shields, expecting her to draw a weapon. She didn't, for she needed none. And besides, couriers weren't in the habit of killing guards. It was bad for business. She breezed past them, quicker than an eyeblink, and was out in the streets once again.

The market was full today. It was the busiest part of the city, which was why she had run here. Throngs of people would make it hard to follow her and one person could weave through quicker than a large group.

"Stop her!" Captain Fault called, chasing after her. He had been waiting outside the alley a few paces away when she had burst through. He was a chubbier man, with rounded cheeks and a balding hairline. He could have snagged her when she emerged, had he not been stuffing his face with pastries.

She winked at him before hightailing it down the road, toward the Barrows. There were a few places she could lose them in there. It wouldn't be too difficult, but she wished a different captain had spotted her. Fault was notorious for not giving up on a mark. Despite his portly appearance, he was a fast little criver.

She had evaded him over a dozen times already. Sure as the sun rose in the morning, she would do it again. It was just a criving pain, was all.

People turned to stare as she ran by. Some moved out of the way, others stood still, afraid to be barreled into, but none tried to stop her. Everyone knew what she was and what she was doing, being a courier from the Post. In a way, she was somewhat like a folk hero to them. At least, that's what she liked to think.

She dashed around a corner, toward the drawbridge leading to the Barrows. Fault and the other guards were hot on her tail, indifferent to the people they shoved aside as they closed in. Fault screamed at the top of his lungs at the guards stationed in the drawbridge tower to raise the bridge, his voice echoing far above the noise and tumult of the market.

A large moat surrounded the Barrows, and unless one climbed into the moat and then up the other side, the drawbridge was the only way to quickly cross. Getting trapped down there was like painting a target on your back, ready to get stuffed with arrows.

Per Fault's orders, the bridge began to rise. Ryan ran harder, wind rolling off her skin and tossing her hair, snatching away the heat of the day. The large piece of wood had risen high into the air, already too high for a normal person to scale and reach.

Power flared in her chest. Too little to be detected, but enough to give her the *oomph* she needed. The muscles in her legs grew bigger and taut as she leapt upward. Her jump took her much higher than someone her size was capable of and for a moment she flew, suspended in the air.

For a moment, she could see a vast portion of the city. The market filled with people. The slums with buildings of various sizes. The Water Gardens and all their beauty. White-fire, she loved this sight. Would she miss it, once she was gone?

Her stomach slammed into the edge of the upraised bridge, and the air was expelled from her lungs. Years of instincts kept her body going and with a grunt, she slapped her hands down before she could fall and thrust herself over the top. Her heart slapped viciously in her chest as she rolled down the other side, and she let out a barked laugh of tension to force herself to breathe. If she had fallen from the bridge, into the small, near empty moat, she would have broken bones. Her Imperia couldn't save her from that and she was no Healer to shrug off injuries so severe.

Behind her, Fault screamed at the guards to lower the bridge. Panicked, they obeyed, turning the wheel that controlled it with all their might. Fault swore at them, slapping them with the flat of his sword, demanding they move faster.

Criver.

"Give up, Fault!" she shouted, rubbing a hand across her stomach as she rose with a wince. It was tender to the touch. "You've yet to come close!"

What followed was a string of language unbefitting a captain, or anyone, screamed at the top of his lungs so loudly Ryan almost had to plug her ears. She chuckled and continued forward, into Everfont's land of the dead.

The Barrows were the least populated area of Everfont, as was proper for a graveyard. The only people that lived there beside the homeless were the morticians, and they kept to themselves almost as much as the people in the Post. The area was filled with ornate tombs and catacombs, headstones and underground graves. Most of it had been built hundreds, perhaps thousands, of years ago, but the custodians were serious and studious about the upkeep. It was the cleanest place in Everfont, save for the Water Gardens, because of their tireless work.

She flicked sweat from her forehead as she turned into one of the catacombs, the largest, descending the stairs by taking them five at a time. The sun was shining, as it always was, a blistering ball of heat in the sky. Once—just once—she would have liked to run in the rain so she could know what it felt like to run in the cool. Or even just to see what rain looked like.

Thankfully, a blast of cool air rushed to meet her as she descended below ground. It was a thirteen-story grave, meant for the storage of those who died without names. Rumors said there were already over a thousand souls buried here, and that was with only the first four floors filled. There was no better place to lose a squad of guards and to frustrate Fault.

Torches hung on the walls illuminated the stairs as she skipped past the first floor, and the second, and the third. Yelling echoed throughout the catacomb as Ryan detoured into the fourth floor. Bodies filled the alcoves and stone coffins cut into the walls, stacked from top to bottom. At the far end of the room, however, was one alcove of particular interest to her.

Ryan slowed as she reached the end of the room. Two sconces with torches set inside burned brightly, illuminating the area, revealing nothing but dust and cobwebs along the far wall. The alcove in the bottom right corner, however, was free from the regular coverings of a lifeless place.

The guards' voices drew closer. They were almost here. Ryan pulled the sconce on the left, and it leaned forward before snapping back into place. There was a loud grinding sound as she dropped to her stomach and squeezed into the alcove, her back grinding against the top and her tender stomach scraping against the coffin. The back wall had shifted to the side, allowing her enough room to shove herself into a dark and hidden passage. She fell into the dark corridor with a grunt just as the wall grinded back into place. Any light that had filtered from the room behind her was now gone and she was left shrouded by darkness.

She leaned up against the now closed entrance and slid to the floor as she sucked in a few long breaths. She used this escape route into the tunnels often. The King's Hand knew of secret entrances to the tunnels below Everfont but had access to few. She had thought this one was safe and undiscovered, but now they would know there was an escape route here.

On the other side, she could hear Fault's voice echoing faintly as he stomped around the floor. Ryan smiled softly to herself. In her mind's eye, she saw an image of him doing his particular brand of waddling and strutting back and forth in front of his men, his face contorted with anger.

"Well, where is she?" Fault demanded. From the way his voice sounded, Ryan could also imagine his face as purple as a poppo fruit.

"She didn't make it to the fifth floor, sir! We were waiting for it!"

"Crives, man! You didn't have men stationed on the fourth?"

Ryan frowned. They had been waiting for her this time, and in this specific catacomb no less. She used it frequently, but not *that* frequently.

Did she?

Regardless, she was getting sloppy if the guards knew to wait for her. They knew she had been using hidden passageways to get around. A few of her more common ones now had watches posted, but there were dozens of passages all around the city. It was easy to pick a new route to run, which she would be doing as soon as she returned to the Post.

"We didn't expect the passage to be so close to the surface, sir. If there was to be a secret passage anywhere, it should be further down."

"You idiot!" Fault screamed. "This was our chance to catch her! We knew where she was going to be running and you still let her slip through your fingers! You should have been waiting on the first, or the second!" There was a thumping sound, and Ryan winced. Someone near Fault would be sporting some nasty bruises. "Search the tomb. *Now.*"

"Sir, we've searched this place half a dozen times. There's no other way out, unless she's a—"

"A what, sergeant? A what?"

The temperature chilled. Ryan closed her eyes, her smile fading, a well of pity forming in her chest for the poor guard. The response was whispered, quiet to the point she couldn't hear it, but she already knew what it was going to be.

Spacer.

Fault's voice was the next to ring out. It naturally carried, and though his tone had dropped dangerously low, Ryan could still hear him through the wall. "A Spacer, did you say, sergeant? A filthy Imperial?"

Ryan swallowed. A Spacer. One gifted with the ability to manipulate space, or time, depending on which gift you were born with. She had never met one before, but she had heard of them. Incredibly powerful and dangerous. If she had been a Spacer, running around Everfont would have been much easier.

Then again, it also would have meant the Seeker was always on her tail. As a Spacer, she could never do what she did as an Amplifier. With the little power she expended now, she could evade his detection. A little boost to speed her in the market. A small burst to help her jump higher than normal. Extra strength to her fingers to help her scale walls and buildings. Never enough for the Seeker to truly find her.

She shivered thinking about him. Her mother had told her stories of the things he did to Imperials in his dungeon. Stories of torture, screams, and blood, of a room so deep and dark the gods could not see. A place where neither justice nor mercy existed.

It was why she had hidden Ryan away. To protect her from falling to such a fate. She had done a good job, for the most part.

Right up until she had been killed.

Don't. Don't think about it. You get distracted when you think about that. You slow down and you can't slow down. If you slow down, the further away your goal gets. Eva needs you.

"I'm just saying what everyone else is thinking, sir. She's been playing us for fools with this cat and mouse game." The sergeant had guts; Ryan would give him that. No one else in the guard, or in the city for that matter, would dare to even think what he had just said.

"That's treasonous talk," Fault spat. "You're implying our King missed an Imperial in the purge? That the Seeker isn't doing his job?"

He had. Within the Post, there lived two Imperials that had slipped through the King's fingers. Her sister, and herself, though she liked to limit that knowledge to as few people as she could. The fewer who knew, the better.

"Perhaps one has been born since the time of the purge," the sergeant said. Ryan didn't know his name and his voice was unfamiliar to her. Fault seemed to get a new one every week, and she never had enough time to learn about them.

There was a shuffling sound, followed by a grunt. Ryan winced as Fault's voice came through next. "Sergeant Tallas, you are relieved of your station, and charged with sedition against the crown. You will be tried, and then hanged for your misconduct, and your family will be sold into slavery."

Ryan rose, hand along the wall to guide her further into the corridor, unwilling to listen to more. Fault was a hardheaded fool, blind to his own inadequacies and faults, which was why it was so much fun toying with him. Perhaps, however, she should take a break from tormenting him. This wasn't the first sergeant Fault had fired, but it was the first he had charged with a crime.

The man would almost certainly be executed, with no chance for appeal, and Ryan shuddered to think of what would happen to his family. She hated the guards—but their families were innocent.

She avoided the thought that it was her fault. People had their places in Everfont. The sergeant had picked his and she had picked hers. They all had to live with the consequences.

The sergeant screamed for mercy as he was dragged away by some of the other guards. His pleas fell on deaf ears. Fault didn't have a merciful bone in his body and Ryan was in no position to help. She had barely escaped herself and if this experience had shown her anything, it was that she needed to lay low for a while. She had the funds to hide for a few months, maybe even a few years, without working, but it would put her that much further away from her goal.

She sighed. Decisions, decisions. Ah, well. She would rather be delayed than dead. She could always make up for lost time, after all.

⤶

Walton was waiting for her at the crossroads.

Even bent over, with a large hump on his back, he was a bigger man than most. It was one of the reasons he was head of the Post guardsmen. His skin was dark, he was missing an eye, and he walked with a pronounced limp. When he was on the streets of Everfont, or in the Post itself, most ducked into shops to avoid him, and others stuck to the outer edges to give him a wide berth.

Despite his rough appearance, and his rougher mannerisms, he was one of the most intelligent men Ryan knew. It was poor circumstance he happened to look like a giant baby cast down the palace walls. However, he had confided in her that his appearance worked to his advantage. Most assumed him to be a dumb giant, incapable of deep thought. They underestimated him, and because of that, he gained an advantage both in battles of fists and of wit.

In one hand, he held a small pocketbook. He had a different one every time Ryan saw him. Honestly, she didn't know where he found them all. There was hardly any literature in the Post and trade had been slow lately.

He held his lantern toward her as she drew closer, squinting at her with his one good eye. "Hey, Walton," Ryan said, raising her hand to shield her eyes from the light. She had been walking in darkness for nearly an hour. White lines filled, then fled her vision as she blinked rapidly, trying to adjust.

He grunted, turning away from her, tucking the small book into a pocket. "Caused a stir."

Walton rarely spoke with more than one word, though Ryan knew he absolutely could if he wanted. It had taken her a while to fully understand what he was saying, but after knowing him for nearly a decade, she had gotten the hang of it.

She fell in step behind him and he began leading her back to the Post. She knew the way but guards were required to escort anyone coming from the outside.

"Fault was after me," Ryan explained, trying to justify the commotion she had caused. "He's been on my tail for the past nine weeks."

"Menace," Walton sighed.

"A menace with power. He charged one of his men with sedition today for suggesting I might be a Spacer."

Walton looked at her from the corner of his eye. She knew what the look meant, and she rolled her eyes. "He would have caught me by now if I was."

Most people didn't know the Seeker's power wasn't absolute. One could expend tiny bits of Imperia without being noticed.

Then again, she supposed anyone who had tried experimenting would have been caught. She only knew because her mother had told her. Memories flitted to the surface, but she shrugged them off.

That's twice in one day. What's wrong with you?

It was common knowledge her sister was an Imperial, but Ryan had managed to keep her abilities secret. If anyone in the Post had known, she would have been ineligible to be a courier or hold the head courier position. Poppertrot suspected there was more to her than she let on, but beyond him, no one had an inkling.

Well. Besides Marle, that is.

The King had ways of finding them. Whenever one used their powers, his hound came searching. No one could figure out how the Seeker found Imperials—but he had an uncanny ability to chase them down once he had the scent.

Most of the general populace assumed the Imperials had been wiped out. Contrary to that belief, some Imperials *had* escaped the purge, with Ryan being one and her sister another. She hoped there were others out there, somewhere, but if there were, their numbers were dwindling. The Seeker was efficient. There could be no more than a handful of them left.

Some Imperials had joined the underground to make a living in the Post. A city unto itself, buried beneath the streets of Everfont. The King's authority didn't stretch down there and there were protections in place to keep the Seeker as well as any other unwanted visitors out. All who sought to escape his justice fled here.

Those Imperials were gone now. Whether they had been killed or escaped was anyone's guess. Ryan only knew she and her sister were the last two living in the Post.

"Which?" Walton asked.

Ryan shrugged. "The new one. He's sacked four since he's started chasing me."

"Crives," Walton muttered. "Idiot."

"Idiot indeed," Ryan agreed. "So, how much of the wager do I get?"

They had a bet board in the Post. Everyone was able to bet which couriers would be caught and which ones weren't. It was a morbid business, as a courier that was caught would go to prison and be tortured for the rest of their lives—but the bets were a way to temper the sadness of losing a member of the Post.

People bet on her a lot. Of the couriers, she was the oldest and the most experienced, as well as the most wanted. Lately, she had been taking more dangerous jobs to the Water Gardens and even up to the palace wall. It netted her more money but was more likely to get her caught. As such, the bets on her rose and she took a cut of the winnings.

She was happy people were betting against her. It made her rich. Richer than she ever would have been had she only been running letters and packages between the walls of the Water Gardens and slums.

"Five."

"Hundred?" Ryan said hopefully.

"Thousand."

Ryan missed a step, her mood sobering. That—that was bad news. Five hundred drops was a lot of money. A little on the high end but still reasonable. But five thousand? It was unheard of.

Someone tipped Fault off, she realized. That's why he was waiting for me. Somebody had gone to the guards and told them where she was going to run to, hoping to make a few quick drops off her. Well, she was lucky they had bungled the job, otherwise she would be rotting in the palace dungeons right now.

Or worse. She shivered, not daring to think about such things.

"Well," she said, a bit shaken from the news, "I won't have to work for a while." Which was a lie. She would always work, no matter what. There were other jobs in the Post that were less lucrative than running letters, but she could make do.

Walton glanced at her, a small smile gracing his lips. "Me neither."

Ryan blinked, then punched him lightly in the shoulder. "You sly dog. You bet on me? How much did you win?"

His smile grew wider. "Two."

Two thousand. Not a bad sum. "And Marle's okay with this?"

His smile vanished and he grunted. "Wants to tax it."

Ah. That was classic Marle. Always wanting a cut of whatever money passed through the Post. It was her right, after all, but she had become a bit greedy as of late. Her skimming off the top had become so bad Ryan had considered taking a break from being a courier, or at least running less expensive packages.

She'll only be Crow for so long, Ryan reasoned with herself. The Crow was only in the position for a single year, and Marle's time was almost up. Honestly, Ryan wondered how she had ever gotten the appointment in the first place. She was a horrible courier and an even worse leader.

A few times, she had almost let spies into the Post. A guardsman sent by Fault, posing as a merchant willing to do business, had made it all the way inside before he was discovered by Dmitri. The Post guards had dealt with him after that. Another time, a young man hoping to curry favor from the King had followed a courier back to the Post after a delivery to the market. The Post guards had dealt with him as well.

There had been other incidents, too. Still, it was impossible to remove a Crow before their time was up. They just had to wait it out for another three months. Ryan could stand to wait for three more months. Especially with the money she had just made.

"How much is Marle wanting to take out?"

"Twenty."

"Percent?" Ryan gasped. "Normal practice says no more than fifteen."

"Bigger haul. Bigger tax. So she says," Walton grunted. Obviously, he wasn't happy with the arrangement either. Crives, Ryan doubted anyone was. A lot of people had just lost a lot of money, and the higher tax would make them even more sour. It would set a poor precedent for following Crows to take advantage of big scores or bounties.

"Wellspring save us from the foolishness of that woman," Ryan muttered. "Does she want to see me?"

Walton nodded.

"Of course she does. Probably to congratulate me on my winnings. Crives, I hate her. Can I tell you that? You won't tell anyone else, will you?"

Walton barked a laugh. "Everyone knows."

"She deserves it," Ryan sniffed, which, even as little as a year ago, would have been something Ryan couldn't picture herself saying. It was like the world had upended and she could barely keep up. Marle had once been her closest confidant. Now they couldn't speak to each other without shouting. Strange how one change in their relationship could upend so much of Ryan's daily life.

The air shifted as they walked. No longer was the long tunnel dank and musty, but instead, she could smell the sweet scent of a roast wafting through the air. Her mouth began to water and her stomach growled.

"Celebration," Walton said grimly.

"What for?" Ryan asked.

Walton sighed and shook his head. He looked worried, concerned, frightened even. "Others tell you."

A knot formed in Ryan's chest. If Walton was worried, things were serious. He had lived through more than five men in the Post combined, and Ryan trusted his judgement. If he thought something was bad, then things were grim.

But why would he be worried about a celebration? She wanted to ask more, but she knew better than to push him. He never said more than he intended to say, and it was impossible to make him budge. It was like blowing air into a sandstorm to stop it from rolling across the desert.

They came to the end of the tunnel. It was a dead end, with a decaying brick wall laying before them. Walton walked up to it and tapped on it with a specific rhythm.

Tap. Tap tap tap. Tap. Tap tap.

He stepped back. One of the bricks removed itself, and a pair of eyes peered through the hole.

"Password?" the eyes asked.

Ryan folded her arms. "You know who we are."

"Whether I know or not doesn't matter, Princess," the eyes twinkled, "You know the rules. No one's exempt. Speak the password or be stuck out there. I'm sure Fault would find you eventually."

"If he does, all of my money goes to Dmitri. You don't get a single drop."

"Alas, whatever shall happen to poor Poppertrot without Ryan's charity?"

"Bumberspinks," Walton grunted, ending their banter. It was a type of vegetable, exotic, harvested from the northern desert. Ryan had never had one, but Walton had, and he said they tasted like garbage. Most exotic or fancy food did, in Ryan's experience.

The peephole shut. The wall swung inward to reveal a gangly creature with arms longer than his body, knuckles dragging on the ground, standing in front of them. Thick fur covered every inch of his body, save for his smashed in face, where two beady black eyes stared back at them.

He was a Trompkin. A kind of creature that had all but been eradicated from the face of Gritt. Those left had been sent to the mines up north to dig up jewels and metals for the King. Poppertrot was, as far as anyone knew, the only one who had escaped such a fate.

"Good to see you home, Princess," Poppertrot grinned.

"You know I hate it when you call me that."

Poppertrot just shrugged, his stupid grin growing wider. Ryan rolled her eyes and brushed past him and into the Post. It was a vast circular cavern, stretching hundreds of feet into the air and hundreds of yards wide. In the center was a large stone pillar, made of cobblestone, that reached all the way to the ceiling. Buildings surrounded the outer walls, stacked on top of one another seven stories high, while throngs of people bustled in the center.

Raucous shouts filled the cavern, and the smells of several different, delectable foods assaulted her nose and made her stomach rumble once again. "What's going on?"

At this, Poppertrot looked down. He was an insufferable annoyance most of the time, but he was nearly as smart as Walton. He and Ryan were friends, for the most part, if only because of the relationship he had formed with Eva. And he, too, was worried. "It's not good."

"Walton said that. What's wrong?"

Poppertrot looked down, shuffling and shifting his weight from one oversized foot to the next. Ryan put her hands on her hips impatiently. "Just tell me. Get it over with."

Poppertrot and Walton shared a look. Finally, Poppertrot sighed and met Ryan's eyes. "Marle's signing a treaty with the King. The Post is his."

⌇

Ryan could hardly see straight as she walked into the Crow's Nest. There were several people inside—partygoers, celebrators, some of the usual folk—and in the back, bruisers, standing at attention near the Crow's door. Their hands twitched expectantly at their sides at the sight of her, hovering near their swords.

They hesitated as Ryan stormed past them, into the Crow's Office. As head courier, Ryan was a member of the Ruling Council, and a high ranking one at that. If they apprehended her it could end badly for them. So, instead of stopping her, they gave each other a nervous look and followed her inside.

Marle was within, sitting at her desk, cleaning her fingernails with a long knife. She was an older woman, fifteen years Ryan's senior, and it was beginning to show. Wrinkles were beginning to wear on her skin and her once youthful gaze was now haggard with age and responsibility. She wasn't an old woman, in comparison to the rest of the world—but for a citizen of the Post, thirty-two was practically ancient.

Across from her, seated at the opposite end of the desk, was Vema. Another of the Post's strange residents, Vema was an abnormal creature called a Grelkath. She was the leader of the mappers, a group in the Post dedicated to running through the endless tunnels that ran beneath Everfont and beyond. Her head was completely bald, with no nose and light blue skin. Her legs were bent the wrong way past the knee, and instead of arms, she had two tentacles that ended in hooks dangling at her sides.

She looked nervously at Ryan, cut off midsentence and glanced between her and Marle.

Marle glanced up at Ryan as the door slammed open, jingling some of the pictures she had hanging on the wall.

"What in white-fire are you thinking?" Ryan hissed, stalking up to the desk. She slammed her hands down, knocking over Marle's empty mug and sending a few quills skittering to the floor. "You sold out the Post?"

"Vema," Marle said, ignoring Ryan. "We'll talk more about this later. Have your people draw the glowing symbol they saw. I'd like to see it in the coming weeks."

Vema nodded and rose from her chair. She gave a quick tilt of the head toward Ryan and toward Marle before pushing herself past the bodyguards and closing the door behind her.

Ryan didn't wait for the door to shut before she continued. "You sand-licker," she spat.

Marle sighed, setting her knife down and leaning forward. "We all knew this day was coming, Ryan. It wasn't a matter of if, but when. Did you know Donovan thought it was going to be him that sold out the Post? He didn't, and so the job fell to me. I've been fighting it for the last nine months."

Donovan had been the previous Crow, despised even more than Marle. Under him, conditions in the Post had gone from good to bad, and under Marle, from bad to worse. "So that's it? You're giving in? Letting the King take us?"

"I did the best I could to protect all of us. The Post is to be made available to all in the city. There will be rich visitors, land development and exploration in the tunnels. With enough drops, we could even make a second Post. It will be like an actual city. The King will grant amnesty to everyone living here and allow them to keep their own property."

Goosebumps ran up and down Ryan's back and she stared defiantly at Marle. "You know amnesty isn't an option for some of us."

Marle raised her eyes, meeting Ryan's. They were cold as they stared back, and Ryan forced herself not to look away. "I'm aware of what I've done. I did it for the good of the Post. Most people living here will continue on as they always have—except now they will be respected citizens of Everfont."

Ryan pushed herself up, barely containing the anger and pain of betrayal inside her. "Except me."

"You can stay down here if you wish," Marle said. "You have enough control to avoid detection."

This couldn't be happening. "I won't abandon Eva, who is also *your* niece, in case you forgot."

The room dropped a few degrees. Marle paused for a moment, her face awash with regret. Little Eva had only just turned seven. She wasn't Ryan's full sister. They shared the same mother, but not the same father. Even still, Ryan had cared for her as if they had been full siblings. You took what family you had in the Post, and you clung to them. That was one of the first rules everyone learned down here.

Except, it appeared, for Marle. Before they had come to the Post, Ryan and Marle had been little more than acquaintances. It was only once they had arrived and with no one else to turn to they became close—almost like mother and daughter.

Yet Marle had grown distant since becoming Crow. She actively tried to avoid Ryan and Eva, tried to avoid being seen with them, and beyond council meetings, Ryan and Marle never spoke to each other.

Perhaps this was the reason why.

"I am the Crow. Family does not take precedence over the Post," Marle said, rising from her seat. "I protect as many people as I can. I weep for the rest." She leaned over the desk and glanced at the bodyguards before whispering, "You know I've already broken the rules for you, letting you be a courier."

"I doubt you'll be doing much weeping," Ryan said, "considering how rich you must be now. How many drops is the King paying you for the Post? A lot, I'd wager. Or maybe not, seeing as you've levied a twenty percent tax on my earnings."

"If you want to have a real conversation instead of throwing childish insults, you are welcome back anytime. My decision, however, is final. I can't risk the Post to save two people—even if they are my own family," Marle retorted with icy fire in her eyes. She snapped her fingers, and the bodyguards stepped forward. "If you had wanted to be Crow and make this decision, you should have fought for the position. Then you could have felt guilty about what needed to be done instead of me."

The bodyguards stepped up on either side of Ryan and grabbed her by the arms. She let them push her gently, but firmly, out of the Crow's Nest. There was nothing left she wanted to say. They escorted her all the way to the front door and out into the cistern.

"Sorry, miss," one of them said as they unhanded her. She brushed off her arms where they had grabbed her, knocking a bit of dirt from her arm. "She outranks you."

"It's all right," she said, closing her eyes and sucking in a deep breath. "You have jobs and families to think of."

The bodyguards nodded, and headed back inside the Nest, leaving her alone on the street. Well, not entirely alone. There were still many people outside celebrating, drinking and having the time of their lives. Their cheers and celebrations echoed high into the air, all the way to the ceiling of the Post several hundred feet above them. It seemed everyone in the Post was there, save for a few couriers and tradesmen. They were the only two groups in the Post allowed to leave the underground tunnels on a daily basis and go to Everfont.

Nobody knew how the Post had received its name. Its origins were ancient, lost to time, and knowledge of its original purpose had long been lost. It served as an autonomous sanctuary from the King's rule. Built right under the city of Everfont, it looked like a large, upside-down cistern made of cobblestone and brick, with a large pillar in the center, appropriately named the Center Pillar. Through there flowed the Wellspring, the only water available to Everfont for hundreds of miles. From the depths of Gritt it shot up, straight into the palace where the King then distributed it to the people in the city.

Some of it leaked through the cobblestone, however, pooling at the base of the Center Pillar. They had built a makeshift fountain around it, and the people of the Post went there for water. It was the only reason this underground community existed. No one could draw from it to fill their bank or pockets, and the water wasn't filtered enough to be used as drops anyway. It was strictly to drink.

No one knew how the culture of the Post had started either. They had no history to tell them how—just traditions that needed to be upheld. There were rumors, however, the first members of the Post had been freedom fighters, revolting against the world above and against the tyrannical kings of old. It seemed not much had changed over the ages.

Now that was all coming to an end. Marle had sold the Post, and everyone down here would become citizens proper. The celebration loudly continued as Ryan walked from the Crow's Nest to the other side of the cistern, where the living quarters were. People gestured at her, inviting her to join, but she couldn't find the heart. Soon, the guards would be down here, and things in the Post would be the same as things up on the surface. And Ryan . . . she shoved her hands into her pockets, meandering home. The entire reason she had come down here was to escape Everfront.

Well . . . not the only reason.

Don't think about that!

She let out an audible sigh, blowing her hair out of her face. Her timetable would have to be moved up. The five thousand she had won, four thousand after tax, would certainly help, but she didn't know if it would be enough. She had been planning on saving for at least another two years before leaving.

She had been planning on taking not only Eva, but Walton, Poppertrot, and Dmitri as well—Marle too, before they had drifted apart. Now, she would have to face the reality she might need to leave someone behind. She didn't know when the treaty would be signed, but it wouldn't be long. A few weeks at most. If she had at least two weeks, she might be able to make enough. Anything less, however, would be impossible.

She blew out another stream of air, anxiety welling within her. Everything changed now, and not just in her life. The Post would change, too. It would be gradual, but it would be unstoppable. It could take as little as a month, or many years—but it would come. The King would squeeze tighter and tighter until the Post was just like Everfont.

Criving Marle and her criving know-it-all-attitude. Ryan resisted the urge to go back and punch her.

"Ryan! Hey, Ryan!"

The voice belonged to Flint, another member of the council. He was one of the most well liked of the Post leaders, mostly because of his wit and charm, but also because he oversaw trade. Everything they enjoyed from spiced meat to vintage wine was because Flint found someone to trade with them—an increasingly rare occurrence. As the King's Hand closed in further around them, fewer people were willing to take the risk of openly trading with what was, for all intents and purposes, a foreign country. For whatever reason, it wasn't illegal to buy or trade with people from the Post—but if a citizen of the Post was caught in your shop, they could shut it down and arrest you for association.

The King had many backward laws. Why people could use services from the Post and buy goods from them and yet anyone from there was considered a criminal, Ryan would never know. It worked to their advantage, so she didn't complain.

"Are you going to come join in the feast?" Flint asked with a broad smile.

Ryan gave him a polite shake of her head. "I'm afraid I can't. I need to head home and take care of Eva."

"At least take some food," Flint said, proffering her a plate. Ryan's mouth watered and she was sorely tempted, but again, she shook her head. To her, the food was tainted. It was the symbol of a deal that would lead to the death of her and her sister. A symbol of the place that had loomed for so long over them, a place where—

Forget. Move on. Don't focus on that. The King can't hurt you anymore.

No. She wouldn't eat.

Flint pulled the plate away and gave her a sympathetic look. "Ah, girlie. It's not all doom and gloom. The King is a foul git, no mistaking that—but we'll no longer be criminals! We'll be able to walk topside and not fear the guards. Our businesses will be legitimate!"

Ryan snorted. "With legitimacy comes the King's taxes—an arm and a leg, and then some more on top. Most of us came down here to be free and it's that freedom being taken from me I'm bitter about."

"Freedom always comes at a cost," Flint said, his eyes glinting in the firelight, "and there's a fine line between freedom and the anarchy we've been straddling for the past few years."

He was in a joyous mood. Crives, they all were. The taxes were still high, that was an issue, but nowhere near as much as the rest of Everfont—it was all part of the treaty. The citizens of the Post would live like kings while the rest of Everfont starved.

How was that justice? Ryan didn't just want her portion of the world to thrive—she wanted everyone to. She would be lying to herself if she said that was her only reason for being outraged—she wasn't so altruistic—but it was part of it. Her main reason, however, was Eva, who would suffer the most from these changes.

Which was why they were leaving. There was nothing more she could do here.

She excused herself from the celebrations and continued on to her house. She was drawing nearer, lost in thought, when someone grabbed hold of her arm. She turned, opening her mouth to berate one of the other residents, then stopped.

It was someone she had never seen before. That fact alone was strange—Ryan knew everyone in the Post. It was a small enough community it was impossible not to. That meant he must have been a newcomer. His attire testified to the fact, as he was wrapped head to toe in long strands of dingy yellow cloth— the mark of a sand sailor. Only his eyes, a deep, vibrant blue, were visible.

She pulled free, rubbing the spot where he had grabbed her and taking several steps back. "Can I help you?"

"Are you God-Spoken?" the man asked.

Ryan blinked, off-put by the suddenness of the question. "What . . . what is that?"

Her eyes narrowed, but she couldn't see his expression behind the cloth. From what she could tell, however, he was dumbfounded. He cleared his throat. "I know it's a sensitive subject, but I'm curious about these things. If not God-Spoken, perhaps Twice-Blessed? You would have to be one or the other to have evaded capture so long. All the Thrice-Gifted ones have been caught."

A madman then. Most sand sailors had to be in some ways. It was a lonely life, escorting people to and from the funnel. Two weeks across the desert wasn't so long a time to spend by oneself, but sand sailors were hunted nearly as fervently as Imperials. It was impossible to settle down in such a life. The only offset was the fact sand sailors made more in a single run than anybody else in the Post made in a year. It made them rich, though Ryan wasn't sure she would trade her sanity for drops. Not only that, she was neither an Elementalist nor belonged to the sand sailor race.

"Enjoy the festivities," she said, striding past him. She left the man standing there, bewildered, as she continued on. In a few moments, her thoughts had moved on and she once more found herself lost in thought as she returned to the subject of the treaty.

"Well?"

Startled, Ryan glanced up to see Walton. The rest of her surroundings suddenly registered in her mind, and she blushed. She hadn't realized she had arrived at her home.

Home was a bit of a stretch. The living quarters of the Post were little more than wooden shacks, stacked on top of one another against the far wall. Ryan's was the third one up, above Poppertrot's and Walton's, but below Dmitri's. The old watchman was sitting on the bottom rung of the ladder leading to her front door. He rose without a word and stepped toward her.

"As bad as I thought it would be," Ryan said with a sigh. "Did the council vote on it?"

"Mhhmm," Walton grunted. He offered her a bottle—Lecruse, vintage. Expensive stuff.

"Sneaky devil," Ryan said, graciously taking the bottle and tilting her head back. It was sweet on her tongue, with a bit of a sour aftertaste. "She waited until I was out of the city to call for it. How many people voted with her?"

Walton held up seven fingers. The gesture only fueled the flame in Ryan's chest. There were fourteen members on the council. In a regular session there were thirteen votes, and the Crow only got one in the case of a tiebreaker if someone was gone. Had Ryan been there, the vote wouldn't have gone through. Normally, you couldn't vote on something unless all the council members were there anyway.

But there were a few clauses, obscure and rarely used, that allowed the council to vote even if some members were missing. Which was exactly what Marle had done. Ryan hadn't read the minutes yet, but she was curious to see which clause Marle had invoked to get the council to take a vote.

"When does she hand the Post over?"

"Four."

"Weeks?"

"Days."

Ryan sputtered mid-sip, spraying wine over the cobblestones in front of her. "Crives! That's hardly any time at all! When does the treaty go to the King?"

"Tomorrow."

This whole thing was moving fast. Too fast for Ryan. Earlier in the day, she had been expecting to have a good laugh leading Fault around, having him chase his tail and end the day with a restful sleep in her bed. The next, she was finding out the entire Post was being sold to the King. All its secrets, all its hidden passageways, all its occupants.

"It's not right," Ryan said, though she wished there was something else she could say. Those three words just didn't seem to convey the injustice of it all. She handed the bottle back to Walton, who took a swig before settling back down on the ladder.

"Eva?" he asked.

Ryan shook her head. "She wouldn't know. She's been inside all day. Or she should have been." Her little sister stayed inside on days Ryan was gone. Most of the time.

"What are you two yapping on about out here?" Poppertrot's voice rang out. He stepped out of his home, onto his deck, and leaned over the railing. "Still worried about the treaty?"

"Still worried about what we're going to do next," Ryan said. "I haven't saved up enough money to get all of us out of here."

Poppertrot clicked his tongue, his entire mashed face moving as he did so. "No one ever saves up enough to leave. 'S just the way of the Post. The people in the Water Gardens can, but not us."

"I was going to change that," Ryan said. "I was going to take Eva, and you, and Walton. We would have left for Niall, or Rim, or Wulfanraast. Anywhere but here."

"But here is where we are," Poppertrot said. "And it looks like here is where we'll stay. Can you imagine trying to make money now the King is going to own this place?"

"Impossible," Walton said.

Ryan agreed. The twenty percent tax on her winnings was unthinkable, but it was nothing compared to the King's taxes. Eighty percent of everything the populace earned went straight to him. Some of it found its way back into the hands of the commoners, but more often than not, it went to his whores and his gold and his palace. His high taxes were the main reason people found themselves coming to the Post.

"Wulfenraast is only a smidge better than here anyways," Poppertrot yawned. "You have to be an Imperial to make anything of yourself there. Eva could make it. The rest of us would be stuck in the sand."

It was a sly remark, meant as a jab at Ryan. She ignored him as he eyed her and knelt down on his deck, his eyes boring into the back of her neck. He had long suspected she was an Imperial and had been trying to get the information out of her almost since she had come to the Post. Ryan didn't understand why. Perhaps it was a desire to feel kinship with someone. Trompkins were also hunted, but instead of being killed, were shipped off to the mines in the north. If Poppertrot ever left and the guard found him, they wouldn't hesitate to take him.

It made Marle's betrayal all the worse. She had sold out the Post, knowing that Eva and Ryan and even Poppertrot would have nowhere to go. This was the last safe refuge in all of Gritt.

Poppertrot continued. He never did know when to leave well enough alone. "After all, we all know what the King does to Imperials."

"What about what he does to Trompkins, hmmm?" Ryan mused, turning the conversation on him. "Shipped off to work white-fire knows where. Do you think he'll do the same to you?"

Poppertrot shrugged. "Not much I can do about it if he does. Unless the treaty is stopped from going forward, not much anyone can do." He looked down at his feet, as if suddenly ashamed. Once, Ryan had heard him mention his family when he was drunk. Through slurred speech, he talked of how he had betrayed them but hadn't shared any details. Whenever they were mentioned in passing, a flicker of guilt and shame passed over his face.

Ryan didn't care what he had done. They all had secrets and demons in their past, and if they remained buried forever, that was fine with her. What mattered was the choices they made, here and now. She didn't care if the Trompkin had murdered his whole family. Poppertrot had been a good, if obnoxious, friend to her and a protector of Eva. That made his past irrelevant.

The three of them fell silent as sounds of the celebration continued to echo all around them. It was impossible to escape the noise. The Post was a large cavern, and any noise would bounce off the walls for dozens of seconds. People were cautioned about whispering secrets—you never knew where they would end up in here, or who would hear them. Across the Post, despite the dancing and cheering, she could make out a few joyful conversations.

She wanted to be happy for them. Truly, she did. As much as she didn't like it, there would be good parts to the treaty. The people down here would no longer be treated like criminals. They could all move freely between the Post and Everfont and they would finally be first class citizens while the job of courier would officially be sanctioned by the King. Truly, the treaty Marle had grafted was for the good of most people in the Post.

It just wasn't good for her.

Walton stood, finishing the last dregs of his bottle before tossing it aside. He rose from his seat on the ladder. "Night," he muttered as he slipped inside his house.

"Goodnight," Ryan said as Walton pulled the door shut behind him. Moments later, the lantern in his window was blown out and his home fell dark. She arced her head upward to look at Poppertrot, who yawned once again. "Shouldn't you be getting to bed, too?"

"I'm thinking of going and joining the celebration," he admitted. "There won't be another one like it. If I am to be shipped off by the King, I might as well get drunk before I do."

That was true. The Post could only be liberated—or imprisoned, depending on your viewpoint—once. For a moment, Ryan longed to go as well. There would be great wine, if the bottle of Lecruse was anything to go by, and the food in the Post was always great. It wasn't too expensive, and there were a variety of great cooks living down here.

But she had other things to see to. She turned and stepped on the bottom rung of the ladder to her home. It wasn't tall, but her stomach still twisted at having to climb. "Have fun then."

"The night is still young," Poppertrot said as she climbed by. "You could come with me. Or you could just come to find Dmitri. I would bet he's come back by now."

Ryan paused. Dmitri would have been back from his route at this point, and he would have heard the news—though Ryan doubted he would join in the celebration. He had as much reason to be sour as she. However, he wasn't so much a fool he wouldn't grab some free food on the way back home. Besides, he would stop in to see her before bed, so there was no use going to look for him.

"Sorry, Trot," Ryan said, continuing upward, keeping her eyes up and away from the ground. "Eva's waiting for me."

"Bah," Poppertrot said. "Babies." He leapt off his deck, landing on the stones with a thud. "Want me to bring you anything?"

"As long as it's not rotten."

"I'll get you the hundred-day eggs then," he said, and lumbered off toward the party. Ryan winced at merely the mention of that ghastly food. Like Bumberspinks, they were a delicacy, and were as awful as they were expensive. She had tried one once—and she hadn't been able to even think of them without her stomach turning ever since.

She finished the climb up to her home, sighing in relief as she stepped onto her deck. For a third story home, she had a nice view of the Post. She could see nearly the whole thing, save for the opposite end that was blocked by the center pillar. She paused on the deck and turned to bathe in the sight.

A city of cobblestone. One of the most unique places in all the world of Gritt. Ryan had always loved it for that uniqueness, the sense of ruggedness the cavern gave off. And it was about to be sold to one of the most money hungry monarchs of all time.

What a waste.

She turned around and ducked inside her home. It was a moderate space, as far as homes in the Post went, with a small front room and two bedrooms in the back. There wasn't room for a kitchen and even if there was, Ryan dared not light a fire for fear of burning her home down. For furniture, she had a small couch, a dining table with two chairs, and a small storage container for snacks and silverware.

A modest home. Ryan didn't need anything else. She was gone most of the time anyway.

"Ryan!" Eva called. The little girl leapt from the couch, flinging the stuffed dolls resting on her body all over the floor. She was a small girl, with curly orange hair and a face that was splashed with freckles. She smiled wide at her sister to reveal a mouth filled with crooked teeth.

"Hey, kiddo," Ryan smiled as Eva tackled her, wrapping her tiny arms around her legs. Ryan reached down and hoisted her sister into the air, throwing her up a bit before nestling her into the crook of her arm. "Did you have a good day?"

"Yep!" Eva said excitedly. "Dmitri came to visit me before he left. And then Walton did, and Poppertrot, too!"

"Oh, really?" Ryan asked with a smile. White-fire, she loved this girl. Her youthful energy and innocence were contagious and, despite news of the treaty, put a smile on Ryan's face. "Who was your favorite?"

"Dmitri, duh," Eva said, as if it were the most obvious thing in the world. And it was. Of the three, Dmitri was the kindest and sweetest. "He seemed a little sad, but he was happy after we played dolls. But Poppertrot played puppets with me, so he was my favorite, too."

"Oh?" Ryan put Eva down, moving to the kitchen and kneeling in front of the storage container there. Inside was some utensils and an assortment of food, mostly consisting of beans and corn, and some salted meat. She picked a small can of beans and grabbed a spoon, ripping off the lid and shoveling large spoonfuls into her mouth. "What kind of dolls did you play?"

Eva's enthusiasm waned, however. She clutched one of her dolls tightly to her chest and lowered her head, swaying from side to side. "You could have gotten some food from the party. I heard they had some."

Ryan shook her head. "I wanted to come see you, sweetheart. You've been alone all day." She scooped up another spoonful of beans and shoved them in her mouth.

"Poppertrot came to play with me. I wasn't alone," Eva said quietly, still looking at the floor. "You don't always have to eat beans. You can buy something nice every once in a while."

Ryan smiled as she shoveled in another spoonful. Setting the can and her spoon aside, she knelt beside her sister and cupped her face. "Eva. Do you know why I eat beans?"

Eva hesitated, then nodded. "Yes."

"Tell me why."

"So that we can stop hiding."

"So we can stop hiding," Ryan said. "I eat beans so we can leave. So one day, you can run free beneath a blue sky instead of living in a damp cave of stone."

"But I like our house," Eva said.

"I do, too," Ryan agreed, "but our home is going away soon, and we have to leave anyway. When we leave, wouldn't you like a home where you can play outside?"

Eva thought for a moment, then nodded vigorously. "Can Dmitri and Poppertrot come, too?"

Ryan smiled and tousled Eva's hair. "I'm working on that. They want to come, but they aren't sure I'll have enough money to go in time. They'll need some convincing."

"I can do it!" Eva beamed, smiling proudly. "I can convince them!"

"Oh, can you? How are you going to do that?"

"I'll tell Poppertrot he can't be my friend anymore if he doesn't come," Eva said. "And I'll tell Dmitri I'll miss him real lots. And I'll make my special eyes, like this." Eva stuck out her lip and looked down as though she were heartbroken. Ryan laughed and tousled Eva's hair. She had seen that look many times and from experience, she knew it was effective.

"Well, what about Walton?"

Eva wrinkled her nose. "Walton's scary. He always grunts and stuff."

"Ah, but Walton would protect us," Ryan said, picking up her spoon and can of beans. Crives, she was hungry. It had been morning since she'd eaten last, and she hadn't had a chance to slow down all day. She might even break out a second can.

Eva cocked her head and looked at Ryan strangely. "Can't you protect us?"

"Once we're out of the city I can," Ryan said. "Until then, we'll need Walton. Which means he has to come along. Understand?"

Eva lowered her face and pouted. "Okay," she said resignedly.
"Good. Now, are you ready for bed?"

At this, Eva let out a low whine, and swung her doll from
side to side. "Already?"

"It's bedtime. Past it, in fact. You're up way longer than you
should be." Ryan finished her container of beans, but her stomach still growled. She would need that second—but she wouldn't
eat it until after Eva had gone to bed. The girl was only seven,
but she was perceptive as a desert hawk. She would have com-
mented continually on how Ryan should have grabbed something to eat.

Ryan would never have said it, but she agreed with her
little sister. Free food was free, even if it was spoils of a deal
she detested. Yet her pride had gotten in the way—though she
would never admit that.

"What if I promise to be really good tomorrow? Can I stay up?"

"No," Ryan said sternly. "Because you'll be grumpy. And we
both know what happens when you're grumpy. Plus, the sand
gators will get you if you don't go to bed."

"Sand gators aren't real!" Eva stuck out her tongue, and then
ran to her room to get changed. Ryan lazily tossed the can onto
the kitchen floor and followed close behind to make sure she
was getting ready for bed instead of playing with her dolls.

"What in white-fire is this?" Ryan said as she pulled back
the curtain to Eva's room. It looked like a sand tornado had
run through. Toys were strewn all around the room and Eva's
bed, which normally should have been made, had the blankets
and sheets thrown in every direction. Clothes had been tossed
everywhere and were spilling out of the closet like a strange
refuse pile.

Eva didn't seem to notice the chaos. She had already pulled
off her clothes and slipped into a nightgown and was hugging
her favorite doll close to her chest. She stood beside her bed,
looking expectantly at Ryan. "I'm ready for bed."

"Not a chance," Ryan said firmly. "Clean up this room first."

"But Ryan!"

"Don't want to hear it," Ryan said, holding up a hand. "Do you want me to get Walton in here, have him keep an eye on you while you clean?"

The wind in the room picked up and began swirling around them. Eva's brow furrowed with frustration and the wind grew stronger. Dolls on the ground began to roll from the force and the door creaked open from the power of the swirling wind.

Goosebumps ran up and down Ryan's skin. "Eva! Stop!"

Eva yelped, and the wind died down. Without a word further, she began stuffing things in her nightstand and cleaning up her toys. Ryan leaned on a nearby wall and watched, making sure her younger sister did as she was supposed to, exhaling softly. The Seeker couldn't sense her sister using Imperia while they were in the Post—that was one of the benefits of living here—but it was never a good idea to test the boundaries. After a few minutes, and some more prodding, Eva had finished, and the room looked at least semi-clean.

"All right, Princess," Ryan pulled Eva's blankets back before laying them down as her sister snuggled in. "Time to sleep now."

"Do I get a bedtime story?" Eva asked, giving Ryan large puppy dog eyes.

Ryan laughed. "Tomorrow, sweetheart, I promise. I had a long day today, and I'm tired."

Eva groaned. "That's what you said yesterday."

"I know," Ryan said, feeling the sting of broken promises. She had been pushing herself hard lately, trying to earn extra money. She was so close; she could almost taste it. Only a few months longer . . . .

Well, none of that mattered now. She would have to figure something else out. "Well, this time, I mean it. I'll read you a bedtime story tomorrow night."

Instead of agreeing, or cheering, or being happy, Eva frowned and turned over in her bed, away from Ryan. She pulled the covers over her head and didn't say anything.

Ryan sighed, but she knew better than to press the issue. When Eva was upset, it was the smartest thing to let her be. Not to mention Ryan didn't have any energy right now to deal with her. She leaned down and gave Eva a kiss on the head before rising. She hesitated in the doorway, wishing there was something more she could do to comfort her sister, before pulling the curtain and heading into the living room.

Immediately, a wave of exhaustion hit her. She flopped onto the couch, stretching out and yawning loudly, before relaxing into the cushions. She was still hungry and was going to eat a second can of beans—but right now she was so tired.

I'll just take a quick nap, she thought as her eyelids closed, *just for a moment . . . .*

⤳

Marle sighed as she sifted through various paperwork on her desk. The sounds of celebration echoed through the Nest, reminding her how alone she was. Many of the other council members had gone to celebrate and she had given her bodyguards leave to join them. She had stayed behind to finish up a few things and go over the treaty once more.

Part of her wanted to join in the festivities. Another part of her trembled at the thought. For her, this time of joy and happiness was bittersweet. She had traded many lives for the coming peace and prosperity. Ryan's. Eva's. Poppertrot, Sul, Tava, and anyone else that was condemned by the King to be sold as a slave or killed.

Would it be worth it? She couldn't be sure. Even now, doubts lingered fervently in her mind. Would the King keep his end of the bargain? How long would this peace last before he eroded and chipped away at their independence? The treaty was explicit that, while they were under the jurisdiction of the King, the Post would be a sovereign state—but no one knew what that looked like. No one alive could remember any other type of government system. Everfont was the last city—now technically kingdom—on the face of Gritt. It had been that way for several hundred years.

Ultimately, however, her loudest and most painful reservations came when she thought of Ryan. She could still remember when she had found the girl, hiding on rooftops in the slums. It was the first time they had met, though she had heard stories of the girl from her husband. Intelligent, but quiet. Determined, but gentle. Fearless, but not foolhardy.

Perhaps that was what had jarred Marle so badly. She had found Ryan sleeping on a rooftop, baby sister clutched in her arms, in one of the poorest parts of the city. Not only had the girl escaped the city guard, and had been hiding on the rooftops of the city, she had also somehow managed to avoid the Seeker *and* kept her baby sister fed for several weeks—a feat men and women much older than her would struggle to do. A feat *anyone* would struggle to do.

It was then Marle realized there was something truly special in her niece. A determination and willingness to do whatever it took to survive. The two had never met before—Ryan's mother had kept her sequestered away from everyone to try and keep the Seeker from finding her. But, in Everfont, you could only hide for so long before the Seeker found you or someone ratted you out for drops.

Marle had taken the three of them to the Post. She hadn't intended to stay but had convinced herself otherwise. She had been thinking of separating from her husband for a while, and this had given her the excuse she needed. He had been a good man when they had married, ambitious, and with plans to change Everfont—but he had grown darker over the years. So dark Marle had begun to fear him more than she loved him.

What would he think of her now? Sad, perhaps. He might even commend her choice. He had always been like that. Willing to be a martyr for the sake of others, willing to stain his hands for the greater good. That quality was the ultimate reason she had left in the end. How long before he decided he was better off without her, all in the name of what was necessary?

The Post had granted them safety for the past seven years, and Marle and Ryan had kept Ryan's Imperia a secret. It had been impossible to do the same with Eva's. The young girl liked playing with the wind, making it swirl around her and others as a baby. There was no explanation for it other than she was an Elementalist Imperial.

That freedom Marle had bought them was now ending. The King would kill them, treaty or no, yet this was the best solution to save the Post. Sacrifice a few for the many, even if those few included family. The more Marle thought about it, the more she was disgusted with herself.

She reached into the bottom drawer of her desk and pulled out a small bottle of wine. She uncorked it and poured herself a glass. She rarely drank—she hated her senses and mind being inhibited—but tonight she needed something to dull the ache inside her. The pain of knowing that despite all her best efforts, she was exactly what she had said she never would be: as cold, heartless, and logical as her husband.

Three quick raps on the door woke Ryan.

She jerked out of sleep at the sound, weariness still blanketing her eyes. Blearily, she looked around, disoriented. The sounds of celebration still echoed outside, with cheering and laughing and roaring. She looked to the small, inexpensive clock they had on the wall to see only an hour had passed since she had collapsed on the couch.

Not much of a nap, she thought sourly.

The knock came again. With a yawn, she rose and stretched her arm into the air. Crackles ran up and down her body as her bones popped. She stepped over the small coffee table to the door, her heart quickening as she gripped the handle. There was only one person it could be, knocking this late at night.

She flung open the door. Dmitri stood on the porch, holding a large sack to the side. He was a handsome man, a few years older than Ryan, though a bit shorter. He had a full head of blond hair, and his eyes were a light green, though he swore on his mother's grave they were blue. It was an argument they constantly had, all in good fun.

He looked her up and down and raised an eyebrow. "Asleep already?" he laughed as Ryan yawned once again, leaning against the doorway.

"It was a long day," Ryan said. He stepped inside and she gave him a kiss. "What's in the bag?"

"Leftovers from the celebration," he said, handing it to her. She took it and instantly caught a whiff of a delectable scent. Her mouth began to water. "I figured you would be too prideful to grab some while it was there."

"Who told you that?" Ryan muttered, opening the sack to peek inside. There was an assortment of several different meats. Pork, beef, chicken and several strips of varbule. "No rolls?"

"They were all gone," Dmitri said, plopping down onto the couch. She took out a strip of varbule, a meat that came from scorch wyrms in the south, and began munching on it slowly. It was her favorite food—rare to have in Everfont, and even rarer to have in the Post. The hunters that harvested it mostly sold their catches to the King. It was fatty, with a strange tang to it and easy to chew. The fact it was being served was a sign the people down here were *really* celebrating.

She couldn't begrudge them for doing so. It had been so long since they had a proper celebration. The holidays these past few years had turned to times of fear and distrust. More and more people had been captured by the guard, sent into the palace to have their secrets pried from them.

Thankfully, it was impossible to enter the Post without first being invited, which was how they had been able to stay independent for so long. The long winding passages made it confusing and near impossible to find the Post without a guide—but there was magic that kept it impregnable. Unless someone was invited in at one of the four entrances, no one unwanted at the Post could come inside. The runes that protected this place somehow knew how to differentiate between friend and foe. Not to mention the guards, like Poppertrot, that would prevent anyone from entering with unknown strangers.

That was all changing. Thanks to Marle.

Ryan plopped down beside Dmitri, extending the sack to him. He raised a hand and shook his head. "I already ate."

Ryan swallowed a large chunk of varbule and shook her head. "It's not proper to eat before a lady."

"Good thing you're not a lady then," Dmitri said with a smirk. It earned him a slug in the shoulder, and he chuckled good-naturedly. His expression darkened and he shook his head. "You've heard the news?"

Ryan nodded. "Almost before I walked in. The party began before I even got back."

"Fools. All of them," Dmitri said. "They're celebrating the dying breaths of the last free kingdom on Gritt."

"We're hardly a kingdom," Ryan snorted, though she shared his sentiments. The Post was the last free place in the world.

Every year, the King's Hand moved further and further inside, eating up at what little space they had. It was only a matter of time before they discovered every entrance into the Post—and then what? They would be trapped in here, forced to pay the King's taxes and be subject to his rule.

It was part of the reason Ryan had been trying so hard to save up. It had always only been a matter of time before this small pocket of liberty vanished. She just hadn't expected the end to come so soon. No one had.

Criving Marle. I hope she burns in white-fire.

"It's the closest thing to what we are," Dmitri reminded her.

"We're more like a village."

"And how many self-governing villages exist in the world?" Dmitri asked. "They all had to pay tribute to someone."

"Long ago, maybe," Ryan said. "There are no villages left anymore. Everyone on Gritt lives in Everfont, or their bones are buried in the desert."

That was a third reason she wanted to leave. Just as the King and his men were steadily encroaching on the space the Post afforded, so too was the desert encroaching on Everfont. No one talked about it, and it was borderline taboo to mention, but every year the sands grew closer and closer to the outer wall. There wasn't even grass anymore, and what trees and plants were left existed within the city walls, shielded by the strange power that kept Everfont cool.

Ryan wondered if the Wellspring would dry up one day. The pillar of water that shot up, right through the center pillar of the Post and all the way to the center of the city. It was the only thing keeping Everfont alive. If it disappeared, just like the grass . . . .

She hoped to be gone long before that.

Dmitri sat back, contemplating. "My point still stands. We may be few in number, but we're still independent."

"Were," Ryan reminded him. "In four days, the treaty will be signed, and we'll officially be the King's subjects."

"Criving sand-licker," Dmitri muttered. He had a long and colored history with the King, more so than most denizens of the Post. He had personal reasons to hate the monarch. Ryan didn't know much, but she did know it had something to do with his parents. When he was staring off into space, he would have a dark look on his face, as if everything had gone cold.

He had told her a little of his past since he had arrived two years ago. His father had been an Imperial that had been caught by the Seeker. That meant even though Dmitri wasn't an Imperial himself, he might have Imperial children. As a result, he had languished in the Seeker's prison for years.

The scars from those times were still fresh in his mind, Ryan knew. Things like that didn't just go away. She would know. There were things in her past she refused to think about. He had shared bits and pieces of what had happened with her, but not all. Ryan didn't ask for details, just the same way he didn't pry into her life.

He would tell her, one day. When he was ready. And she would tell him everything, too, once they were away from Gritt. Maybe, then, they would be able to heal from the things that had happened to them. And maybe—just maybe—they could start a family together.

Sad to say, neither of their stories were unique. There were hundreds of others in Everfont who had personally suffered at the hands of the King. Children who had parents ripped from them and had been left to fend for themselves. Others who had escaped slavery. There wasn't a single person here that didn't have a colored history, which led the way to another unspoken rule of the Post. Don't ask about another's past. What's done is done and the future is all anyone needs to be concerned about.

Dmitri turned to her suddenly, his light green eyes focused and intense. "How much do you have saved up?"

Ryan blinked. "There may be enough, with the winnings Marle owes me. I can afford a ticket for myself and Eva and Walton . . . but I still need a bit more for Poppertrot."

Dmitri ran a hand through his hair. "How much?"

"Seven thousand drops."

Dmitri swore. "Crives. That close?"

Ryan nodded. She had been saving ever since she came down here. Almost eight years. "The winnings gave me a large boost. If Marle wasn't taking so much out in taxes, we could be preparing to leave tomorrow."

Another reason to hate the current Crow. Marle truly was the worst choice the council could have made. She would have even preferred Swim, leader of the sanitation branch of the Post, and he was a complete fool. "How much do you have saved?"

Dmitri bowed his head and shook it. "Not enough. The job today barely gave me fifty."

Ryan nodded, and sighed. They were both couriers, but they got paid more depending on how dangerous the job was. Ryan was the fastest of all the couriers and took all the dangerous jobs, which netted her a hundred drops each, before Marle taxed them. Dmitri, on the other hand, was one of the slower ones. The jobs he took were less dangerous, but also didn't pay as much.

Fifty drops would barely buy one a night at an inn. A bit of an exaggeration, but it was a pittance compared to what they needed to spend to leave. To pay a sand sailor to take them across the desert to the funnel, where they could leave to a better place.

It was a hundred thousand drops each. A fortune large enough to buy one a comfortable life in Everfont, or a life of luxury in the Post. Yet it said something about the state of the world that there were those willing to pay it to escape the city. No one from the Post had ever managed to, but many high-ranking citizens in the Water Gardens had.

"Sul was captured as well," Dmitri added.

Ryan grimaced. Sul was the sand sailor they had lined up to take them to the funnel. Most sand sailors were twitchy about transporting Imperials, due to tales of the Seeker chasing them across the desert. They had picked him because he had no reservations about who he transported. He would get them through the funnel before the Seeker could chase them.

The fact he was captured was damaging, but it wasn't the end of the world. They could find another sand sailor—provided they didn't tell whoever it was Eva was an Imperial.

She would worry about that later. "How much do you have saved up?" Ryan asked again.

Dmitri mumbled something Ryan couldn't quite make out. When she leaned closer to hear, she shrunk at the words.

"Eighty thousand," he said, his voice hollow.

Sweat pricked the back of Ryan's skin. Together, they still needed twenty-seven thousand drops. At the speed Dmitri delivered, that was nearly a year's worth of wages and a quarter of a year for Ryan. Any other time, she would have celebrated being only twenty thousand drops away. That would have meant only a few months of work. Now, however, they only had four days left.

Four days to make twenty-seven thousand.

Four days to escape to freedom.

"Could we sell our homes?" Ryan asked.

Dmitri shook his head. "We'll barely make ten thousand on these shacks. We chose to live here because they were inexpensive."

"What about a loan?" Ryan said desperately. "We take one out for twenty thousand."

Again, Dmitri shook his head, more vigorously this time. "Sand sailors won't take them. They put a special mineral in the water to mark loaned drops. Brokers and banks are notified if you take a line of credit."

Ryan sat back, wracking her brain for ideas. Twenty-seven thousand. Surely, there was something they could do to come up with the money. They had worked so hard, only to come up short at the finish line. . . .

An idea popped into her head. There was one last way to make that much. One, dangerous, lucrative way to make it. She would have to do it, and there was a high chance she would be caught. But if she succeeded . . . .

Dmitri seemed to sense what she was thinking. He shook his head vigorously. "No. No, I'll figure something else out."

"We could be gone in two days," Ryan argued.

"Not if you get caught," Dmitri said. "Do you know how long couriers get thrown into the King's dungeons for? It will be double for you if you're lucky. If not, you'll be executed. And then who will look after Eva?"

"The treaty will be signed in four days," Ryan argued. "It would be the last thing they expect. If I don't do it, we're stuck in the mud." Already, she could see it working. A little planning, some misdirection—she could be in and out with no trouble. "Besides, Eva would have you, and Walton, and Poppertrot."

Dmitri stood abruptly, shaking his head as he stepped over the coffee table. "This conversation is over, Ryan."

Ryan stood as well. "Dmitri, I'd rather be dead than live under the King's rule. This is our last chance. If we don't take it now, we'll be stuck here for the rest of our lives." *And I'm dead either way.*

She didn't say that last part.

Stubbornly, Dmitri continued to shake his head. "I don't want that for you. I don't want that for us. I wouldn't be able to live with myself if you died trying to get us out of here."

"But—"

"No," Dmitri said firmly. "It's too risky, and we've come too far to stop now. You and Walton will go ahead. Poppertrot and I will stay behind to earn our way and we'll join you in a few years."

Ryan bit her lip. It was a lie. The King not only taxed eighty percent of what the people made, he also taxed eighty percent of what they spent. Whenever an item was bought in Everfont, you had to buy it for nearly double what it was worth to keep up with the King's taxes.

Which meant that buying a sand sailor from Everfont instead of the Post would cost one hundred and eighty thousand to leave instead of one hundred thousand.

In other words, it would be impossible to leave.

Still, Dmitri looked determined. Ryan knew better than to argue, so she let herself slump back down onto the couch. "Just think about it. It's an easy fix. And we have to leave before the treaty is signed."

Dmitri opened his mouth, intending to say something, then closed it. Finally, he sighed and leaned down to kiss her. She let him, and his lips grazed softly against hers in a chaste, yet invigorating, tantalizing kiss.

"Good night, Ryan," he said, pulling away and opening the door.

Ryan rolled her eyes. So typical of him to avoid a conversation he didn't like. Yet it was too late to stop him, and she was too tired to pull him back. "Good night, Dmitri," she said softly as the door closed behind him. She reached into the sack he had given her, pulled out a piece of pork and munched slowly on it. The sleep that had wearied her earlier was gone, replaced with nervous anxiety.

Four days.

Four days to come up with the money they needed to escape this hell on Gritt.

Criving Marle.

⌒

The screaming started just when Ryan was falling asleep.

It was a rough, guttural sound, echoing through the walls, filled with primal fear. Ryan shot up in her bed, adrenaline coursing through her body. For a moment, she forgot where she was—then, her vision cleared and she found herself lying on her couch, in her front room.

The scream came again, louder this time, followed by some mumbling and some whimpering. Ryan sighed and threw off the small straw blanket she had draped over her body. She yawned before standing, little cracks tingling up her spine as she stretched. She stumbled toward the door and slowly pushed it open, so she didn't wake Eva.

Outside, the Post had gone mostly dark. The lamps had been dimmed, and there was only a faint green glow to light the way. Light never truly faded in the Post—the cistern always glowed with that strange, green light, and there were always people moving in and out while carrying torches. This night, however, there was next to no one roaming through the cistern. She guessed most of them were all sleeping, exhausted from an evening of drinking and partying.

Except one.

The scream came again, louder this time, clearer now she was out of her home. Ryan winced at the sound and began climbing the ladder next to her home, up to Dmitri's shack, ignoring the fluttering in her stomach as she ascended. There were nine shacks in a stack, and Dmitri's was the one right above hers, so she didn't have to climb too far.

There was a fourth scream, though this one wasn't as loud and was hoarser. She stepped onto Dmitri's porch and quietly opened the door as a whimper came from within. His house had even sparser decorations than hers—the front room was entirely empty, save for a small painting on the far wall he had earned as payment for one of his jobs. It was an unusual painting, one that depicted a strange, lopsided building, with a large white sheet hanging from several poles, resting on a desert of dark blue sand, with a dingy and lumpy grey background. It was so old, the oil that had been used to create it was flaking off in so many places, the original picture was barely discernable. She gave it only a passing glance and went straight to his room, where he slept on the floor with nothing but a blanket over him.

His eyes were wide, yet blank as he huddled in the corner, clutching the blanket to his chest. He whimpered as Ryan drew close and knelt in front of him.

"No. Get away!" he yelled, pushing himself further into the corner. Pity welled in Ryan, but she reached out and gently put a hand on his shoulder. He shuddered at her touch, whimpering and whining as she lowered herself next to him.

"Dmitri. It's me," she whispered softly. "It's not real. You're dreaming."

"No. You're lying. You're going to kill me," Dmitri whispered, his voice a quiet, shrill pitch. Tears of terror streamed down his face, and he looked blankly at her. A shiver ran down Ryan's spine. His nightmares were often like this—he would stare right at her, but he wouldn't *see* her.

She shifted her weight and scooted in close to him. "It's me. It's okay. You're just having a bad dream."

He stiffened as she leaned against him. She gently guided his head to her chest and began to stroke his hair while she hummed a small song. It was one Walton had written and, when he was drunk, sung for her. She didn't remember the words, but it had a soft, slow tune that reminded her of a lullaby. She hummed it to Dmitri whenever he became like this.

Gradually, the tension left his body. His shoulders sagged, and his breathing became even. Ryan continued to hum, closing her eyes as she leaned up against the corner. She continued to slowly stroke his hair. A few moments later, he stiffened, and she knew he was awake.

"Another one?" he whispered.

"Mhmm," Ryan hummed. He had told her what his night-mares were about, once. It was always the night his father was killed. Ryan had witnessed some terrible things in her life—most in the Post had—but to relive them in her sleep, nearly every night, was something she could hardly fathom.

Dmitri sighed and pulled away. Ryan shivered as his warmth also left, and she wrapped her arms around herself to stave off the chill air.

"Thanks," he mumbled, pulling the blanket around himself and huddling underneath it.

Ryan stood and stretched once again, letting out yet another yawn. "You should get a bed. You'll sleep better."

"Can't. He'll get me," Dmitri said, his gaze distant and hollow. He was probably still thinking of his nightmare. Then, realizing he was awake, added. "We'll be gone soon anyway. No point in wasting the money."

Ryan couldn't argue with him there. They were so close to their goal, it would be pointless for him to get a bed, and he refused to sleep on her couch with her. She wanted to argue with him, but decided he was right. Plus, she wanted to get back to sleep.

She leaned down and kissed him on the head. "Goodnight."

Chapter Two

U P AND AT 'EM! EVERYONE GETS AN ASSIGNMENT!"
Ryan yelled.

The couriers lined up near the eastern exit, each and every one of them yawning and stretching and wiping sleep from their bleary eyes. It was always an early day for them, regardless of parties or holidays. At six, you were expected to be standing at attention, awaiting your assignment for the day.

Today, however—today, no one was ready besides Ryan and Dmitri. They had been the only two to go to bed before the celebration ended and it showed in their straighter postures and brighter eyes. Though they were more rested than the others, Ryan still felt a twinge of weariness from dealing with Dmitri's nightmare, and she could see the same feeling reflected in his eyes.

You reap the consequences of your actions, Ryan thought humorlessly as one of the younger couriers fell asleep standing up. His head began to fall forward and he jerked awake, much to the amusement of the others. He shook his head, muttering under his breath.

Ryan sighed. She wouldn't be giving out any dangerous assignments today. There would be some complaining, as the less dangerous jobs didn't reward as many drops, but it was nothing she couldn't deal with. It was part of her job as head courier to make sure no one took more than they could handle.

"It's another day, another job. Let's hurry and get to it," she said, passing out the envelopes.

The couriers were a special branch of the Post. Unlike everyone else, they were the only group, besides traders, to leave on a consistent basis. They delivered packages, letters, and other things for the residents of Everfont, to the residents of Everfont. It was cheaper than using the King's delivery service, and more private. All mail that entered the public mail system, on order of the King, was read and inspected for contraband or propaganda. There were many who had been thrown into prison for "treasonous communication." Often, it was nothing more than a trumped-up charge to get rid of a political rival, or someone the guards had a grudge against.

So, people paid for the privacy the Post offered. And while it was illegal for the courier system to exist, it was not illegal for the residents of Everfont to use it. Ryan often wondered why the King didn't just throw everyone in jail that used them as a service, or make a law banning or fining people for doing so. Thankfully, he had yet to do so, which meant they had a steady stream of income and work. At least until he decided to change his mind.

"Why do we gotta work today?" one of the couriers, Razo, whined. "The treaty's getting signed. In four days, we'll be a legitimate postal service."

"Because these four days are our last chance to make money without having our cut gouged and flayed. And the people we deliver for pay so their mail isn't read. Once the treaty is signed, they lose that privilege. We need to deliver everything we can before then," Ryan said. "We have four days to earn as much as we can before the King comes in to take it all. Let's not waste it."

"I've already got enough money to eat for weeks!" Gut, one of the larger couriers, yelled from the back. "If that's all we're working for, let me get some sleep and come back tomorrow!"

Ryan held up a stack of envelopes and waved them around in the air. "the Post waits for no one. We've got good people paying better money to see us deliver these. It's not about you anymore, it's about them."

Normally, Ryan would give each courier anywhere from five to ten envelopes a day, depending on their danger level. There were twenty couriers in total, with thousands of letters waiting to be delivered. Today, however, she only gave out a maximum of four. Dmitri was the only exception, whom she gave eight.

Let's hope he can handle it, Ryan thought as she pulled two out for herself. She had picked each of them early this morning. They were both very dangerous—she would be delivering letters to the mansions in the Water Gardens—but they were both lucrative. A thousand drops a piece each.

Once everyone had received their charges, they broke for the day. Ryan went to leave through the east exit, but Dmitri caught hold of her arm and pulled her back.

"Did you need something?" Ryan asked, raising an eyebrow. In response, Dmitri snatched the envelopes from her message bag. Ryan groaned and wrenched herself free from his grip as he read the names.

His eyes narrowed. "The Ardor of the East? And Morgia the Merchant?" His nostrils flared as he looked at her. "Are you insane?"

She snatched the envelopes back and stuffed them in her bag. "We need money. I picked the ones that paid the most without being too dangerous."

"Too dangerous?" Dmitri muttered. "Any delivery to the Water Gardens is dangerous. You're going to get yourself caught. Maybe even killed."

"That's the way of the world, I suppose," Ryan shrugged. "People die every day and today I might be one of them."

"You are hopeless." Dmitri shook his head, then sighed, and scratched the back of his neck. He looked at her from the corner of his eye, a wry smile on his face. "Just be careful, okay? Make sure you tell Walton where you're going. Maybe you'll be able to earn a few drops off some bets."

"Not likely, after yesterday," Ryan grinned. After her unlikely escape, even with a trap set for her, few people would be betting on her now. She doubted in the next four days she would make even a thousand drops from the bets.

Unless I take that *delivery.* The one no one would ever take. The one that paid over a hundred thousand drops, enough to pay for a single person to leave. The one that required her to go where she swore she would never return.

It would be suicide to try.

Dmitri leaned in and gave her a peck on the lips, and she squeezed his hand before they departed. Ryan left through the east exit, while Dmitri left through the north. Most of his deliveries would take him to the slums, where the guards were fewer, and it was easier to blend in.

Anxiety always gripped her when they left each other. Around Dmitri, she was safe. Around him, if she wanted, she didn't have to be a courier or an older sister. She could just be her.

That didn't stop her from putting up those various masks when they were alone together. It was just instinct. She had lived so long working without any breaks and had dedicated so much of her life to caring for Eva, she wasn't sure *who* she was anymore. But she was excited to discover herself, with Dmitri, once they left Everfont.

She stepped outside the Post, the wall sealing behind her. Walton stood outside, leaning against the wall. He gave her a slight head nod as she passed. "Where?"

She flashed the envelopes. "Water Gardens."

He nodded. "Good."

He would update the bet board. Those who worked in the Post proper would see it and would take bets on which couriers would get caught and which ones wouldn't. Few would bet on her capture, which would dampen her income—a quarter of the money she made came from those bets. Some people said she was blessed by the guardian of white-fire, that anyone who touched her skin would be burned and she could easily slip away.

If only that were the case. . . . All she had to rely on were her wits and quick reflexes, along with some of her other talents. The ones she kept hidden, even from some of her closest friends.

⁓

Samuel walked through the slums, head tilted high, spear at his side. As he walked, men and women cowered, running into their homes or down roads so they could avoid him. Guilt pricked at his conscience, but he couldn't help how the world was. People were afraid of the King's Hand. It was just the way of Everfont, and it ever would be.

They said it was a great honor to be part of the King's Hand. They were the men and women that kept Everfont safe from crime and disorder, that made the streets walkable and safe. At least, most of them. He was a lower-ranking guard, but even still, that was a great honor.

He had been born in the slums, to the crime-ridden streets beyond the outer walls, where the heat of the sun could be felt more acutely. Most of the neighborhood he had grown up in was gone now, swallowed by the desert. Being afraid of being mugged, fearing that once he walked out the door he would receive a knife in his ribs, had been the thing to set him on the path to joining the King's Hand. He had wanted to protect the people and make a change in Everfont. It had required a lot of sacrifices. Long hours, years of training and abuse at the hands of his superiors.

Disavowing his parents.

That part had stung. It had been the final step on his path to joining the guard, before they would swear him in. His ma and da . . . they weren't bad people. Like most, they lacked the will-power to pull themselves out of the slums, to bear the amount of punishment Samuel had needed to succeed. However, they had encouraged him in his dreams, pushing him toward success. It had broken his heart the day he had been forced to swear them off, forever.

Most who had lived outside the outer wall didn't like the King, his parents included. They lived like outlaws, ruffians, and thugs, unregulated due to the lack of guards. Samuel had shared much of that attitude until he had joined the guard and he had found the beauty of order and security. His parents had been proud of him—but they had still hated the King and his laws.

"Can't have relations outside the outer wall," Captain Fault had said. You could have family inside the city, but not without. "Especially ones that are so vocally against the King. Conflict of interest."

It was one of the many burdens of being part of the King's Hand. He had chosen his sacrifices. All that was left was to live with them.

He hadn't seen them in nearly ten years and the distance had broken him. He often wondered if they had made it into the city, beyond the reach of the desertification. Somedays he liked to imagine them, setting up their little sand pearl shop, selling the different small cakes his mom made, or his dad working on houses in the city to get by. Sometimes, he liked to imagine himself there with them, kneading dough alongside his ma or fixing holes in walls with his da.

Things could have turned out differently had he taken a different path. Strange, that one small decision had changed his life irrevocably.

Something stirred to his right. He snapped to attention, barely able to see the fruit that was flung at him. He ducked and it sailed harmlessly past his head, splattering into a nearby woman. She gasped and stumbled, but Samuel paid her no heed. He was too busy looking for who had thrown the item.

There! Further down the street nearly twenty paces away, two youths were fleeing down a small alley, casting backward glances at him.

"Halt!" he said, raising his spear and running toward them. They paid him no heed, intending to get lost in the crowds on one of the other main roads—but Samuel was too quick. Years of training had made him swift and agile, and he easily made his way through the throng of people separating them. The boys yelled in fear as he entered the alley. They scrambled to get away, but Samuel was quicker than lightning in a desert storm. He let his spear drop and grabbed the two of them, one with each hand, and twisted their arms.

Something had snapped inside Samuel, being in the King's Hand. Maybe it was the beatings, maybe it was the constant harassment. Maybe it was the feeling of hopelessness he wasn't actually making a difference in Everfont. Whatever it was, the young man who had once thought he could change the city had been buried deep, leaving someone behind much like the other guards. That buried part of him screamed as he twisted the youth's arm so far it began to crack, causing the boy to whimper with pain.

This wasn't what he had become a member of the King's Hand to do.

"Assault on a King's Hand. They'll see you hang for that." Samuel's mouth and voice worked on their own and he felt like he was watching someone else take control of his body. As if he were no longer in control and he was just a mindless doll, jerked around by the strings attached to him.

The boys' eyes widened with fear, and they struggled to wrestle themselves free, but it was no use. Malnourished and skinny, they barely had any muscle to pry themselves free from Samuel's grip. Samuel, on the other hand, enjoyed the comforts and food of the barracks, where he could train and remain well fed.

He had wanted to change Everfont.

"Please, sir," one of the boys whimpered, falling to the ground. "We were just angry, is all. The King's Hand took my da the other day and my ma has to resort to being a nightsheet to get us by."

Samuel heard the words, empathized with them even. There had been a time when his da had run out of work and his ma had considered becoming a nightsheet. Terrible, dangerous business—but they had come through all right in the end.

"That doesn't give you an excuse to attack a member of the King's Hand," Samuel said, jerking the young man up by his arm. There was a loud pop in his shoulder and the boy cried out. Outside the side street, on the main road, people hurried by. If they didn't see anything, nothing was happening.

"Stop, stop!" the other boy said. "You're hurting him!"

In response, Samuel jerked him up, too. There was another loud pop, and the second boy began to cry, tears streaming down his face. The inner Samuel, the one that had wanted to make things change, wept bitterly. The outer Samuel, however, wasn't finished. He raised the boys up by their arms and gave them cold, disdaining looks. "I was like you once. A gutter rat. But I never threw things at the King's Hand, because I knew they were there to protect people and I was grateful for it."

"You ain't no protector," the second boy said, struggling to keep tears from his face. "You're nothin' but a bully!"

"A few broken arms, and I won't turn you in for a hanging," Samuel said, reasoning that if he delivered the punishment, someone else wouldn't have to. If someone else had caught them, they would have taken them back to the barracks, and Fault would have executed them. Attacks on the King's Hand were intolerable. So, in a way, they were lucky it had been Samuel they had attacked and not someone else.

The second boy moved, so suddenly Samuel didn't have time to react. He flipped a knife out from his waistband with his free hand and plunged it toward Samuel's chest.

Normally, the blade would have bounced off. Street-made knives and daggers weren't strong enough to break through the armor the members of the King's Hand were given. Yet Samuel's eyes widened with surprise as the dagger pierced the cuirass and plunged through his armor and ripped through his skin.

The pain was instantaneous. It flared up his side and down his leg, as though someone were taking his skin and twisting it repeatedly. He coughed and dropped the boys, unable to breathe. The boy had struck a lung, and blood began to pour through the wound, drowning him.

The boys clambered to their feet, nursing their wounded arms, already hurriedly walking away to leave him for dead.

Samuel wasn't going to let that happen.

A surge of adrenaline rushed through him. Without so much as a grunt, he leapt toward them, ignoring the spear he had tossed to the side. He wouldn't need it for this. The boys turned in surprise as he tackled the one who had stabbed him. The two of them, assailant and guard, fell to the ground, flopping on the cobblestones before Samuel came out on top. The boy started to say something, but Samuel couldn't hear as he wrapped his fingers around the boy's neck and squeezed.

This was within his rights. Blood had been drawn. As a member of the King's Hand, he was authorized to defend himself. Blood continued to pour into his lungs, but he held his breath. If he coughed, he might lose his grip and the boy might get away.

It was over in seconds. There was a satisfying snap and he let the boy flop to the ground, vacant eyes staring upward. The other boy began to moan with horror, rooted in place, with glazed-over eyes as he stared at his unmoving friend. "You killed him, you killed him, I can't believe you killed him . . ."

Samuel unwrapped his fingers from the scrawny neck and spat blood to the side. Before the King' Hand, he wouldn't have hurt a fly. He had joined to make Everfont a better place and to help others. But there were things you learned in the King's Hand, things that normal people wouldn't understand. That sometimes, taking a life was necessary, for the greater safety of Everfont.

There was little religion in Everfont. His parents had taught him of the invisible third moon, Phoron, who saw all acts, both good and bad. Most, however, considered the idea of a god or deity wishful thinking—but when Samuel felt the life leave someone's body, he swore he could feel their spirit pass through him, and that sensation more than anything else told Samuel there was a divine power.

How did that power feel, knowing he was a murderer? the voice inside wept. The voice of his younger self, filled with faith and righteous desire.

He ignored it. That voice only brought confusion.

"Help. Help!" the other boy cried, his voice laced with hiccups and sobs. He tried to run but tripped over his own feet. Still unable to breathe, Samuel coughed blood as he rose and put a foot on the other boy's neck. The boy squirmed and tried to get free, but it was no use. Samuel pressed down, and a moment later the boy stopped moving.

On the main road, people walked by without looking. The rule still applied—if they didn't see it, nothing was happening. That was the way to keep yourself safe on the streets. To avoid attention from the King's Hand. After all, no one wanted to end up like the two boys at Samuel's feet.

He began coughing violently, trying to clear the blood from his body. The blade had struck a clean hit—not only had it gone straight through a lung, Samuel was sure it had nicked a rib, too. He would be dead within minutes, drowning in his own body fluids, if he didn't get help soon.

He closed his eyes, panic welling up inside his chest as he considered his options. He could breathe, if a little, and he might be able to make it back to the guardhouse. The chance was slim, however, that even if he did, they would be able to help him. He could stay here and enjoy his final moments. Anyone else would have been dead from a wound like this.

Or . . .

He sucked in what little breath he could and looked to the front of the alley, then to the back. No one was watching. He was far enough away from the palace it might not make a difference.

So, he reached inside himself, and willed the wound to heal.

Being an Imperial was a strange thing. When you were born with power, you knew it. All his life, Samuel had known he was different. His scrapes healed quicker than others'. Scabs nearly never formed, and bruises only lasted an hour or two. It wasn't until he was older Samuel had realized he could will wounds to heal as well.

It was dangerous, for the Seeker would find you if you used it. No one knew how, but he could. Samuel had often wondered, however, how he had survived so long while he had used his Imperia. He had come to realize that, while the Seeker could sense you if you used a lot of power, he couldn't sense it in small bursts.

The ability had served Samuel well in the King's Hand. Minor healings allowed him to recover quicker from broken bones, from fatigue, and from a variety of other things. He could work longer, get paid more, and make the streets of Everfont a safer place.

This was dangerous though. He had never healed a lung before, and the Imperia required would be more than Samuel had ever used in one instance. If he used too much, he might draw the attention of the Seeker—then, he would be hunted for the rest of his days until he was caught and dragged into the depths of the palace. He had heard tales of what the Seeker did to people, and each and every one filled his head with nightmares.

But it was that or die. So, with a grimace, Samuel chose to live, hoping against hope the Seeker wouldn't sense him. He reached inside himself, gripping that well of power lying within him, and let it flow to his chest.

The effect was instantaneous. Blood drained from his lungs, and the throbbing in his chest stopped. He sucked in a large gulp of clean air, his breaths no longer ragged and short. Inside, he could feel the lung stitching back together, followed by the muscles around it and finally the outer layer of skin. Within moments, the wound was gone, leaving nothing but the hole in his armor and a few spots of blood as evidence of what had happened.

He wiped the blood away from his armor and glanced around. He waited for a moment. Then two. Then three. The Seeker didn't appear.

He breathed out in relief before going to pick up his spear. He glanced regretfully at the two young boys, who lay lifeless in the alley. He would need to write a report on what had happened. A lot of paperwork, tedious but not hard. Once he had filed it, there would be street cleaners who came by to take care of the bodies. Until then, they would lie there as a reminder to to all; the King's Hand existed to protect the people.

He left the alley, satisfied with the job he had done. Satisfied the streets were a little safer because of him.

※

There were a few stops Ryan had to make before she delivered her packages.

She had told a partial lie to Dmitri. While she was going to deliver Morgia's and Ardor's letters, she wasn't going to do it today. Instead, she was delivering a few minor packages to the marketplace. The jobs didn't pay much but they were easy, relaxed routes, and Ryan needed the time to think.

It would also be dangerous for her to tell the people of the Post where she was going. She didn't know who was ratting her out, but someone was feeding information to the King's Hand about her deliveries. For now, it would be best to lay low until she could figure out who it was. Yet she couldn't do that for long and she might not find out who the spy was at all. Either way, she was on a timer.

Four days before the treaty was signed. There was still lingering resentment toward Marle for her actions, but most of it had passed overnight. Stewing about it would do no good and was just a waste of energy. She could find a way out of this—hopefully.

She arrived at her first stop, a small shop only two stories high, doubling as a house, that specialized in woodworking, on the east side of the city just below the Barrows. Bore was the man who ran it and he often placed and received custom orders for materials through the Post. He was one of the few craftsmen allowed to sell down there. Most merchants were forbidden, as it was nearly impossible to differentiate ally from foe unless you were a resident.

She opened the door, a small bell announcing her arrival, and pulled a small envelope from her back pocket. She had ten of them today that would take her from east to west across the city.

The front room was small, but not uncomfortably so. Wooden figurines, tools, and other trinkets hung on the walls, a testament to Bore's skill. Ryan moved to look at a particular piece that had been here for nearly three years, a carving of the palace.

The upper part of the piece was form perfect, an exact representation. The lower half, however, was missing details and he had added things in that weren't there.

Not surprising. No one outside the Palace walls, save the King's Hand, knew what it actually looked like. The common rabble wasn't allowed in.

Bore emerged from the back, wiping his hands with a towel. Ryan stepped away from the carving, giving him a small smile. His eyes widened as he saw her, and he grunted in surprise.

"Ryan?" he said, leaning over the front counter. "By the Wellspring, it's been a long time. I thought we'd seen the last of you once you became the head courier. What brings you here?"

Ryan handed him the envelope. "Running deliveries today, Bore. I put you first on the list. I know you like yours delivered early in the morning."

"That I do. I'm surprised you remembered," he said. He turned the envelope over in his hands, eyebrows knitting together before he nodded and tossed it on the counter. "Delivering to me though, that's a bit beneath your station. Did you get demoted?"

"No. Just needed a break."

Bore blinked, then laughed. "You? Take a break? Ryan, you work so much it becomes a sin. Plus . . ." he leaned forward and lowered his voice. "You must be getting close by now."

Ryan nodded. "Close enough. I'm only a few thousand drops away."

"Then why make a delivery here? I only pay a hundred drops for my deliveries," Bore said, folding his arms.

Ryan glanced behind her, then sighed. "I was nearly caught yesterday."

"Had to happen eventually," Bore shrugged.

"They were waiting for me. Someone told them where I was going to be."

Bore was silent for a moment. "There's a traitor in the Post?"

"Must be," Ryan said. "I lied about where I was going today to throw them off the trail."

He scratched his chin, thinking deeply. "That's bad news for all of us. I thought the Post had protections in place to prevent that kind of thing from happening. Doesn't it?"

Ryan paused, thinking. Did she tell him the protections were failing? He was an honest man—it was why the Post worked with him—but there was always the risk he let something slip.

She had lied to Dmitri about where she was going. She could omit a few facts from Bore.

"We don't know what's wrong. We have some people looking into it," she said.

"Tell them to hurry. I can't afford for the King to find out I sell to your people," Bore muttered. "He'll throw me to the Seeker."

Ryan didn't say anything. It was a common fear among the people. The Seeker had become the harbinger of death in the minds of every citizen of Everfont, including her own. However, the Seeker didn't take or kill regular people—he only attacked Imperials. Besides that, those that traded with the Post were rarely charged with crimes. It was criminal to belong to the Post or live there—it wasn't criminal to deal with its residents.

"I have a few more deliveries to make. It was good to see you again," Ryan said.

"Take care of yourself out there," Bore replied. Ryan waved goodbye as she walked out, back into the smoldering sun. She reached into her pocket and pulled the next envelope out, idly bending the corner as she reexamined the address. She already knew where she was going, but it was a nervous habit of hers to double check.

It was to one of their main food suppliers, Delvin. They grew food in the Post, but most of it was sparse and wasn't able to feed their population. They had to supplement it through imports, and Delvin was one of the few people left in Everfont who owned enough land to grow crops. Thankfully, he was friendly to their cause and gave them first pick of everything—which meant they got the best.

Ryan liked him. He was rich enough to live in the Water Gardens but chose to live in the lower markets. He said it was because he liked helping the common people. It had been a while since she had seen him and she was looking forward to the visit, even though it would probably be brief. He was a busy man and didn't have much time for idle chatter.

Shoving the envelope back into her pocket, she made her way through the crowds. People hustled and bustled through, bartering, and moving from one stall to the next. There were many homes in the lower market, and nearly all of them sold something in the way of food or items. It was the only way to survive.

"Please. Can't you give me any food?"

"Crive off, kid, I can't afford charity. If I give some to you, I have to give some to all of the other worthless sacks of bones. You'll all be over me like flies. Go find someone else to beg from."

Ryan's pace slowed. To the right, past the throngs of people that were always in the market, a small child stood on his tiptoes near a poppo stand. His skin was tan, and his clothes hung loosely off his bony frame. His arm was extended as far as it could go, trying to reach one of the delicious fruits. The stand owner, who was wiry and thin himself, had pulled them all out of his reach.

"I haven't eaten in three days," the boy said softly. "The dispensary is closed for the week. Please. I only need a little one."

"Not my problem," the man said, slapping the child's hand away. The child slumped, letting his arm fall to his side. He fell to his haunches and lowered his head, staring hopelessly at the ground.

"Hey! Hey, get out of here!" the stand owner yelled. He cursed as he rounded the side of his small shop, kicking at the boy to shoo him away. The boy didn't move, instead letting the old man jab him in the ribs. The poor lad probably didn't have any energy left.

Ryan winced, remembering the times she had been like that once. It had been after . . .

Right before Marle found me. That's when. Nothing else.

There was little she could do to help the boy. If she bought him the poppo, it would do nothing but stave off the hunger until tomorrow, and that was if he got to eat it all before some other larger child stole it from him. There was no telling when the dispensary would open again either. They were only given so much from the King to feed the homeless, and it was a pittance against the masses.

Still . . .

She sighed and pulled out a small five-drop pouch. She always tried to keep twenty on her in case something happened. "Kid. Come here."

The boy looked up, his eyes filling with hope. He shuffled over as Ryan knelt down and proffered it to him, the water sloshing around inside. "Will five drops be enough?"

"Try ten. They're the best poppos in all of Gritt, and I've got mouths to feed," the stall owner sniffed. "You're not going to buy it for that little boy, are you?"

Ryan scowled and pulled a second drop pouch off her belt. She rarely spent the money she brought with her. She only carried it in case of emergencies. "What's it to you?"

"It's a hopeless cause, is why. Are you going to feed him tomorrow, then? And the day after that?" The shop owner reached for the pouches. Ryan passed them off. He opened the tops and sniffed the contents, dabbing a bit of water out to taste. He eyed her suspiciously before removing a magnifying glass and a plate from beneath the stall.

Ryan rolled her eyes but bore the scrutiny. Checking for fake drops was common practice, and there was a simple way to do it. Any and all legal drops were filled with a mineral known as mildrite. Translucent, it was invisible to the naked eye, but under a magnifying glass, the edges were easily visible. Without mildrite, water was just water and couldn't be used as money. If anyone wanted to *really* check to see if drops were counterfeit, there were charts depicting proper mildrite to water ratios—but nobody went that far. Most of the time, it was easy enough to tell with just a magnifying glass.

Ryan had once wondered about the lack of counterfeit. Other members of the Post had been quick to tell her that mildrite was odorless and tasteless, while other minerals could easily be spotted as fakes.

It also allowed the King to control how much money was in circulation. It was unknown where mildrite came from, but everyone knew what little there was available was stored safely away in the palace.

"No," Ryan said. She picked the best poppo out from the bunch, one without any bruises and with a nice purple sheen, and handed it to the boy. His eyes shined as he took it, almost reverently, with his trembling hands.

"Then why feed him today?" the stall keeper asked.

"Because that's all I can do today," Ryan said. She turned away from the shop owner and looked down at the boy. "Eat it fast, or the other kids will try to take it from you. All right?"

"I know, miss. Thank you," the boy said. He wrapped his arms around her neck and she around his small back before he scampered off, disappearing into the crowds.

"Feh," the shopkeeper snorted, clearly displeased, but he said nothing more and returned to relaxing in the shade of his stall. Ryan kept her gaze focused on the direction the boy had run for a moment longer before turning on her heels and continuing to her next delivery.

She couldn't do much. But that wasn't an excuse for not doing anything at all.

The rest of the deliveries were fairly boring. Delvin wasn't at his shop, and Ryan talked to his assistant instead. The rest of the letters were to people Ryan either didn't know or hadn't had much experience with. It took her the entire day, however, as there had been two guard patrols she had needed to avoid. By the time she returned to the Post, it was well after dark.

Walking in was a different experience than yesterday, more akin to how things normally were. There were no loud sounds of celebration, no large cookfire in the center. Most were already safely inside their homes, asleep for the night, ready for another day of work tomorrow.

She dropped her update off at the bounty board. Walton raised an eyebrow as she explained she had lied about where she was going, but just gave a nod and disqualified her from receiving any winnings. Since she had gone to a lower-risk area, it nullified any bets placed and anybody that bet on her would have their drops returned. There was also the added penalty of receiving a lower percentage of winnings the next time she went on a delivery, but it was a price she was willing to pay for extra safety. Satisfied she had done all she needed, she returned home, excited to finally have some rest.

Eva was waiting for her. "You're late."

"I am," Ryan said, tousling the girl's hair. "Did you play with Poppertrot today?"

"Yeah. He took me into the tunnels."

"Did he now?" Ryan asked, pulling open the cupboard and taking out a can of beans. Poppertrot wasn't supposed to leave the Post at all. It wasn't an official rule, but one that was more for his own safety. There were many guard patrols in the tunnels, searching for an entrance into the Post. If they found a lone Trompkin wandering the halls, they wouldn't hesitate to take him and send him off to the mines.

Poppertrot was Poppertrot, though. Rules didn't apply to him if he didn't want them to.

"How far did he take you?" Ryan popped open the can and began shoveling in food. The beans were bland, but they tasted like heaven after a long day. She flopped down onto the couch and Eva followed her, snuggling close into the crook of her arm.

"Not far. We just played chase in front of the entrance. Poppertrot said he had to keep it open, or we would get locked out, so we didn't play long. Walton was there, too, but he didn't play with me."

That made Ryan feel better. Poppertrot was strong, but Walton was skilled. If they had been attacked by multiple people, Walton would have been able to fend them off long enough for Eva to get to safety.

Still, wandering around the tunnels was dangerous. She would have to tell Poppertrot not to do that anymore. Or at least for the next three days.

She looked at Eva, who was stroking the head of her pet doll. At the corners of the room, the wind whipped around different objects, causing drawings Eva had done or the flimsier fabric on her toys to flutter. When not focused, her sister had a hard time controlling her Imperia.

Once, they had tried draining it. While in the Post, they had used up all of Eva's Imperia, causing a small windstorm in their home. It hadn't taken long. The more you focused, the more energy you could release in small bursts. The hope was it would be drained enough that, if they used just a little every day, Eva could go unnoticed in Everfont.

Their hope had been misplaced. Eva had said she hadn't felt any different the next morning. Ryan had even tested the theory on herself, and found that whatever energy she released returned after a good night's sleep. There would be no way to conceal themselves.

We're going to have to leave as soon as the treaty is signed, Ryan thought. If they didn't, that meant the Seeker would find them. But it also meant they would have to leave the others behind. Ryan only had enough drops for three of them.

Dmitri and Poppertrot would be left. Walton was a fierce warrior, more skilled than any of the rest of them. Ryan had asked him to come along as a bodyguard of sorts. They wouldn't know what awaited them on one of the other worlds, but skill with a sword would protect them no matter where they were.

However, Ryan didn't know if she had the strength to leave her family behind. That was what she considered the others. Marle had been part of it, too, until she had become Crow. Ryan had already left one life behind—could she do it again, this time leaving those she loved?

A knock came at the door. Ryan tensed as Eva hopped off the couch and ran to open it. Ryan rose and dusted herself off as Dmitri stepped through. Eva let out a squeal of joy. He laughed and picked Eva up with a smile, swinging her by her arms once before putting her back down. "You're still awake?"

"Ryan hasn't put me to bed yet," Eva said proudly.

"That's a bit irresponsible, wouldn't you say?" Dmitri said with a grin. He cast a sidelong glance at Ryan, who folded her arms and rolled her eyes. "Don't worry. I'll tuck you in. Do you want a bedtime story first?"

"Yes, yes!" Eva shouted, hopping from foot to foot with unbridled excitement. She grabbed Dmitri's hand and towed him into her room. Soon, his muffled tones could be heard throughout the house. Ryan sighed and began picking up the various dolls strewn about the house, throwing them into the small toy bin in the corner.

I can't leave him, Ryan thought. *Not just for my sake, but for Eva's, too.* The girl looked up to him, saw him as a brother, like Poppertrot, or maybe even a father figure. It would break her heart if they left Dmitri behind.

Criving Marle. If the woman had just waited for Ryan to be gone before signing the treaty, none of this would have happened.

Dmitri emerged from Eva's room a few moments later, pulling the curtain closed behind him. He had a small smile on his face, but there was a coldness and a pain in his eyes as he helped pick up the remaining toys. Ryan didn't say anything. This wasn't a conversation she wanted to start.

It was going to happen anyway.

"You lied to me," Dmitri finally said as they worked beside each other. His voice was a whisper, but it carried the weight of a guttural scream. It wasn't an accusation, either, but a statement of fact.

Ryan winced. She hadn't thought it, but a part of her had hoped never to hear those words from him. Dmitri was one of the few people she had hoped never to lie to. "Yes."

"Why?" he asked, his voice hoarse. He didn't sound angry—just confused and hurt.

"I didn't mean to. I intended to do those deliveries today," Ryan said, throwing the last of the toys into the bin and placing her hands on her hips. "I just . . . wanted to be safe."

Dmitri nodded. He reached out, enveloping her in his arms as she rested her head on his chest, returning his embrace. "I understand. I want you to be safe, too. But . . ."

"I know," Ryan whispered. "It won't happen again."

"Promise?"

"I promise," she said. She meant it. She had thought it would be all right, that both she and Dmitri would brush it under the rug. But there was a gut-wrenching guilt gnawing her, and she had no desire to feel that way ever again.

Dmitri nodded, satisfied. They finished cleaning up the room before they sat down on the couch. Ryan nestled in close as he stroked her hair. She loved it when he did that.

"Where did you go instead?"

"The marketplace," Ryan said. "To Bore's, Delvin's, and a few others. It gave me time to think about what we're going to do."

"Did you think of anything?"

She hesitated. "No."

Dmitri sighed. "Me neither."

The two of them were silent for a while longer. They both knew what that meant. They had talked about that possibility long before today, but neither had ever thought it would become a reality.

"I'll follow after you, when I can," Dmitri said. "Maybe a year or two. We'll have to coordinate where to go."

"I think Rim would be our best option," Ryan said. She forced her tears down as she was forced to confront what she had been trying so desperately to avoid. Dmitri would have to be left behind, as well as Poppertrot.

Now wasn't the time for an emotional outpouring. She could do that later, once she was safe. Right now, she needed to be strong for both of them. "We have a few maps. It'll be easier to find each other there. I'll leave my leftover drops for Poppertrot. Hopefully he can save up and the two of you can come together."

Dmitri nodded, a faint smile on his lips. "You may want to give them to me. You know how he spends his money on wine. But we can talk more about it later. Will you leave tomorrow?"

Ryan shook her head. "We'll leave the day of the treaty. There will be less guards and it will be easier to slip away then. We should be protected by the Post until then."

"Mmm. Good plan," Dmitri said softly. "Let's enjoy the time we have left then, shall we?"

"Yes," Ryan said, twirling her fingers into his. The tears were still fighting to come out, but she wouldn't let them. She would *not* ruin her last few days with Dmitri crying like a silly little girl.

〜

Marle rarely got a restful night's sleep anymore. It was part of the job. Crow was always the first to arrive and the last to leave—and it seemed she was always the last to finish her work, too.

There was so much to do . . . the mappers had delivered a report to her desk about the strange engraving they'd found. It glowed in the dark, and to some, it felt malevolent. To others it felt comforting. No matter what anyone thought, no one had any idea what it was. Many were asking her to reach out to Imperia experts on other worlds to see what secrets it held. Some believed it may even have been the source of power for the Post itself.

Marle had to admit, she was intrigued . . . but they didn't have the resources for such an excursion. Their finances were balanced on the edge of a cliff—one wrong move, one disaster, so much as a slight breeze, and it would push them over the edge. The King was clever, and he was squeezing them dry. Little by little, he was taking away what freedom they had left.

He wouldn't come outright and do it. That would make them martyrs. No, he wanted the Post to come to him. To submit and acknowledge him as their ruler. That was essentially what the treaty said—he had won, and they had lost.

They needed the treaty. Fewer and fewer vendors were trading with them. The King's Hand cowed them, and some had been given generous deals regarding taxes *not* to trade with the Post. Their food supplies were rapidly dwindling and what little they could grow was not enough to sustain everyone. Marle hated to admit it but coming to an agreement with the King had been just the out she needed.

All it cost was the trust of her niece.

Instinctively, she looked in the direction of Ryan's home. There was no window in her office, but she knew exactly where to look. Part of her felt guilty for what she had done. In signing this, she had saved the Post, but condemned her family—but that was part of what being a ruler was about. If her husband had taught her anything, it was that. In the end, she had become just like him.

Ryan will find a way to survive. She always does, Marle told herself. The girl had a natural hardiness to her, an undying tenacity that carried her forward. If her suspicion was correct, this treaty would harm her much less than she let on, though Marle had no proof of that. All she could do was wait and see until Ryan played her hand.

Until then, she would continue to protect the Post as best she could.

‿

The next morning was much better than the one before. All of Ryan's runners were rested and at attention. They received their assignments without complaint and were gone within the hour. Even Dmitri, though tired, was looking chipper. He hadn't screamed in his sleep last night, and any night he didn't sob and yell was a good one.

"Where are you headed today?" he asked. They were two of the last few couriers still in the Post. The others had already gone out on their deliveries.

"On the board, it will say I'm attending the markets," Ryan said, idly rifling through different envelopes. She needed to do a higher-paying contract today. Though they had already decided she would be leaving Dmitri and Poppertrot, she wanted to leave them with as much money as she could. "But I'll be heading somewhere else."

"Want to tell me where?"

"I think it's best if no one knows for now," Ryan said. When Dmitri frowned at her, she leaned in and gave him a quick peck on the lips. "It's not that I don't trust you. I'm just being extra careful."

"Sure, sure," Dmitri said doubtfully. His tone was morose, but he was quick to plaster a grin on his face. He jogged over to Walton, who was updating the bounty board, before heading into one of the tunnels.

Ryan watched him go, her heart twisting in her chest. Perhaps they should have taken the day off to spend together, but she knew that wasn't a possibility. It just wouldn't feel right to stop working right before the end. Plus, Ryan wouldn't know what to do with herself if she didn't have anything to do. She hadn't taken a day off in seven years.

Finally, she decided she would deliver to Ardor and Morgia, the two people she had been going to deliver to yesterday. They were both high paying, and both were expecting their letters soon. She shoved the two envelopes inside into a waterproof container, given to her by Fogvir, and then placed it carefully in the messenger bag.

"Off?" Walton asked as she passed into one of the tunnels. With the bounty board updated, he had begun his patrol.

"Mhhmm," Ryan said, patting her messenger bag. "You?"

"Mmm," Walton hummed. And that was that. The two of them parted ways to finish their work for the day.

༄

The Water Gardens was the richest place in all Everfont, save for the palace itself. Everfont was built in a circle, with an outer wall that separated the people from the desert, and then an inner wall that separated the poor from the rich. Finally, there was a palace wall that separated the rich from the King.

The Water Gardens was that place in between the inner wall and the palace wall. Merchants who had made hundreds of thousands of drops, retired captains from the King's Hand, funnelers that had been rich when they came here—all of them resided in the Water Gardens.

Not only were the Water Gardens rich, they were also new. It had been less than a decade since the inner wall had been flooded and cultivated to create such a paradise. Some said the King had sacrificed his soul for the magic to create it. Others said it was the work of a secret group of Imperials working for the King. And others still thought it was the result of some kind of strange invention never before seen in all of Gritt. No matter what anyone thought, however, everyone wanted to live there.

Ryan didn't think the entire place being flooded was natural, but that didn't matter. The Water Gardens weren't only beautiful, they were also safer than the rest of Everfont. Even the air was cleaner. There were less people, and, above all, there was an abundance of water. An endless supply of money to drink, but not to sell. There were strict conditions on which residents of the Water Gardens could store water. It was, after all, the city's currency.

The rest of the city struggled. They received a daily allotment of water from the King, harvested from the Wellspring in his palace. It was fought over, rationed, and even sold illegally. In the Water Gardens, however, there was more than enough to go around. So much, in fact, that it coated the entire ground with a small layer of water, like a giant puddle. Trees grew in this area of fertility, as did grass, and there were even small rivers that ran between houses big enough to swim in.

It was decadence in the extreme. While Ryan didn't blame people for wanting to live here, she did blame them for taking part in such a system. People on the other side of the inner wall were dying of thirst, unable to get enough to drink, while in here people could stoop down and scoop a handful of water into their mouths. There was more than enough here to share with the regular populace, yet the King ordered they only be given so much.

Nearly four years ago, there had been a revolt. People had climbed over the walls and into the Water Gardens, desperate to slurp up as much water as they could. The rivers had turned red for days when the King's Hand finally put a stop to it. It was just the latest in a long line of failed attempts to oust the royal family and ruling class.

I really hate that man, Ryan thought as she entered the Water Gardens over the southwest wall. It was the least guarded portion of the inner wall, yet today security seemed even less stringent than normal. With the grace of a sun swan, and a little bit of Imperia, she easily scaled the inner wall and dropped to the other side.

On this side, it was easier to see the spires of the palace, sticking up over the palace wall. Ryan's stomach churned at the sight, and she looked away. Deliveries here were always hard because she was so close.

Just focus on the job. You've done this a hundred times before. Get in, get out.

The ground pressed and depressed as she sidled to the nearest house, purposefully looking everywhere but at the palace wall. It was a modest home with a hedge that ran around the length. Water squished between her toes as she walked, and grass tickled the bottoms of her feet as she fell to her stomach and squeezed beneath the hedge. There was just enough room underneath for Ryan to squeeze under and remain hidden, while still having a clear view of the path before her.

There were no guards that Ryan could see. Most would be at the unveiling of the treaty, which would be announced to the people today. The King had invited the entire population to come see and hear of the unity between the Post and Everfont. Rumor had it he would announce a weeklong celebration, beginning on the day the treaty was signed.

It was precisely the reason Ryan had chosen to come today. There would be fewer people here than in coming days—far easier to remain unspotted. A large portion of the guards would be gone as well, used as extra security to protect those at the unveiling of the treaty, with few left behind to patrol. The Water Gardens were large and with the right maneuvering, it would be easy to avoid them.

She poked her head out from underneath the hedge, raising a hand to block out the sun. She was right next to the main walkway that ran straight to the palace wall, though there was a mile of distance between the palace wall and the inner wall. Much of the space between was used as farmland. The Ardor of the East lived close, near the palace wall, so she would need to make her way up there eventually.

Morgia, however, lived closer to the inner wall, and her letter would be far easier to deliver than the Ardor's. Once Ryan was sure there were no guards coming, she slipped out from underneath the hedge, sucked in a deep breath, and dove into one of the small rivers and let herself be towed downstream.

The transportation system in the Water Gardens was complex, to say the least, and Ryan barely understood it. A portion of the water from the Wellspring was carried by a strange propulsion system to the walls, then released in a steady flow to water the area. It all flowed back down to the center, where the palace was, where it was then recycled through an intense filtering process. The water wasn't meant for drinking, but it was clean enough one could.

Normally Ryan would have traversed the rooftops of a given area to get where she wanted to go. It worked in a population-dense area like the slums, but the houses here were too far and few between. The only quick and reliable method of remaining unseen was to let the current take her where it would. Thankfully, she had delivered enough letters here to know how the river flowed and how to take advantage of it.

She didn't let herself linger in the river for too long. Once she had flowed a safe enough distance inward, she removed herself and rolled underneath another hedge. There were many surrounding the manors here, and the river was an excellent mode of transportation. The water was crystal clear, however, so if a guard happened to be walking by, she would easily be exposed.

She allowed herself time to regain her breath and enjoy the cool water soaking into her clothes and rolling across her skin. Morgia's house wasn't too far now—Ryan could see it, a little further down the stream. All she would need was to fish the envelope out of her bag and stick it in the crevice of the door. Then, she would be on her way.

Like most homes, Morgia's had a large hedge surrounding the outer wall. Unlike most others, however, hers had a small tree in the backyard. They were a rare commodity in Everfont. It proved Morgia's brilliance as a merchant that, not only had she moved into the Water Gardens as a commoner, but she had procured one of the rarest plants in the world to adorn her yard.

It still baffled Ryan, as she crept up to Morgia's door, how complacent the people were in the system they lived in. Here she was, delivering a letter Morgia had paid one thousand drops for. A letter. All because the King's Hand previewed every message and every package that went through their own courier system.

It made her hate the King all the more.

Still no guards. Hastily, she removed the letter from her message pack, her fingers wetting the outside a bit, and she shoved it into a small receiving box. Morgia was a repeat customer that used their service often—mostly to discuss discreet business deals she didn't want the King knowing about. Once the letter was inside, Ryan hastily slid under the hedge, and looked around. Not a guard in sight.

Ryan scooted out from the hedge and rose, looking around suspiciously. The entirety of the Water Gardens were empty. No guards. No people. Nothing.

Where was everyone?

Unease formed within her stomach. Casually, she walked down the walkway, toward the palace. At any moment, she expected someone to jump from their hiding place and say "Aha! We've got you!" but nothing of the sort happened. In fact, the longer Ryan walked, the more she realized she was completely alone here.

Any other person would have taken it slow. And on any other day, Ryan would have allowed herself to. Instead, she broke into a run, water splashing up behind her heels as she made her way toward the Ardor's house. These two jobs were normally a full day affair of waiting and hiding and waiting some more. However, it looked like she was going to finish in less than an hour. If that was the case, she could return to the Post, grab some more jobs, and make some more drops.

Still, she kept a cautious ear to the wind, expecting someone to jump out at her. But no one did. She made it all the way to the palace wall without incident, somewhat winded from her running. She leaned up against it, taking a moment to rest, before continuing to the east gate.

She had to admit, it was pleasant to run deliveries without the stress of being caught. She still had to worry a little bit, but the more she walked, the more convinced she became all the guards had been assigned to watch over the treaty announcement.

She arrived at the eastern palace gate, and she pointedly ignored its grandeur and ornate architecture. The Ardor's house was nearby, off to the left, and that was where she focused her attention. Being so close to the palace wall, it was one of the bigger manors. It had no hedge around it, but it stood three stories tall, with many windows and an ornate front door. He didn't own a tree, like Morgia, but the beautiful way his home was designed made up for it. Like Morgia, he too used the courier service often. He and his secret lover passed messages through the Post.

Ryan withdrew the letter from her messenger bag and dropped it in the receiving box. And just like that, she was done.

She exhaled and turned to look out at the Water Gardens. Water flowed toward her from every direction, sparkling in the sunlight. Grass and plants, foreign objects in the desert world of Gritt, stared back at her, swaying gently in a breeze she hadn't noticed was there. It was . . . peaceful. Peaceful in a way Ryan hadn't experienced many times before.

"Wonderful day to be out for a stroll."

Ryan started. She was about to run away when the voice registered in her mind. She breathed out, slowly, and the goosebumps across her skin began to fade. She turned to the sound to see an old, withered man sitting atop the palace wall, looking down at her.

Cackler. The old man she had hidden behind yesterday.

He was unique among the citizens of Everfont, in that he was the poorest in the city, yet he could go anywhere he wanted without being accosted. He was simply a facet of life here that everyone put up with in a similar way to the Seeker. It was a mystery how he moved from place to place, however—no one in the Post had ever seen him moving in the tunnels and despite his untouchable status, the guard were forbidden from letting him through the various gates around the city.

Most assumed him to be deaf and blind, but that was how he wanted to be perceived. Ryan was one of the few people that knew the truth—he was in full possession of his faculties and was neither blind nor deaf. He possessed a shrewd, if not eccentric, mind.

She knew because he was her father. Memories flashed through her head, but she sucked in a deep breath and shoved them aside.

"What are you doing here?" she asked.

Cackler chuckled, sliding down the wall. He splashed down beside her, crouching down onto all fours like a frog. He was an odd one—for the past seven years he had been like this. Ryan had never been close to him, even as a child. He had spent a few nights of passion with her mother and then left, only stopping in occasionally to see her. He had stopped coming altogether before she had turned five, though she had occasionally seen him in the general vicinity where she grew up. Her mother had kept her hidden away, as far from other people as possible.

He ignored her question and straightened, raising his arms high into the air as he yawned. He was lanky, and Ryan often wondered if he didn't have Trompkin blood in him. The thought made her sick. That would mean she was part Trompkin as well, which would imply that somewhere down the line, she and Poppertrot shared a common ancestor.

She shivered. She liked Poppertrot well enough, but she wouldn't want to be part Trompkin, no matter how distant a relation it was.

"I saw your boyfriend. He was heading toward the palace last night. And today."

Ryan sighed. Her father didn't like Dmitri very much. He had told many lies about him over the years that were demonstrably false. One that said he was working with the King. Another that he had met with the guards. She figured it was his idea of trying to be a father. They had to hate boyfriends. Normal fathers did at least.

"What are you doing here, Cackler?" she asked again, impatiently this time. She was already wasting precious moments that could be spent doing another delivery and earning drops.

"Enjoying the peace. While it lasts."

"You mean while the guards are gone?"

He nodded. "This place isn't as busy as the slums, but it's still noisy. You can barely hear the voice of the river when everyone's talking and there are guards stomping around all over the place. Then I'm reminded how lucky we are to have this place at all. Twenty years ago, it didn't exist. All the water was hoarded in the palace for the King and his family. Oh, how times have changed."

Ryan darkened as she stared out at the water. "Now it's just hoarded for the wealthy."

"Progress is progress. Once, the water belonged to a single family. People used to be slaughtered by the dozens trying to get into the palace—and then the Water Gardens, once they were around—just for a sip. Now, it belongs to many. After enough time, it will pass to the common people, too," he paused. "And these people aren't wealthy, Ryan. They just pretend to be."

That was true. Despite her father's insanity, and lack of hygiene, he could be incredibly wise. Those who lived in the Water Gardens had most of their drops taken by the King. They were allowed to live here because they paid the King's high taxes, but, they probably owned as much as the people outside the inner wall. "Do you think the water will really extend to the poor, too?"

"Not if they all bathe as frequently as me. The filters couldn't handle it." Cackler raised an arm and sniffed his pit, making a disgusted face. "It's been a few months."

Ryan waved a hand. "There's plenty of water here. Have at it."

"And ruin the crystal-clear rivers?" Cackler said, mortified. With his mouth agape and his eyes wide, he looked as if she had suggested he walk barefoot on boiling sand.

She sighed. Some days, it was hard to believe she was related to this man. Then again, she could see the resemblance. They were both tall, and while she wasn't skinny because of her muscle mass, she was limber. There were even some similarities between their faces, though she would never admit it. She wanted to maintain the mindset she was pretty, albeit in a rough way.

"Are you ready, Ryan?" Cackler suddenly asked.

Ryan snorted. "For what?"

"For the change that's coming."

Shivers ran up and down her spine. "What do you mean?"

Cackler turned to her; his eyes filled with sorrow. "the Post is being sold."

She folded her arms and stared him down. "I'll be gone before then."

"Oh? You've finally saved enough money to take you and your friends?"

"Nearly. I'm just a few thousand short," she lied. He smiled, and somehow, she knew he didn't believe her. It was the most infuriating thing—Cackler had an uncanny ability to see right through her. Perhaps that was part of him being her father—he knew her better than she knew herself.

"Mmmm," Cackler said, "and have you found a sand sailor to take you?"

Ryan hesitated. She hadn't. It was another thing she still had left to do, and she gave a slight shake of her head.

Cackler, instead of taunting or making fun of her, patted her gently on the back. "I would hug you, child, were I not so filthy."

"Then why don't you take a bath?" Ryan muttered.

"Because this is part of my disguise," Cackler murmured. "The King lets me alone because I'm a dirty old man. He doesn't remember what I was because all he sees is the madness and the squalor. In a way, it blinds him."

"Sounds like a high price for freedom," Ryan said, inching away, breathing through her mouth. His stench was appalling.

A mix between rotting fruit, mud and sweat. Had she been in his place, she would have been drowning herself to get clean.

Cackler nodded. "Men will sacrifice a lot of things to be free. As I'm sure you're well aware," he said with a knowing smile. It vanished a moment later. "If you can, Ryan, I would leave today."

Ryan shook her head. "I don't have enough to take everyone."

"Pardon my language, daughter, but crive the others. You take yourself and your sister to the funnel and you find a better life," Cackler said in an uncharacteristically somber tone, squatting down and running a single finger through the water. "The King is close to achieving his goals and nothing will stop him from pushing forward. He won't until he is sure all the Imperials are gone—and he knows you and your sister are still out there. That's why he is signing the treaty with the Post. So he will have a clear way of removing you."

Ryan bristled. She knew he was trying to warn her, knew he was trying to help her. "I can't just leave the people I love." She was unable to keep the bitterness from her voice.

Cackler sighed. "You still haven't forgiven me?"

"No, I've forgiven you. Otherwise, we wouldn't be having this conversation," Ryan said. She turned on her heels, walking the length of the palace wall. There was an entrance to the Post in the Water Gardens, though it was rarely used because of how frequently this part of the area was patrolled and how close to the palace it was. "I just don't want to be anything like you."

Cackler shrugged. "I did what I thought was best, and what I needed to survive." His voice was already growing distant as she walked away. "I love you, Ryan. With all my soul. Remember that when you're finally free of this wretched place."

That . . . that stung a little. It opened wounds Ryan had been trying to forget for a while. She held back tears as she walked, running her hand along the wall at chest height before finding the spot she wanted. It wasn't long before her hand passed over what she was searching for—a small indent, barely notice-able unless one was looking for it. She pressed down and the wall rippled, revealing a small passage leading into the tunnels below.

Only a denizen of the Post could use this. Somehow, the runes that protected this particular entrance knew who lived there and who didn't. If anyone else happened upon the indent, they would think it inconsequential. Even if they did manage to open it somehow, they would still need someone to let them in once they arrived at the Post.

Within the small entryway, a long set of stairs led deep into the earth. She took one last look at her father, who was waving enthusiastically, before stepping inside. The wall shut a moment later, leaving her enveloped in darkness, trapping her in the tunnel.

This entrance could be opened from the outside, but not from within. Otherwise, Ryan would have used it for all Water Garden deliveries. She had tried several times to find some kind of lever or button, anything, that would make it open but to no avail. Eventually, she had given up and now only used it as a way to exit the Water Gardens. If she ever met the person who designed it, however, she was going to strangle them. Why make a door that only opens one way?

She mulled on her father's parting words as she descended. What did it mean to love someone? She loved Eva, and Walton, and Poppertrot, and Dmitri, and she supposed she loved her father. But did that really matter, in the scheme of things?

She didn't doubt her father loved her. His constant visits once she had fled to the Post and advice he tried to impart showed on some level he did care for her. It just wasn't the kind of care Ryan had needed. She had wanted a father to play with her, to love her, and to protect her. Most important of all, she had wanted him to be there when it mattered most.

That time had long since passed.

Despite not doing much work, she was suddenly tired. Her conversations with her father often left her that way—drained and ready for bed. Still, he gave her a lot to think about. She could leave today if it was just her and Eva. If she did, however, she would never forgive herself for leaving Walton and Poppertrot. Still . . . freedom was at her door.

No. She wasn't her father. There would be no trip to the funnel if Walton, Poppertrot and Dmitri weren't coming with her. Shrugging the thoughts from her mind, she began to jog down the stairs. If she hurried, she could still take another job or two to earn some extra drops and put her closer to her goal.

Chapter Three

IT WAS THE AFTERNOON WHEN HE CAME FOR SAMUEL.
Sweat beaded Samuel's forehead. He was alone, in a small
shack, huddled on the ground in the corner. Light filtered in
through the spaces between the doorframe and boards that
made up the house, illuminating the area just enough that Samuel could see the outline of the home.

With a sickened feeling he had walked back to the guard barracks, worried he had used too much of his Imperia and the
Seeker would sense him. He had been right. The man—that
thing—had been waiting for him, just outside the King's Hand
barracks. Dressed in all black, fabric wrapped around his face,
and in a billowing robe—the very effigy of death himself. He
had been looking for Samuel and Samuel had known it.

Now all he could do was hide. Hide, and hope the Seeker
didn't find him.

He was in his parents' old home, outside the city walls. The
desertification had reached all the way to the outer wall and
any vestiges of civilization outside the city were beginning to
fade away. Houses had crumbled, their foundations destroyed
by the shifting sands. What little remnants remained were half
buried and would soon be lost completely. The people, if they

had survived, had moved inside Everfont for better protection—better that, than to die from the heat.

Samuel's family had been different. His father's shack still stood because his father had found a spot with a firm stone that lay just beneath the ground. He had chosen his spot carefully, knowing eventually the desertification would reach them. He had built the house in hopes of weathering it and still being able to find work out here.

He had been wrong. The desertification had progressed much faster than anyone had expected, and the small villages had been quickly swallowed up. It was so hot, corpses littered the ground outside, completely dried out.

In the shack, his father's shriveled corpse sat hunched over the dinner table he had made. His skin had become leathery and clung to his bones, the air too dry and hot for him to decompose. There was a grave marker for his mother in the back. Samuel presumed his mother had died and then his father had simply lost the will to keep living.

He hadn't visited them. The King's Hand had forbidden any visits to people beyond the outer wall. It hadn't *really* been his fault, or so he told himself. Yet a small measure of guilt pricked at him as he huddled in the corner, staring at the corpse of his father. There was a chance he could have saved him, had he come back.

But he hadn't. Now, he was stuck here, hiding from the most dangerous man on Gritt, with no family and no friends to rely on.

Sweat continued to build all over his body. The summer sun burned bright in the sky, seeming to set the very air on fire. Out here, in the outskirts, they didn't have the same type of protection Everfont possessed to deflect the heat away and form a protective bubble. The sand had become blistering, hot enough Samuel could feel it burning through even his shoes.

It hadn't always been this hot, though. When Samuel had grown up here, the air had been warm, but not dangerously so—still livable. Amazing what ten years could do to the landscape. The desertification was moving quicker and quicker, and Samuel couldn't help but wonder how much longer Everfont had left before Everfont's protection gave out and the desert took over. Hopefully, the Seeker would be deterred from seeking him in the heat. He wore all black, and even in the safe confines of Everfont, his outfit would soak up the sun and cause discomfort. Samuel expected the Seeker would wait until nightfall to come find him—but by that time, Samuel would already have a head start.

He would make for the funnel on foot, the portal leading to Rim, or Niall, or Wulfenraast. Worlds beyond that of Gritt, where the Seeker would be unwilling to follow. It was a foolish idea—the funnel was on the other side of the desert and no one alive had made the trip on foot—but it was better than any prospects he had left to him in the city. He had briefly considered seeking refuge in the Post, but as a member of the King's Hand, he would have been denied entry. They hated his kind.

He would walk at night and find shelter from the sun during the day. His biggest dilemma was water. Even if he could find a cave or a tree to take refuge beneath, it was a weeklong trip to the funnel on a sand sled, which could cross hundreds of miles in a day. Samuel wagered the journey would be much longer on foot, which meant he could be walking for as long as an entire month, with no sure oasis along the way. He would have to take it on faith he could find something. That hopefully some divine presence out there was watching out for him.

His parents had raised him with a belief in the gods. Or rather, a god. Phoron, the third moon. He was invisible, unlike the other two, for his light did not illuminate the physical world, but rather, the spiritual one. If one were to drink of his teachings and eat of his works, one could attain peace and enlightenment, even in the hardest of times.

The King's Hand had beat those beliefs out of him. It was the last thing they had broken him of. First, it had been his compassion. Then, it had been his reason. Third, it had been his family relations. And last, it had been his religion. How grateful he had been for that, for there were times in the King's Hand when he had known, in the back of his mind, Phoron looked on disapprovingly. The third moon was the god of good will and self-improvement—not the god of beatings and authority.

I've been improving. Haven't I? Samuel tried to justify his actions. It wasn't his fault the King's Hand had made him the way he was. They did that to everyone, eventually. There were some strong men who resisted, but Samuel hadn't been one of them. He had just wanted to protect the people of Everfont. They had taken that belief from him, too.

Yet now, hiding from the Seeker, Samuel had no other options left. He gulped, fearing his prayer would go unheard. Fearing Phoron would turn a blind eye to him for the actions he had taken in the King's Hand. He could only hope the third moon understood it wasn't really his fault. He had been forced into doing it.

Please. Save me.

"Praying for help?"

The door slammed open, scattering sand through the air, and in stepped the Seeker. Tall, menacing, unperturbed by the heat, he was every bit the nightmare the stories said. Not a single bit of skin was exposed—he wore a black mask that covered his eyes, long black pants, black boots, black coat, and black gloves. He even wore a black hat.

Samuel screamed and grabbed the sword lying beside him and pointed it at the man. His terror was exacerbated by the fact the Seeker had seemed able to read his thoughts. His arm trembled and a low whine escaped his throat as he yelled, "Stay back! Stay back, or I'll do it!"

The Seeker cocked his veiled head, unperturbed as he stepped further into the shack. "Do what?"

"I—I'll kill you!" Samuel said, his hands quivering as badly as his voice. He knew the words were empty threats even as he spoke them. This man, this . . . thing was unkillable. It had been stabbed and burned and beaten, suffocated and hanged—nothing stopped it. Yet he was acting on instinct. He could not be taken by this thing. If he let that happen, he would disappear into the depths of the palace, never to be seen again.

The Seeker didn't laugh at his words. Instead, it spread its arms and legs wide, like a star in front of the doorway. "Then do it."

Samuel blinked. His hand shook and he gulped, expecting some kind of trick. Yet the Seeker continued to stand there, unmoving. Hesitantly, Samuel stepped forward. Still no reaction.

"Hurry, please," the Seeker said softly.

Something in Samuel snapped. This thing was here to kill him. Well, he wouldn't let it! With a roar, he dashed forward and plunged his sword into the Seeker's chest, right where his heart would be. The Seeker stumbled backward from the force of the blow, into the sunlight. Samuel took a few steps back as a wave of heat washed over him, pouring in from the open door.

Perhaps . . . perhaps he would be the one to kill the Seeker. Perhaps this time, the sword would work. There were no such things as immortals. Everyone and everything could be killed in some way or another. Samuel might be able to return to Everfont after all.

The Seeker tilted his head down at the sword protruding from his chest. He fell to his knees and made a strangling sound in his throat, before falling facedown on the sand. He twitched momentarily, then stilled, his body cooking in the sun.

Samuel froze, dumbfounded by his luck. At any moment, he expected the Seeker to say it had all been a trick, that he was still going to capture him. Several seconds passed. Seconds turned into minutes before Samuel finally began to suspect the Seeker wasn't getting up.

He wiped sweat from his brow and stepped over the corpse. The stories had been exaggerated! No one actually believed the nonsense the Seeker was immortal. He was just a skilled fighter, a lucky combatant. Besides, Samuel was a Healer. The Seeker couldn't kill him anyway. Any damage the man inflicted, he would just heal. Truly, he had been a fool to be afraid.

He lurched forward as something ripped into his back, severing his spine and bursting through his chest. He gaped down at the tip of the sword piercing the front of his shirt, now slick with blood. He tried to speak, but the words wouldn't come.

He was lifted into the air, his weight pushing him further onto the blade. The Seeker lifted him high, then swung the sword. Samuel's body slid off the steel, and he fell to the ground, his blood beginning to coat the sand. Instantly, he began healing, reknitting the torn bones and flesh. Feeling returned to his legs and mouth and he reached forward to pull himself away even as his skin was burned by the scorching sand. Skin on his cheek peeled away, flaking to the ground, only to be regrown seconds later.

"Not so fast." A foot pressed into his back, pinning him. Samuel grunted as the Seeker grabbed him by the hair. Without so much as another word, he began dragging him back to Everfont.

"Let me go," Samuel groaned as a nameless terror filled him. "Please."

The Seeker didn't respond. He just kept walking, tightening his grip on Samuel's hair. Samuel weakly tried to reach up and smack away the Seeker's hand, which earned him a kick in the ribs and another in the stomach. The wind rushed out of Samuel and his ribs cracked. He tried to curl into a ball, but his body was yanked outward as the Seeker continued on, unbothered.

"Please," Samuel tried as soon as he could breathe, tears in his eyes this time as he sucked in large gulps of air. "Please. You don't have to do this. You can let me die in the desert. The King will never know!"

He wasn't expecting a response. But the Seeker looked down at him, and said, "Would you like to walk to the palace on your own? Or do you want to be dragged?"

For a moment, Samuel wondered if the Seeker was deaf. Then he understood—the Seeker had heard all these pleas before. To him, this was just another day.

Samuel was going to die. There was no changing that. All that mattered now was how long he could delay it and with how much dignity he could muster to face his execution.

He feebly stood up, rubbing a hand over his now sore head, and fell in step beside the Seeker. The Seeker nodded, and together, they walked toward the city wall.

Samuel couldn't help but notice the cut fabric in the Seeker's clothes, where he had been stabbed. There was no wound there, not even a scar. In fact, aside from the tear in the clothes, it was as if he had never been stabbed at all.

～

Poppertrot waited, as he did every day, at the entrance to the Post.

He guarded the eastern entrance, one of four for each point on a compass. There were many entrances to the tunnels beneath Everfont, twisting and turning, many unexplored—but there were only four entrances to the Post, meant to be guarded at all times. Even if one wandered the tunnels enough to find the Post, they could not enter until one of the guardsmen let them in.

So, there was always someone on duty. For the east, that someone happened to be Poppertrot.

It was a dull job. Lackluster, endless and, in his mind, next to worthless. Sometimes he brought Eva out to play, but that was merely a temporary fix for the boredom. The entirety of his existence was spent, waiting to open the door for someone with the correct password. The runes prevented the Post from being opened from the outside and so there absolutely had to be someone to open it—but Poppertrot didn't want to be that person.

Still, it beat working in the mines to the north, outside of the city. His cousins and family and friends were there. Trompkins were larger, stronger, and faster than humans and were desirable for their labor. The King had harvested—enslaved was too tame a word for what the King did—his kind to mine jewels and money and other things from the desert and there were hardly any of them left in the city.

He looked up, across the way, to his home. Right above it was Ryan's, where little Eva—a girl that saw nothing but the good in him—was playing with her dolls. Poppertrot assumed that was what she was doing. There wasn't much else to entertain a seven-year-old girl in the daytime.

She believed in him, as only a child could. Ryan, Walton, Dmitri, Marle—they were all suspicious and wary of him, and with good reason. There were no other Trompkins in the Post and even if they didn't think it, they unconsciously wondered what he had done to escape. More than one person had accused him of making a deal with the King to sell out the Post, and Marle had hinted she believed he was capable of such betrayal.

He was. He had done so before, and if he needed to survive, he could do it again. The question he kept asking himself was— would he?

He kept his gaze focused on Ryan's house, thinking of small little Eva. How broken she would be if he did to her what he had done before.

Movement on the other side of the cavern caught his eye. His attention flicked toward the far wall, to the entrance guard on the other side. The man was nothing but a dim speck to him from this distance, but Poppertrot could see the wall opening. His eyes narrowed and he rose from his seat, trying to get a better look. No one was supposed to come back for at least another three hours.

A figure encased in steel came through the door. Then another, and another, and another. Panic filled Poppertrot as he realized it was the King's Hand. His voice caught in his throat as he tried to yell, but another rang out in the cavern.

"The King's Hand are invading! To arms! To—!"

The scream was cut off as the entrance guard was quickly cut down, a sword shearing his head from his neck. The King's Hand shouted orders, waving their swords and fanning out into a defensive position. Poppertrot cursed and opened the door he guarded, shouting for Walton. The large man appeared a moment later with a questioning expression. It fled when he saw the other side of the Post.

"Crives," the old man muttered. He lowered his spear, grasping it with two hands and jerked his head at Poppertrot. "Grab the others."

"You're going to fight them on your own?" Poppertrot said. Walton shrugged and stepped forward, but Poppertrot pulled him back. "They'll kill you."

"I know," Walton said. He pried himself out of Poppertrot's grip and ran forward.

Fool.

Poppertrot froze. It was just like before when they had come for him. They would find him and take him to the mines, along with the other Trompkins until the day he died. It was a fate he had run from all his life, and he wasn't going to stop now. He turned back, stepping through the doorway and staring at the dim darkness of the endless tunnel. Someone could run for days through the complex. The tunnels didn't just run under Everfont but stretched for miles across Gritt like a maze. He would hide until the commotion died down and then return.

But something stopped him this time. He turned back and looked across the Post, at the small home above his. The guards were moving closer to the housing complex, and they had rolled barrels into the cistern. It was hard to tell from this distance, but it looked like they were using them to light torches.

With horror, Poppertrot realized they were filled with oil. They were going to use them to burn down the houses.

And Eva was inside.

He hesitated. It would be a simple thing to run and hide. It would require no more of him than what he had always done. Yet, he found himself unable to move his feet, as though he were a sand gator stuck on land.

Shouts rang out as the guards patrolling the tunnels returned. Steel met steel, echoing through the entire cistern as several residents of the Post that owned weapons had joined in to defend their homes. Still, Poppertrot stood, looking into the empty corridor that stood before him, torn by his decision.

He stiffened and turned back. Without giving himself time to doubt or time to breathe, he sprinted for the houses. He let his mind go blank, for if he thought at all he would falter. The King's Hand were already setting fire to the first one, and the flames were spreading rapidly, consuming the wood like a man who had crossed the desert consumed water. People cried out as they fled from their homes, straight into the waiting guards, who were quick to tackle and shackle anyone trying to push past them.

Poppertrot didn't care about any of that. He was returning for one reason and one reason only. As he drew nearer, one of the King's Hand saw him approaching. The man shouted and several of the King's Hand swiveled to face him. Some readied arrows and fired, but they went wide. Others drew their swords and formed a line, ready to meet him.

Poppertrot sucked in a breath. With all his strength, right before he reached the wall of King's Hands, he slammed his feet into the ground and pushed with all his might. Had he been a human, such an action would have been suicide.

But he was a Trompkin. He easily cleared the line of guards, sailing over their heads and landing on the porch of Ryan's home. The wood where he landed cracked beneath his feet, and his momentum carried him forward into Ryan's home. The wall groaned and bowed, but thankfully, it held.

An arrow thudded into the wood near Poppertrot's head. He paid it no mind as he stumbled forward, bursting through the front door. Eva yelped and held a stuffed animal in front of her, as if to ward him away. She sat in the corner, clutching as many of her dolls as she could possibly hold. Her eyes filled with terror, but they lessened at the sight of him. She pushed herself to her feet and ran to him, wrapping her trembling arms around his legs.

Finally, he let himself think. Any doubts he might have had vanished at the sight of this little girl, this child, who needed him.

He would not abandon his family this time.

"Come on, princess," he said, scooping her up in one arm. "Time to go."

Bravely, she peeked over his shoulder to see what was going on. "What's happening? Did you do something bad?"

"Not me. Someone else," Poppertrot said, grabbing a few of her dolls. He picked her favorite three—a sand gator, a sun swan, and Mr. Tinn, who was a small version of a human man dressed in sand sailor garb. He would have tried to take them all, but he didn't have a bag. Crives, he should have grabbed one before he got her.

He couldn't believe he was even thinking of that. Smoke began to waft into the room. The Post had been invaded, for crives sake, and he was worried about dolls?

He paused, eyebrows knitting together as her question registered on a deeper level. Someone had to have let the King's Hand in. There was no other way they could have entered. Who had done so?

It didn't matter. What mattered was getting Eva to safety.

He ran out the door, shoving the dolls into Eva's hands and pushing her head down into his shoulder. Smoke billowed upward, obscuring the cavern and rolling hot across his skin, coloring his fur black. Flames licked below them, tickling Poppertrot's feet as they rapidly pushed upward. The fire had already spread across the base of the stacked houses. It had nowhere to go but up and it was rising fast. Through the smoke, Poppertrot could see a few of the King's Hand point at him and shout.

"Hang on to Mr. Tinn," Poppertrot muttered, patting Eva on the back. She clutched her dolls tighter as Poppertrot backed up a few steps. His legs tensed and he pushed off, springing forward with all the strength he could muster. He leapt off the porch, soaring far over the guards and landing on the cobblestones below. He bent his knees to absorb the impact and let out a grunt. Behind him, the King's Hand rushed forward, swords raised.

"Don't let them get away! We need that girl!" someone yelled. The voice sounded frighteningly familiar. Poppertrot had the feeling he should have known who it belonged to, but he didn't have time to think about it. The King's Hand had begun to surround him.

He reacted on impulse. He swung his free arm around, and it connected with the closest guard's head. His helmet, and skull, crumpled beneath the blow, bits of red, brown and pale skin squishing out from the flattened helmet as the man dropped to the floor. Trompkins were stronger than humans and their bones were denser. It was easy to forget that fact when Poppertrot spent so much time around them, but the brown, spongy material oozing from the man's helmet was a stark reminder.

In his arms, Eva convulsed at the sight. Crives.

"Look away," he growled. She buried her face in his shoulder as more guards approached. Several others broke away from rounding up Post citizens fleeing the fire to help stop him. On the other side of the cavern, the guards and denizens of the Post had been pushed back, forced into the center of the cavern. Already some had begun to flee, running for the three exits the King's Hand had not entered through.

Poppertrot tried to run, breaking into a sprint for the exit he had been guarding, but it was too late. He skidded to a stop, clutching Eva tighter to his chest as more guards arrived, pointing spears and swords at him. They closed ranks, forming a circle and pushing in tighter.

Nowhere to go.

He clutched Eva as tightly as he could without hurting her, wrapping both arms around her. There was nothing more he could offer than his body as protection—and it wouldn't be enough.

At least . . . at least I didn't run this time.

What a fool he was. But strangely, he was a fool at peace.

He stared defiantly at the circle of men around him, his upper lip curling into a snarl. There wasn't enough room for him to run and jump over them. "Come on then, you criving sand-lickers. Be done with it."

"No!" someone else cried. A young man pushed through them with a grim look on his face. Poppertrot's heart hardened at the sight of him and suddenly, he understood why the voice had sounded so familiar.

"We take them with us. The King has need of them."

Poppertrot opened his mouth to speak, to demand answers, but something slammed into the back of his head. He stumbled, a breathy wheeze escaping his lips as the cistern went dark. Somehow, he managed to hold onto Eva as he fell, turning to shield her from the fall. She cried as he slammed into the ground and a moment later, she was ripped from his arms. He tried to hold onto her, but a boot to his chest knocked the wind out of him.

A moment later, everything went black.

〜

Walton lying face down in the tunnel was the first thing Ryan saw when she returned to the Post.

He was near the entrance, his spear on the ground at his side. The door was open, and a dim orange glow poured out of the Post—unusual, since it was usually lit by a bright green light. Not only that, but the entrance should have also been closed. As she drew nearer the smell of smoke wafted by her nose, almost overpowering.

Something's wrong.

She ran forward, falling to her knees beside Walton. She turned him over and he let out a soft groan. His clothes were torn in several places, charred in others, and there were cuts on his abdomen and arms—but nothing life threatening. Relief flooded through Ryan, quickly replaced with anxiety and questions.

"Walton." She shook him. "Walton."

His eyes fluttered open at his name, focusing on Ryan before closing. She felt his pulse. It was strong. A purple bruise was forming on his temple.

Relief ran through her and she sat back. Nothing life threatening. He had probably been knocked out. It wouldn't be the first time. He would be fine, with enough rest.

She rose and warily walked into the Post. She could come back for him later. Entering the Post proper, however, caused all thoughts of helping Walton to flee from her mind.

There was nothing left.

The homes built along the outer wall had been torched. Burned to a crisp, there was nothing left but charcoal black remains. Several corpses lay sprawled on the ground and there were cracks in the center pillar, while the fountain that held their water had been broken, with water pouring onto the ground. Broken swords were strewn everywhere, as well as random assortments of other items. Some, Ryan recognized as baubles for Babblyn's knickknack shop.

What on Gritt happened here?

"Ryan? Ryan, is that you?"

Ryan turned, baffled to see Marle as well as a dozen other residents approaching. They looked battered and beaten, and some had soot on their faces while others nursed injured legs and arms. Marle looked worse than most, nursing a large cut on her arm. Blood ran down her entire left side and her right eye was swollen shut, while soot covered most of her face and clothes.

"What happened?" Ryan asked, bewildered.

Marle opened her mouth to speak, then looked down and blew out a gush of air. The others all looked away. Ryan scanned each of their faces and a pit opened in her stomach. Poppertrot and Eva were not among them. Dmitri wasn't either, but she shouldn't expect him to be. He was safe somewhere in Everfont, delivering packages.

Her stomach dropped as Marle studied her carefully, weighing her words. She had an idea of what Marle would say before she said it, but that didn't make the news any easier.

Finally, Marle answered. "The King's Hand came."

Ryan stared at Marle, shocked. "No. No one can enter the Post without an invitation." But it made sense—why there were no guards in the Water Gardens. Why her deliveries had been so easy today. The King's Hand had been taking part in a raid.

A raid on the Post. Something that had never been done before, in all their history. An impossibility that no one had ever considered.

"The runes are weakening," Marle said softly. "It's why we needed the treaty. The Post is dying and only amnesty will save our people."

"the Post is dying?" Ryan struggled to keep her voice down. "the Post is a cave, Marle. A criving cave. Caves can't die."

"A cave made into a safe haven by Etchers," Marle responded, "with runes that would eventually lose their power."

Ryan's face twisted into a snarl, though she knew Marle was right. The runes, engraved on the cistern walls and throughout the city long ago, were what made the Post a place beyond the King's reach. They prevented anyone unwanted, anyone with ill intent, from entering unless invited in by a resident. Everyone knew one day, they would fail, and the last safe place on Gritt would be gone.

Ryan had never thought it would happen while she was alive.

She composed herself, shoving her emotions away. She could grieve later. Now, she had to focus. "Did they take prisoners?"

Marle hesitated, then nodded. A cold chill spread through Ryan's chest. Eva's body wasn't among the dead. Somehow, she had made it out of the burned homes, only to be taken by the King's Hand. An image flashed through Ryan's mind of her little sister, alone in a cell, crying and frightened by what was happening.

The promise she had made came back to her mind. Eva would have been expecting a bedtime story tonight, the same one she had been pestering Ryan to read for weeks. Dmitri had read to her yesterday—but it should have been Ryan. She had been putting it off, always saying she was too tired.

Now it was too late. Guilt washed over her, and her knees almost buckled at the weight slamming into her.

"Who else did he take?" Ryan asked hoarsely, trying to change the subject. There was no time to be weak. She had to be strong. If she acted quickly, she might be able to undo some of the damage.

"Council members," Marle said. "Some of the sanitation workers. Many of our scouts."

"Poppertrot?"

Marle's silence was enough. Ryan turned away from her and ran a hand through her hair, trying to remain calm, before turning back. "The treaty was supposed to prevent this."

"I thought it would."

"It didn't," Ryan snapped. She jabbed a finger at Marle. "You were supposed to protect . . ." her voice faltered. "You were supposed to protect the Post."

She had been going to say us—but Marle hadn't been protecting her or Eva for a long time now.

Marle's face hardened. She was leaning on her left leg, nursing a wound, but she drew herself up to her full height. Ryan was still taller, but the effect was immediate. A pit opened in Ryan's stomach and the people behind Marle began to cower. The older woman had always had a way with crowds, able to read their emotions and guide them where she wanted. It was one of the qualities that had made people consider her for the Crow position.

Don't be afraid, Ryan thought, gritting her teeth and meeting Marle's eyes with fiery defiance. There was nothing Marle could do to her.

"If you're so dissatisfied with the work I've done, why didn't you become Crow?" Marle hissed, stepping in close, so close their noses were only inches apart. "The council wanted you to take over. But you declined. You forfeited any right to criticize my actions the moment you ran away from this responsibility."

"You know why I couldn't. This isn't about me; this is about you. You led this place to ruin. You let my sister be captured, and Poppertrot and the others," Ryan said, her anger spilling over. She had declined being Crow because of Eva. Because she had been planning on leaving. Because she never wanted to lead and didn't even want her place on the council. "Maybe they were able to force their way in because of the treaty. Did you think maybe that was what weakened the runes?"

"You have no idea what you're talking about. Poor Ryan— always the victim. If you knew half the secrets I know, you wouldn't judge me so harshly," Marle snarled. She stepped away, however, trying to conceal the hurt in her eyes. For all Marle's faults, she really did care.

If there was anyone in the Post that could hurt Marle, it was Ryan.

Marle turned her back on Ryan, clearing her throat to address the remnants of the Post. "I have a plan."

"Yeah? What's that? Going to continue with the treaty? Cut your losses and save whoever's left?" Ryan said.

Marle ignored her. "We're going to retreat into the tunnels. The guards won't find us further down. When they give up, we will return and rebuild."

Ryan snorted. "Where? Surely not here. Not with the runes failing."

Marle said nothing. Ryan continued. "You never think ahead. We would have to raise an army to keep the King's Hand out. Constant patrols, constant payment of drops. The Post was already hanging by a thread before this happened. You want to start from scratch? You're out of your criving mind."

She turned and began walking away. She was wasting time here. Speaking with Marle would get her nowhere and she needed to save Eva and Poppertrot. If Eva revealed what she was . . .

Don't think about that. Eva is older now. She knows better and has better control. At least, that was what Ryan was hoping. If Eva was scared, who knew what she would do or how long she could keep control? A single slip and it would all be over.

Poppertrot was with her. If luck was on their side, maybe he would even be in the same cell. He would help keep her calm, but he could only do that for so long.

"Where are you going?" Marle called.

"To save my sister," Ryan snapped over her shoulder. Marle called out a response, but Ryan didn't care to listen. Anger boiled beneath her skin at her aunt. If only she had run this place better, if only she hadn't made that criving treaty, maybe Eva would still be here.

However, Ryan's anger was nothing compared to the rage she felt at herself. The guilt that had settled in the bottom of her gut like a rock. She could have avoided all of this had she just left when they had the money. She had enough drops for her and Eva, but she had decided to stay. Just saving her sister wasn't enough. She had needed more.

It was her fault this had happened. Her father had been right. She had been a fool to stay.

She didn't leave the Post immediately. She headed for the storage building, which, thankfully, hadn't been burned down. It was where they kept the different packages and letters the couriers delivered. She was surprised to see Dmitri's painting there, placed gently on the ground, but paid it no mind as she rummaged through the various items awaiting delivery. It only took her a moment to find the specific envelope she wanted. It hadn't moved since the day it arrived.

No better time to deliver this than now, Ryan thought. She was likely to die anyway. Securing it in her messenger pack, she left the storage room and headed for the exit.

She left the way she had come. She forced a smile as she saw Walton, leaning against a nearby wall, breathing heavy. He had his spear leveled in her direction but dropped it when he saw her.

"Welcome back," he said gruffly.

Ryan could have laughed at the nonchalant welcome. He could have died, and that was all he had to say? "Are you all right?"

"Fine."

"Are you sure?"

He nodded.

Ryan sighed and folded her arms. "They took Eva and Poppertrot."

Walton looked down, and Ryan felt a pang of sympathy. Knowing Walton, he would already be feeling guilty. It was his job to protect and defend the Post from those trying to get in. He would view this attack as a failure of his duty. The fact they had taken prisoners would have doubled his pain.

"Was the Seeker with them?" Ryan asked.

"No."

That was a relief. If the Seeker had been here, that would have meant he knew there were Imperials living in the Post. Since it was only the King's Hand, there was a slim chance they knew what Eva was, if she kept her powers in check. They would put her with the other prisoners, beneath the palace, instead of taking her to the torture halls of the Seeker.

Ryan patted Walton on the back as she passed. "I'm going to go get them. Don't beat yourself up. Find us a sand sailor while I'm gone. We'll need to leave as soon as I spring them. See if you can get them to lower their price. They might be more willing after this raid." She paused. "Tell Dmitri what happened and where I am. He'll want to know."

Walton nodded and wandered back inside the Post, out of sight. Ryan continued down the tunnel, heading for the west exit. That would deposit her near the outer wall of Everfont and she had a few friends she would need to see before she stopped in at the palace.

She sucked in a breath before breaking into a run. Everything had changed. Her carefully laid plans had been torn asunder and her sister had been taken. All the things she feared most had happened.

In a way that was a good thing. Now, she had nothing to lose.

∽

Samuel awoke to cold water being splashed on his face. He jerked up, suddenly aware of the cold air on his skin, and the steel around his wrists. He didn't even remember falling asleep. He and the Seeker had walked to the walls of Everfont and then . . . and then nothing.

Even still, he knew where he was. Damp air filled the space around him, as well as the stench of death. There was a green eerie light that filled the air, and though it was dim, the bloodstains on the floor and walls were unmistakable. He shifted his legs and realized the stone beneath him was wet.

The Seeker's lair. A place spoken of only in hushed tones and whispers. A place as frightening as the Seeker himself. A place no one had ever seen, and no one had ever escaped from.

He blinked the sleep from his eyes, becoming alert and aware. Strange bits of paper were scattered on the floor and Samuel shivered as he touched some with his foot. They had a leathery feel to them, and he drew his legs as close to his body as he could, so he didn't brush up against them. He didn't want to think about what they might be.

"You're awake?"

Samuel lurched backward at the sound, letting out a small gasp. There, in the dim light, he could make out the form of the Seeker. It was impossible to see any features, as he blended in with the darkness, but Samuel could just barely see his outline, shuffling about. In front of the Seeker was a table, with various instruments strewn on top of it. And strangely, a stack of papers.

"I like it when people are awake for this part," the Seeker said softly, as though he were offering comfort to a child. "It makes it less lonely."

"You're a sick criver," Samuel said. He was surprised at the boldness of his words. All his life, he had feared the Seeker. But now he had been caught, there was nothing he could say or do that would save his life. He might as well say whatever was on his mind. "Everyone hates you. Everyone fears you."

"I know. It is the burden I must bear, for the sake of the people," the Seeker agreed, much to Samuel's surprise. "But I am much the same as you."

"We're nothing alike," Samuel said, but his blood ran cold. Hadn't he said something similar earlier about the burden of being a King's Hand?

As if reading his mind, the Seeker spoke. "Did you not kill those two boys yesterday?" he said. "You could have arrested them. Sent them away with a warning. Anything but bashing them against the stones."

"They were criminals," Samuel growled, but the argument sounded weak, even to him. *I was just protecting Everfont! That's all I was doing!*

Was it really? They had been young boys, doing stupid things as young boys do. They weren't really a threat. Most people in the slums were harmless, but Samuel had treated them as if they were dangerous murderers.

Samuel began to weep as he realized what a fool he had been. The King's Hand had taken him and twisted him into something he hated.

He was responsible for the actions he had taken. All the atrocities he had committed, in the name of protecting people and serving them, would be weighed against his soul in death. The teachings of the third moon spoke of people like him, saying if they did not see the error of their ways, they would be thrown into a place even worse than white-fire. How ironic, then, that a sense of self finally returned to him, here, in this dank, hopeless prison. That when the moment he could see clearest was his darkest, when no time was left to him to change.

The Seeker seemed to sense his dismay. "I see the change in your soul. You regret what you've done. Don't worry. It's natural for you to feel that way, at the end. All men make mistakes. Often, we become the very things we hate. The more you focus on something, the more like that thing you become."

"Can you read my mind?"

The Seeker chuckled. "I'm no Memorist, flitting through memories and thoughts at a whim. I've just been alive for a very, very long time. And people have a certain . . . color to them, when they pray." He lifted a silver pair of clippers and snapped them three times in rapid succession. Samuel winced. The sound they made was like steel being dragged on steel.

He turned to Samuel. Samuel tensed, pressing himself up against the cold wall at his back. "Please. I could help you."

The Seeker drew closer, brandishing the large pair of clippers. "There is nothing you can do that would help me."

"W-we could be allies. I could help you catch other Imperials!" Samuel licked his lips. A moment ago, he had thought he was ready to die. After all, no one escaped the Seeker. Staring at those clippers, however, had changed his mind. His would not be a quick death. It would be long and painful, something he was not ready for.

The Seeker shook his head. "You are one of the last, and soon, the remaining two will be brought to me. Beyond that, what I do is an evil thing. I capture the innocent and I send them to the afterlife when they have done nothing to warrant death. It is a burden I must carry alone."

Samuel blinked. "Then . . . why are you going to torture me?"

In the darkness, Samuel could have sworn he saw the Seeker smile, even behind the fabric covering his face. "You, my friend, are not one of the innocents. You are stained, as am I. Don't worry—I won't kill you yet. You still have a story to tell me."

He lowered the clippers, placing them over one of Samuel's toes.

Samuel began to scream.

Chapter Four

It was late afternoon by the time Ryan made it to Fogvir's.

Most of the streets were empty. He lived in the slums, in the southwestern part of the city, and there was never much traffic here. Most people chose to stay at home during the day to escape the heat, and those that didn't had jobs that required them to work late hours.

Had she been anyone else, the local thugs would have been on her in an instant. Couriers were known in the less desirable parts of the city, however, and she had made many runs here herself. The street gangs left her alone out of respect for her job. That, and she was no dainty thing to be taken advantage of. Once, a pair of young men her age had tried to take her things. They had both walked away with broken hands.

She found the shop she was looking for and quickly stepped inside. There was no need to fear the local street gangs, but there was reason to fear the guards. Patrols were rare in the slums, but it was best not to take chances. If they spotted her, it would be a never-ending chase now that the Post wasn't safe. What little hope she had of rescuing Eva and the others would be gone.

Does it matter anymore? she thought glumly as she walked up to the store counter. Behind it, a small man with thick-rimmed spectacles was tinkering with a strange device. Now the protection of the Post was waning, her days here were numbered. Until she left, she would always need to fear the Seeker.

Perhaps she could draw his attention away from Eva. Lead him on a fierce chase and buy herself some time to think and some time to plan.

Who was she kidding? She had run out of time the moment that treaty had been signed.

She cleared her throat. The little man behind the counter jumped and swiveled around, a small metal object in the shape of a sphere in his hands. He squinted through his thick-rimmed glasses, scrunching up his mouth and drawing his lips into a thin line. "Ryan? White-fire, woman, don't scare a man like that! You nearly had me jumping out of my own skin!"

"You didn't hear me come through the front door?" Ryan asked.

"You know I don't hear anything when I'm working on something," Fogvir muttered. He set his device on the desk behind the counter and hobbled over to her. "It's been a long time. Six months, maybe?"

"Seven, actually." The last time she had come, she had been looking for something to help Eva sleep better. Fogvir had given her a concoction to take in the evening that had done wonders, in trade for a package delivered.

"Seven? White-fire, I must be going mad," Fogvir muttered. "But you didn't come here to reminisce about old times. You need something."

Ryan shook her head. "A favor."

He shook his head and clicked his tongue. "A favor. That's how it always starts. I'm assuming this is for a delivery?"

"Not exactly," Ryan said. She leaned over the counter and stared Fogvir straight in the eye. "I need to break into the palace."

To his credit, Fogvir didn't blink. He normally didn't. The small man had a strict policy of providing services without questions asked, something for which Ryan was grateful. This, however, was an unusual request and expectedly, he asked, "Why?"

"They took my sister." The words felt like bile in her mouth. It was hard to believe, even though it had happened several hours ago. She was still having trouble digesting the information. "I'm going to get her out."

Fogvir stared at her for a long time. Mixed emotions flashed across his face. Surprise. Anger. Pity. He turned away from the counter and scratched his head while letting out a long sigh. "Ryan . . . I know you've done a lot of difficult and dangerous things—"

"Don't say it," Ryan said.

"But breaking into the palace isn't just difficult and dangerous. It's insanity. I might be able to get you in, but there's no way in white-fire I could get you out, too."

"I can get myself out," Ryan said quietly.

Fogvir snapped his attention toward her. The pieces of the puzzle clicked together in his eyes, and he let out a slow whistle before running a hand through his thinning hair.

"I see," he breathed. "This is it then?"

Ryan nodded. "Marle made a treaty with the King. The Post will be his in a few days. After that, there'll be nowhere to hide."

Fogvir nodded his understanding. He was the only person in Everfont besides Cackler and Marle that knew her secret. "You'll want to watch out for the Seeker then. You'll be wanting a cloaker."

He moved to the back of his workshop, disappearing from view. A chill ran over Ryan's skin, and she closed her eyes to try and calm herself. She had been trying not to think of the Seeker ever since Eva had been taken.

Everyone knew of him. He hunted Imperials and when he found them, he dragged them to his torture chambers supposedly hidden somewhere beneath the city. It was said thousands of Imperials had died down there, their screams unheard by any except the demons that lived beneath the sand.

Even the common folk feared him, though they had no reason to. He didn't hunt anyone but Imperials: The people who had been born with magic, that had the gift of gods running through their veins.

Ryan was one of those. An Amplifier, or so she was called, with the ability to increase in physical strength and speed and to stave off fatigue as long as she had enough power to pull on. Her sister was a different kind of Imperial, an Elementalist—an Imperial with the ability to control earth, wind, air and fire, as well as a few other things.

If Ryan didn't hurry, her sister would panic. When her sister panicked, she instinctively used her Imperia, which would draw the Seeker. Once he found her, there would be no stopping him.

Ryan had to prepare for that possibility. That maybe, just maybe, he might get to her first. If that was the case, she would tear this city apart, brick by brick. She would kill everyone in the King's Hand, and even the King himself, to save Eva. Whatever it took to keep her out of their hands.

Fogvir returned with a sleek metal sheet in his hands. It looked like a blanket, save for the fact it was made of metal. He placed it on the counter, gently pushing it toward Ryan. "Here. This should help you get into the palace a bit easier."

Ryan took it. It wasn't very large, and when folded up, would just barely fit inside her messenger bag. It was meant to be worn as a cloak and somehow it would obscure the wearer from the Seeker. She had borrowed it from Fogvir once when she had used too much Imperia and the Seeker had caught her trail. It would have been useful to have running around the city, but the way it reflected sunlight made her stand out like a sore thumb.

Not to mention the fact Fogvir had charged her an arm and a leg to use it. Forty thousand drops to borrow for a single day. It was such an exorbitant fee, she had considered taking her chances with the Seeker tracking her.

"What else can I get for you?" Fogvir asked.

"Do you have anything that will melt steel?" Ryan asked hopefully. She was going into a prison after all. She would prefer not to waste time picking locks on cages. She could likely rip the prison doors off as well, but she didn't want to waste any Imperia, nor did she want to make any noise. The quieter she could slip in and out with Eva and Poppertrot, the better.

"Melt steel, hmm?" Fogvir scratched his chin thoughtfully. "How quickly do you want it to melt?"

"Seconds."

"Just a moment," he said, and began rummaging through different drawers underneath the counter. After a moment, he popped back up, holding a vial of black liquid. "This ought to do the trick. Be careful—if it gets on you it will eat through your skin, fat, muscle and bone in under ten seconds."

"How sturdy is the vial?" Ryan asked, tucking it away inside the metal cloak.

"It can't be broken. Made of some special material I got from Wulfenraast when I visited. Cost me a fortune in drops. It's known as rimeline, but I think it's a silly name for it."

"You went to Wulfenraast, and you didn't stay?" Ryan muttered. She had forgotten how rich Fogvir was. He didn't look it, but he probably had as much money as the King. The people depended on him for his inventions and his genius. Despite his wealth, he chose to live in a humble shop, in the poorest part of Everfont.

"This is my home," Fogvir said, just as Ryan knew he would. "Couldn't leave it if I tried."

Ryan shook her head disapprovingly. She would never understand Fogvir. They had had this conversation many times, and each time, Ryan had left feeling baffled. Gritt was a dying world, and Everfont was a dying kingdom. It made no sense why anyone would want to stay. But Fogvir did, and so Ryan tried to avoid the conversation altogether.

"Do you have anything that can kill the Seeker?"

Fogvir laughed. "You know he's unkillable."

"Wouldn't stop you from trying to find a way to kill him."

"I am not a merchant of death. I tinker, and I dabble in various instruments—but I don't build things that kill."

Ryan raised an eyebrow. "You've never thought about it? Not once?"

Fogvir looked away guiltily. "Thinking is much different than doing."

"And you've never done any research?"

Fogvir hesitated. Ryan pressed. "You can show me. It would help me rid this city of a menace that needs to be killed."

"The Seeker is a necessary evil, though not one I agree with. Besides, he's only a menace to certain kinds of people. If I help you, he will know what I did, and I will become one of those people that needs to fear him."

"Not if I kill him before he finds out what you did."

Fogvir blew out a long puff of air. "He can't be killed. At least, not with the tools and items I currently have available for you. He's an Imperial Healer, and a strong one at that. With all the practice he's had, strengthening himself, it's no wonder he can heal so quickly."

Ryan blinked, unsure she had heard Fogvir correctly. "You said . . . he's an Imperial himself?"

"Yes, yes," Fogvir said impatiently, as if it were common knowledge, already moving to the back of his shop. He gestured for Ryan to follow this time and she slid across the counter and through the door to his workshop. It was larger than his actual home, with a tall ceiling and a wide-open space. Several tables were covered with knickknacks and shoved against the walls, while various gadgets were strewn about the floor alongside random assortments of papers. There was a large metal tube, big enough a person could fit inside, sitting at the back. "How do you think he can be stabbed and beheaded and burned without dying?"

"Blessed by the gods, maybe? Or a demon?" Ryan said. She had never really thought about it. Her whole life she had grown up fearing the Seeker, fearing she might get caught, but not once had she thought about how he did what he did. It was assumed he always had been and always would persist. He might have even been something from a different world.

"No god would bless a man like that. There's something not right with him, and that's putting it lightly," Fogvir said. He kicked aside a few metal objects, wading through piles of what Ryan could only describe as junk, until he came to a large chest covered with dust. He dragged it out and blew on it, sending a plume into the air.

Ryan felt her stomach turn. An Imperial, murdering Imperials, under the King's order. "Couldn't we expose the King, then? Show him that he's a sham for using Imperials?"

Fogvir shook his head as he produced a key and shoved it into the chest's golden lock. It clicked open and he tossed the lock onto a nearby desk. "No good. The Seeker has been a part of society for several centuries now, even before he came to Everfont. His mythology is ingrained in our culture. Even if we did expose the King, it wouldn't change how people fear him. They would rationalize him as something other than an Imperial. And even if we did kill him, the King could just create another Seeker."

"How could he create another Seeker?"

"He'd just have to find one," Fogvir said. "Imperia is not a mystical power that only a few are blessed with. There are thousands upon thousands on other worlds beyond Gritt, and I'm sure there are thousands and thousands of Twice-Blessed Healer-Soulseers. All the King would need to create another Seeker is time. The more one uses their Imperia, the stronger they become. It's like a muscle in that way. The Seeker has been using his Imperia for longer than even I've been alive, and as a result, his healing is nearly limitless. The King would just need to find another Imperial like him and train them for a few decades. Give them enough time and they would eventually be as powerful as the Seeker we have now."

"But it would still undermine the King's authority," Ryan said, troubled by Fogvir's explanation. If Imperia was like a muscle, she was vastly undertrained. Looking inside, she could see a reservoir of power within her, and it seemed like a lot. However, she barely used her Amplification. What would the Seeker's Imperia look like, if she could see it? "If the people know he's using Imperial Healers, he'll be labeled a hypocrite. People will be motivated to fight back. If he's no longer sustained by the people, his rule will collapse."

Fogvir shrugged. "The people are beaten down. Centuries of revolt have left the spirit of the people broken. No one would attempt a rebellion after the last attack on the Water Gardens." The small man shuddered. "Besides, he has the King's Hand. It doesn't matter if the people support him or not. Those that don't will be hunted down and thrown into the dungeons. Most are not willing to sacrifice their lives and families for a cause they don't think is worth it. You were too young to understand the devastation after the attack on the Water Gardens, but it was catastrophic. Thousands died."

"You don't think they would want to overthrow our tyrant of a King?" Ryan asked.

"Tyrant or no, he keeps things stable." Fogvir squinted at her through his thick glasses. "Technically speaking, he could be called the king of the world. Did you know we're the last kingdom on the face of Gritt? A city that's only a kingdom because it's the last vestiges of civilization?" He spread his arms. "People on Rim would call our small living space barely larger than a village. There are less than thirty thousand people in Everfont."

"It's that way because of him!" Ryan said. "His rule is choking the life out of this place. People work to feed him and his! He killed all the Imperials, his own people, because he was scared of the power they held!"

Fogvir shook his head sadly. "I've been to the palace. I've looked at the ledgers. Most of the money he takes is going to research of how to stop the desertification. He certainly doesn't have enough power to cause that and he has no reason to. Why cause the death of a kingdom you rule? As for the Imperials . . ." Fogvir trailed off with a distant look in his eye. "He had his reasons. But it wasn't because he was scared."

Fogvir sighed and adjusted his glasses. "Most men do terrible things when they gain power. The King is no different, though you would be surprised to know he is better than most." Ryan snorted in response, but Fogvir continued. "It's the truth. I've traveled to Rim and Niall both, and in each there are men who commit twice the atrocity and brutality of our monarch, despite being in much better circumstances.

"I digress—you didn't come here to talk about my travels or talk about politics." He flipped open the lid to the chest. Inside, it was mostly empty, save for a small dagger resting at the bottom. It was green in color, ornamented with carvings of creatures that were unfamiliar to Ryan. She felt a chill run through her back as Fogvir grabbed it and handed it to her.

This was no ordinary weapon. She could feel something inside of it, something familiar yet altogether different. It wasn't malevolent, nor was it holy—at least, she didn't think it was any of those things. It just . . . was. "What is it?"

"Something to delay the Seeker," Fogvir said. "It's made of sourblock. If you stab the Seeker with that, it will keep him down long enough for you to escape. If he's chasing you."

"Where did you get this?" she asked, turning the blade over in her hands. She ran her thumb along the edge, admiring the craftsmanship.

"Careful. That weapon is more dangerous than you know. Even a small cut can drain Imperia. Cut a regular person and it will make them lethargic," Fogvir said. He gave Ryan a wide berth, cautiously keeping his eye on the dagger as if afraid she would stab him with it. "And I acquired it in trade while in the City of Kaius. It's a city on Rim. The dagger is the first of its kind, a prototype, which is why it won't outright kill him. I've been working on replicating it, but progress is slow, and I have other projects to work on."

So, not from Gritt. It was an otherworldly weapon then, the likes of which would not be found above or below the shifting sands beyond Everfont. "How does it work?"

"Like any other weapon. Just stab him. It will drain most of his Imperia away, rendering him unable to heal. As I said earlier, however, he is powerful. You will have to leave it embedded inside his body somewhere for its effects to fully work. Otherwise, it will only incapacitate him for a matter of moments."

"Nothing else?" Ryan asked. She blinked as a wave of drowsiness washed over her. It had been a long, exhausting day, finding out her sister had been taken, as well as Poppertrot, and finding the Post in shambles. She had yet to take a break. Perhaps she needed one.

Fogvir laughed. "The blade will do the rest." He handed her a sheath and she slid the blade in, carefully minding the edge. "Do try to knock him out first, though. Stab him in a non-lethal part of his body and he'll simply pull the blade out."

She stuffed it in her messenger bag, alongside the cloak and the acid, wondering how on earth she would knock the Seeker out—or get close enough to stab him for that matter. "Anything else you can give me?"

"There are plenty of other things, but none of them will be useful for what you're planning," Fogvir said.

Ryan rolled her eyes. "In terms of payment?"

"You'll be leaving as soon as you rescue your sister?"

"Yes."

"This will be our last transaction, then," Fogvir said, seeming wistful. He thought for a moment, tapping his chin, before he let out a sigh. "You won't be around much longer, so I can't trade you for a favor. All in all, I'll have to charge you. Fifty thousand drops."

Ryan's stomach turned. That was a lot of money. The items Fogvir had given her were useful, there was no denying that—but they were transitory. She would use the acid to break through the cell doors and she would have to leave the dagger in the Seeker. The cloak she would keep, at least. Still, it felt like throwing drops away. "Fifty thousand? Isn't that a bit expensive?"

"The equipment you're holding is easily worth four times more than that. I'm giving you a deal. Since we're old friends," he said. Ryan could see the truthfulness of that in his eyes. He wasn't trying to cheat her. These things were genuinely valuable, and more than that, she needed them.

Ryan sighed, and pulled a broker's note from her bag. It was no matter. She didn't have the money to take her and all her friends away anyway—and drops were worthless to her save for that purpose. She wrote the amount and handed it to him.

"You'll need to redeem that at the Post. It won't work anywhere else." Then, she slid over the counter, leaving them on opposite sides. She was about to leave, but turned back to Fogvir, hesitating. "You could come with us."

Fogvir shook his head. "Ah, lass. This place is my home, and I'm disinclined to leave it."

"You've said that before. You've also said it's dying. The desert will overtake it in a few years. There will be no place left for you."

"Not if I can make a difference," Fogvir said. "Remember, I disagree with the King's methods, but our goals are the same. I help you not to undermine him, but because I know your goals are just as noble as his."

"I don't understand you, Fogvir," Ryan threw her hands out to her sides, frustrated. "You're a good man. I don't see what you see in the King when he's killing people like me just for being alive. You're a talented, rich man. You could have made a difference anywhere. Why here?"

"Because this is where I want to be."

"That's the part I don't understand," Ryan sighed. She raised a hand in thanks, and he responded in kind as she stepped out the front door. An orange glow still tinted the sky. She hadn't been in there very long. A few people were still out on the streets, more than before, but still not nearly enough to blend in with.

It would be best if she could try to sneak into the palace under cover of night, but the more time she wasted, the more likely Eva would use her Imperia. In recent years, she had become better about controlling her outbursts, but she was still a child. Right now, she would be in the King's dungeons with everyone else, growing cold and afraid. It was only a matter of time before she let something slip.

Ryan found an entrance to the underground tunnels and ducked inside. No use walking about in Everfont when she could cross most of the distance underground in a short amount of time without being spotted. The easier she could make this on herself, the better. As she walked, her mind wandered, and thoughts of Poppertrot, Dmitri, Walton, and Marle flitted into her mind. They had been a team. The five of them. Working to escape this criving hole and to find a better life for themselves. They had found and clung to each other, each one with dreams of doing something different. Walton wanted to open a school for young children. He wanted to teach reading and writing. He would never tell anyone, but Ryan knew he secretly loved poetry.

Poppertrot wanted to travel. It didn't matter where, but he often spoke of going to distant lands where the jungle was so thick you couldn't breathe, and mountains so tall they touched the heavens. Above all he wanted to travel to Wulfenraast to see the lava fields and the never-ending oceans. He didn't want to live there, of course, but he did want to visit.

Dmitri wanted to find the legendary Ambrister and train beneath him. There weren't many legends of other worlds beyond Gritt that reached Everfont, but Ambrister's had. The man was said to be a weaponsmith of unparalleled acumen, and Dmitri had wanted to apprentice beneath him and become a sword master with no peer. He said it was to protect those he loved, but Ryan suspected he also wanted to show off.

And Marle . . . Marle had wanted to find a family. A real one. Her old husband was still alive, but she had left him. He had chosen other things over her, gradually growing distant until finally, she left. Once, when Marle had been drunk, she had confessed she wanted that life again. To settle down in a small, modest home, with a someone who would wrap his arms around her.

And then . . . then the criver had thrown it all away for a few extra days. Finding Eva had been kidnapped had been hard but learning Marle had betrayed them by proposing that stupid treaty . . . that stung more.

Ryan could deal with her enemies causing pain. She couldn't deal with it when the pain came from someone close. After all they had dreamed together, after being let into the depths of Ryan's ambitions, Marle had been the last person Ryan expected to turn on them. It had been so unexpected. Of anyone, Ryan had expected Poppertrot to be the one with spite in him—but not Marle.

Marle had never been weak until becoming Crow. Once that happened, it seemed every negative quality she possessed had come to light. Ryan had seen a new version of her, one that was cowardly, selfish, and abrasive. Hard to believe they had been thick as thieves once.

Ryan grimaced. It still hurt, thinking about what had happened. And it had all happened so quickly, too—everything within the last two days. How quickly the state of the Post had been upended, her small little bubble of life pierced by her supposed friends and the King's Hand.

It didn't matter. There had been wrenches and bumps thrown into her plans before. Times when she had felt all hope had been lost and every time that happened, she had come out on top. She had come too far to stop now, and she would be tossed into white-fire before she let it end like this. No matter what happened, Ryan *would* escape this place with Eva, Dmitri, Walton, and Poppertrot. And if she didn't, she would die trying.

The orange glow had finally begun to fade from the sky by the time she came out of the tunnels. She had chosen an exit in the market, the closest one to the palace. Unfortunately, there wasn't one that led directly in—she would have to sneak over the inner wall as well as the palace wall, something no courier had ever been able to do.

Before she did that, however, she had someplace to visit.

She stepped out cautiously, the cloak wrapped around her shoulders with the hood up. It blocked the edges of her vision, obscuring her peripherals, but that was a small price to pay to remain hidden from the Seeker. She wouldn't have the cover of night, however. The cloak would shine like a lamp in the dark, attracting the guards to her like moth to a flame. Her only option would be to move as quick as possible.

With her Imperia freely available to use, she bounded onto a nearby building with ease, landing hard on the rooftop and kicking up dust. It felt good to brazenly use her gift—an untethering of sorts. Yet at the same time, she couldn't help but feel a prickling at the back of her neck, or a twisting of her stomach. Was she being foolish, so flagrantly using her powers in the open?

Perhaps. Perhaps not. If there was any time to do so, it was now, when she had nothing left to lose.

Her detour didn't take long. She bounded over the rooftops, closing the gaps between them with ease. She could even leap entire streets. There were no guards posted on top of the walls or buildings to watch for someone traversing them, so she was able to move freely. The only concern she had was that of guards on the streets below—and she had their routes and patterns memorized to avoid them easily enough.

After a few minutes, she came to a small spot on a roof in the south of the market, just on the edge of the slums. Unlike most rooftops in the city, this one was not barren, which made it stick out like a tree in the desert. In the western corner, a small tarp had been propped up by a few sticks, and a sand-covered blanket lay sprawled beneath it, crusted over from repeated exposure to the sun.

Ryan knelt down, almost reverently, as she stared at the small space. This—this was where her life had truly ended, as well as where it had begun. When she had been forced to flee with Eva, to protect her from the Seeker. To anyone else, the tarp and blanket would have seemed nothing more than worthless pieces of fabric. To Ryan, they were filled to the brim with emotions and memories.

And failures.

She had only been on her own for a month. This was where they had slept. Day after day after day of stealing food and finding wet nurses willing to feed Eva had taken its toll. At first, Ryan had tried to steal drops—but she had been beat for that. Food had been easier to steal and people seemed to care about it far less. She would then sell it to street rats or pitying nobles for drops and use that to pay wet nurses. Once, she had resorted to selling herself as a nightsheet—but only once. The memory sent shivers up and down her arms and she quickly banished it from her mind.

Looking back, it seemed a miracle she survived as long as she did. A ten-year-old girl, no skills, no resources, and no family—just determination to keep her and her sister alive.

The constant running and fear had taken its toll on her, however. Finally, she had broken. Finally she had made a mistake of being seen by the guards, and the larger mistake of not losing them when they tailed her. She had thought they would leave her alone once they saw she was a gutter rat.

She had been naïve. And horribly wrong.

She gripped the blanket as she saw the King's Hand that had found her sleeping on the rooftop in her mind's eye. There had been two. One wrested Eva from her arms even as the baby cried out with fear and confusion, while the other shoved her to the ground, whispering what he was going to do to her and her sister. Never had she heard such vile, cruel, and disgusting things leave a man's mouth before or since.

Ryan pulled the blanket to her chest, remembering the deadness that had spread through her even as her body filled with Imperia. She had known the Seeker would find her, but at that moment, she hadn't cared. It had been the only option left to her. Let the guards have her and her sister—or fight back.

She had learned two important lessons that night. The first was that she didn't have the luxury of being selfish. Others only had to worry about themselves. Ryan had to worry about herself *and* Eva. Rest, comfort, and any desires or dreams she had would be foregone until her sister no longer needed to fear the Seeker and the King. It was a promise to herself that she had vowed to keep.

The second was a different kind of lesson. A realization about herself, as she watched the light leave the guards' eyes. Like candles in a gust of wind, she had snuffed them out without hesitation or mercy. It hadn't been personal—it was just what had needed to be done to keep herself and Eva safe.

She would do anything to protect her family. And if that included killing another, one that would do her harm, then so be it.

She pulled away from the blanket, wiping the sand from her hands. Ryan had failed in her promise to herself to protect Eva by letting her be taken. She would have failed back then if Marle hadn't found her right after she had killed the guards. She turned to the palace, staring at the walls that rose around it, obscuring all but the very top of the rounded spires. Beneath those walls, under the palace, lay the dungeons.

If Ryan had to, she would tear them apart at the foundations to mend that promise. She stepped forward, ready to meet her destiny.

You could leave. Alone.

She stopped dead in her tracks. It had been a thought pressing at the edges of her mind for some time, always whispering. Would anyone really blame her if she left? She had done all she could do, sacrificed so much of herself, to protect Eva and get them off Gritt and away from Everfont. More than that, she had even intended to take others with her as well.

It wasn't her fault everything had fallen apart at the end. She had fought against an unfair world stacked against her and lost.

She sucked in a breath and shoved the thought away. She was all Eva had. Life had thrust that responsibility on her at a young age, and though she had chafed at it, she had never abandoned it; and she wasn't about to do so now. She would *not* be like her father, who had thrown away his family for personal gain.

"I will save you," Ryan whispered as she looked at the palace. Resolve strengthened, she once again gripped her Imperia and bounded off across the rooftops.

It took her less than ten minutes to arrive at the inner wall. Scaling it was easy, and like earlier today, she crossed over where there were few guards watching. Some had been assigned back to their posts, but the Water Gardens were mostly still empty. Most of the guards were probably resting from a day's worth of hard work. Those that weren't were probably still in the tunnels, hunting down members of the Post.

That made her job easy. Crouching low to the ground, she flew across the Water Gardens, water squishing beneath her feet, grabbing hold of her Imperia to make herself faster. She didn't use a lot—just enough to push her limits beyond her regular capacity.

A guardsman stepped out from behind one of the homes, directly in her path, squinting at her.

She leapt into the air. He gasped, his cry cutting off as she slammed into him. He grunted as they tumbled to the ground. She got her arms around his neck and began to squeeze, shifting the power of her Imperia from her legs to her arms. He thrashed beneath her, trying to pry free and call for help.

Her muscles grew. Veins in her arms began to bulge as she grew two, then three, then four times stronger than normal.

From the old tales, there was more she could do. Once, she had heard of Imperials that could Amplify clothes—that is, if someone wore them, the wearer would become stronger. Ryan had experimented with that once but had had no success. It seemed only the basic abilities of an Amplifier were available to her.

But oh, how strong that made her.

The guard beneath her began to slacken, his strength spent. His arms fell to his sides as his eyes closed, his head lolling to the side. Ryan gently placed him down, face up, so his mouth wasn't covered by water. Though there was little light, she could faintly see his chest rising and falling.

Good, she thought as she continued onward. She didn't want to kill anyone—most of the King's Hand were rotten to the core and weren't the kind of people Ryan had ever wanted to meet— but they did have families. They were men outside of their role as the enforcers of Everfont, and she would not take a father or mother from their family while working to save her sister unless absolutely necessary.

The same logic didn't apply to the Seeker, or the King. If the opportunity presented itself, she would happily kill either of them.

She reached the palace wall. The outer wall was nearly twelve feet tall, and the inner was double that. The palace walls, however, were close to seventy, and obscured all but the spires and rounded roofs of the palace. Not only that, they were also smooth as butter, making them nearly impossible to climb for anyone without rope.

Ryan was different. With her increased strength, her fingers would be able to dig into the stone and she would be able to scale the sheer face. Such a feat would have been impossible without the cloak—the Seeker would have been on her in moments.

Drying her fingers on her pants, she pressed them into the wall and flared her Imperia. Strength entered her fingers and she pressed them into the stone. For a moment, she met resistance—then the rock crumbled beneath her fingertips.

Grinning, she climbed, increasing the strength in her fingers further. They sunk into the rock, making small indents as she ascended. The skin began to rub away from her fingers, leaving small droplets of blood, but she couldn't stop. If she did, she would lose time, or worse, look down and fall. Her Imperia made her stronger and she might be able to draw on enough to survive hitting the ground, but it wasn't something she wanted to test.

Thankfully, the climb didn't last longer than a minute. She reached the top of the wall and perched on the edge to look inside at the palace itself. She had sworn never to think or look at the place again—yet necessity was the one thing that rendered promises obsolete. Peering down in the dim moonlight, and for the first time in seven years, she allowed herself to look at it without hate or malice.

Welcome home.

Beautiful as a description didn't do it justice and neither did large. The closest thing Ryan could come to describing it was grand, and even that was an inadequate word to be attributed to such a magnificent building.

The wall didn't obscure the tallest parts of the building, of course, and everyone in Everfont had seen the ten rounded roofs on the pillars of the palace, as well as the spires that stretched high into the sky. None of the common folk, however, had seen the full majesty of the palace hidden behind the walls. It was a shame, in Ryan's opinion.

It was built of the shiniest metal she had ever seen. It glowed gold, even in the moonlight, sending out shimmering yellow rays. There seemed to be hundreds of windows, each one adorned with jewels and ornate, unique carvings. The doors were large and made of wood, enough that you could have built two or three homes in the Post.

A nice exterior, to hide the wretch inside.

She shook herself free of her stupor and began to climb down the other side—slower than she had risen. She wouldn't have another opportunity to gawk at the palace—this might be the last time she ever saw it from the outside—but saving Poppertrot and Eva was more important than sightseeing.

She reached the grass surrounding the palace and scurried across it to the front door. Surprisingly, there were no guards, but in retrospect, that made sense to Ryan. No one was strong enough to climb the palace wall, and besides the front gate, that was the only way in.

Still, she wasn't in the clear just yet. The palace was large and she had very little insight of the design. Though she had spent her youth there, she had been confined mostly to her rooms and hadn't been able to explore. She didn't doubt she could spend hours doing so now, trying to find the dungeons—but time was short. Plus, there was also the chance there could be guards inside, waiting for intruders.

She grabbed the front door and pulled. It was at least six times her size in both height and width, yet it moved as easily as sand in the breeze. It swung open silently and she hurried in, pulling it closed behind her.

Cool and humid wind met her as she entered. To her right was a waiting room and to her left there were three doors, each leading to somewhere Ryan knew not where. In front was a grand hall, with a large geyser roaring up close to the ceiling, before crashing back down. Ryan knew what it was even though she had never seen it before.

The Wellspring. The source of all life in Everfont. The palace was built right on top of it, so its residents had full access to its life-giving contents. It shot high into the air, almost as tall as the palace itself, before falling into a large pond that extended into the ground. Fine mist coated the area around it, rolling across the ground in waves.

Ryan stepped up to the natural wonder and peered into the depths. Some of the water from the Wellspring fell on her as she stared into the transparent depths. She was surprised at how deep it was. The size of the pond had been artificially expanded, but even still, it looked much larger than she had expected. The bottom seemed a great distance away, distorted, and small.

She tore her gaze away from the Wellspring, reminding herself of her purpose.

Think, she told herself. There had to be a way to find the dungeons. From what she remembered, they weren't on the ground floor, neither were they on the second. Perhaps the third? But no, no that wasn't right either. The King lived on the third. It wouldn't be there. Too many options, and her memory was hardly what it was. So that left the fifth, sixth, seventh and the basement floors, all of which had so many rooms she could search forever and still not find them.

Moving away from the Wellspring, she backtracked and went to the waiting room, which was the size of a regular room. Might as well finish her delivery while she was here. She could worry about finding the others in a moment.

On the far wall was a large bookshelf that extended to the ceiling, along with several tables and soft, luxurious chairs. She ignored those and instead moved to the books and pulled one from its place, titled *The Selfless Man's Charge*. As a child, she remembered the King reading this often, and it was less dusty than the other tomes. She pulled the envelope from her pocket and slipped it inside the front cover, then left it on one of the tables.

The instructions had said to deliver the letter to the palace. An absurd request—no mail entered the palace walls. However, the sender had been anonymous and had explained there was no time limit for the delivery—only that it should be done at some point. Most in the Post had seen the letter as a challenge—would anyone dare to attempt a delivery to the King's doorstep?

Returning to the Wellspring, she began to pace while she examined the water. Now that was out of the way, all that was left was to find the others, something she still had no idea how to do without taking until morning.

The simplest solution would be to find a guard or a servant and force them to give her directions—but then she would have to cart around a hostage. Even if she did find Eva and Popper-trot, there would be no way to keep the servant from crying for help unless Ryan knocked them out or killed them—and the thought left a distasteful feeling in her stomach.

The people here weren't evil. They were just trying to make a living. It was best to involve as few people as possible.

So, who, then, could she use as a guide?

An idea sprung to her mind. A dangerous, reckless idea. But, it was the only one she had. Removing the cloak from her back, she knelt at the side of the Wellspring and drew from her Imperia.

⌐

The Seeker remembered the day he was born.

He couldn't even remember the name he had been born with, so much time had passed—but that first memory, that first speck of intelligence, was clear as day. It had been messy. Painful. Darkness, followed by blood flowing around him, and a sudden burst of light. After that, everything was a bit fuzzy. As a boy, he had been told his mother had died in childbirth, an event not uncommon in those days. His father had beaten him for it, nonetheless. Had told him if he hadn't been such a terrible child, his mother wouldn't have died.

The Seeker had been inclined to believe him. Surrounded by bloodstained walls and fingernail-scratched floor, he could still hear his victims crying out for mercy, their whimpers echoing through the halls. No one heard them besides him. They were so far underground the Seeker wasn't even sure the gods could hear the screams.

He knew if his father could see him, he would have given him a good thrashing, maybe even killed him. "Your obsession with blood isn't healthy," he had said. "You're a Healer, but that doesn't mean you should use your power recklessly," he had said. "Don't cut yourself just to see the blood," he had said.

The Seeker had tried to stop. Truly, he had tried. He wanted to be a good boy for his father. He had resisted the urge for days, and it built up for so long until he couldn't stand it anymore.

Then, he killed. He still remembered the first time. It had been in the slums of Aredine, a city lost to the desert several centuries ago. In the dead of night, he had gone looking and had found an elderly woman, half dead from starvation and cold. At first, she had thought he was there to give her some free drops.

How wrong she had been. Her death had gone unnoticed for days, and when someone finally said anything, no one had really cared. She had been a nobody. But the thrill of the blood leaving her body, coursing out of her veins and onto the Seeker's hands, watching the color leave her form, had been a rush he had never forgotten. It reminded him of the day he was born. So wet, so disgusting—yet at the same time, exquisite and enlightening.

That moment had been the only moment the gods had allowed him to share with his mother. He had been seeking more like it ever since. Moments where he could bask in the gore, let it slide over him, so he could feel close to his mother once more. He was sure had she survived, she would have protected him from his father. She would have loved him, despite the monster he was.

His murders had continued from that day. Over and over, he lost the struggle within to resist his urges—and every time he relented, every time his hands plunged into the flesh of another, his heart soared as he felt closer to the woman that had died to give him life. When the elation had passed, however, he was left with nothing but guilt and shame—and so the cycle continued.

His father had always suspected his son to be the one committing the murders, but never had proof. How could a boy with no eyes kill so many people? Yet the lack of evidence hadn't stopped the beatings. The Seeker could still remember those vividly as well.

The toll of losing his wife and having a murderer for a son proved too much for the Seeker's father, however—and he passed before the Seeker was even five. With no one left to hinder him, the Seeker had stalked the streets of Aredine, preying on anyone unfortunate enough to cross him.

When he had been born, Aredine had already been on the edge of the desert and by his ninth year, nearly everyone had left. The stragglers left behind, the Seeker finished—then he fled to the city of Kindling. There, tales of a phantom in the night had already spread. They had called him by a different title than "the Seeker" back then—but their terror was the same.

Kindling eventually went the same as Aredine, lost to the desert. The Seeker fled to two more cities, those also lost to the desert, before arriving at the last place on Gritt that had yet to fall prey to the shifting sands. The slums of Everfont had been the perfect hunting ground for him. At least, until the kings of old had found him.

"Please . . . please, stop."

The Seeker turned around, looking at the member of the King's Hand he had captured. It was an interesting dilemma he faced. The man was an Imperial Healer, and the Seeker had never caught one of them before. Most had escaped in the early days of the purge. They had the capacity to heal, as he did, from any wound inflicted on their body—provided they were nourished well enough. If the Seeker kept this man well fed, he could torture him for as long and as often as he desired.

That meant more blood. More time with his precious mother. More time to feel loved.

But . . . he turned away, suddenly guilty. This man was not deserving of such treatment. No one was. It wasn't right of the Seeker to use another for his own selfish purposes. He had been taught better than that and if his father saw him, he would get a beating. He bowed his head, remembering his father striking him over and over and over. All because he had been an Imperial.

He straightened. Things weren't like that anymore. The kings of Everfont had seen his value, even if they were always afraid of him. He had been used as an assassin for several decades now—maybe longer. Time was irrelevant to him. The latest king had even expanded his duties and he was able to hunt more often, and in so doing felt close to his mother. So, the Seeker he was.

He would do his job, and he would do it well. And he would try not to exult in the joy it gave him, to see another die. A man shouldn't be happy to kill. But a man also shouldn't deny his gods-given pleasures and desires. So it was that the Seeker was thankful for his job as assassin and executioner. He could be a sanctioned murderer, so long as he only murdered Imperials.

He grabbed a knife from his table of instruments and stepped toward Samuel. He had had his fun with this one. The man looked at him with terror and shriveled up, trying to appear as small as possible.

Then the Seeker felt it.

He froze steps away from Samuel. Goosebumps raced up and down his skin and he took a step back. Someone . . . someone was using Imperia. Here. In the palace.

The King.

The Seeker dropped the knife and ran up the stairs, through the tunnels. The King was the only one who saw his true talent, who had true need of him. If he died, the Seeker would be alone, with no justification for his murders. No higher purpose to the slaughter.

He would *never* return to that.

⤺

Ryan retied the cloak around her shoulders and moved out of the great hall. Her movements were lethargic as she stopped at one of the pillars, struggling to breathe evenly. She wasn't used to using so much Imperia and it was more draining than she had expected. . . . Still, she couldn't stop to rest. With a resigned sigh, she began climbing.

The last place people ever thought was to look up. People typically looked for hiding holes, behind dressers and hidden doors—but rarely did they ever look in the rafters. The knowledge had helped her repeatedly escape the King's Hand and others that would have done her harm. Thankfully, the ceiling here was a mixture of white, grey, and silver, and with her cloak on, she blended quite well, which added another level of protection.

With her fingers comfortably digging into the plaster, she waited. The thought crossed her mind that maybe she was being foolish. Using her powers to draw out the Seeker? Walton would have a fit and Dmitri would have called her crazy. Poppertrot would have approved, though Ryan wasn't sure his opinion really counted.

It took less than twenty minutes. The black figure strode into the great hall, an anxious spring to his step. He stopped at the place Ryan had used her Imperia and cocked his head, confused. He stared at the spot for a long time until finally knocking on a nearby door. After a moment, a disheveled-looking man in a guard uniform answered, his face growing pale as he saw the Seeker. They exchanged quiet whispers and although Ryan couldn't hear what was being said, the message was clear.

The guard hastily removed himself from the room and headed further into the palace. After him, two women, hardly dressed at all, exited the room. They kept their heads down as the Seeker watched them leave through the front. Once they were gone, he swung back around and continued to stare at the spot Ryan had used her powers.

Then, he too, waited.

Ryan clung to the ceiling, almost not daring to breathe. This was the closest she had ever come to facing the Seeker. Chills ran down her arms and sweat beaded her skin. All it would take was for him to look up and squint, and he would see her.

He didn't. He just continued to stare at the ground, as if confused by what he saw. He was a middle-sized man—he wasn't tall, but he was by no means short. He had broad shoulders, and though his face was covered by a mask, Ryan could tell it was more of an angular face. The whole time he stood watching the ground, he didn't move. He didn't sway from side to side, as most people would, and he did not pace or scratch his head.

He stood like a statue. Unmoving, as though he were dead.

A second round of chills ran up and down Ryan's arms. Crives, the stories weren't too far off from the real thing. Even just sitting here, she could tell this was a man—or thing—she didn't want to mess with.

After what felt ages, the guard came back, the King following closely behind. He had a disheveled appearance, and he was wearing a robe wrapped loosely around his frame. He was barefoot and had a slight pinkish expression on his cheeks that grew redder when he saw the Seeker. The Seeker, upon seeing the King, got down on one knee and bowed his head.

"Leave us," the Seeker said to the guard, his voice louder than before, though it was still faint and barely discernable above the sound of the Wellspring crashing around itself. The man was all too happy to oblige, quickly locking himself in the room he had come from, leaving only the King and the Seeker in the grand hall.

"I trust you have a good reason for interrupting me," the King said flatly. He didn't yell, but his voice was laced with anger, annoyance, and a twinge of fear. Even being ruler of Everfont did not preclude him from the terror the Seeker inspired.

If the Seeker noticed the King was afraid of him, he didn't show it. He rose and gestured to the floor. "There's an Imperial in your palace." His voice wasn't what Ryan had been expecting. It . . . sounded normal. A flat, not too high, not too low kind of voice. Not gravelly, like a demon either. Just . . . a voice like anyone else.

"An Imperial?" The King's eyes narrowed. "Impossible."

The Seeker shook his head. "They used their powers right here. I can see it lingering—the color. A great burst of energy."

"Are you sure you aren't just seeing things?" the King asked angrily. "You told me it's an imprecise art."

"It was a powerful wave," the Seeker said softly. "I felt it all the way down in my chambers."

The King was silent for a moment. "Then shouldn't there be a trail?"

"The Imperia residue coalesces here, and then stops," the Seeker said. There was a dangerous, scared edge in his tone.

The King understood the implication immediately. He looked sharply at the Seeker. "You think someone knows what you are?"

"There are ways to hide from Soulseers," the Seeker said, "but few know them."

The King swore. "If they know to hide from you, why use their powers? They could have gone undetected."

The Seeker frowned. "A distraction," he breathed softly. "They wanted me to be distracted."

"From what?"

"I'm not sure. Perhaps an assassination attempt, or a thief come to steal treasures."

The King shook his head. "There is nothing to steal. If they had come to kill me, they would have been done with it already. It has to be something else." His eyes narrowed. "I thought you had finished off all the Imperials left in the city."

The Seeker lowered his voice. Ryan was already straining to hear them over the sound of the Wellspring, but now it was impossible to hear.

The King growled, displeased with the answer, but he didn't raise his hand, something that was uncharacteristic of him. He was a brutal ruler, known to beat men and women for the slightest inconvenience.

Or so it was said. Ryan had never experienced such beatings as a young girl and her mother had never sported any bruises. In fact, that came from the many rumors that milled around the Post. Ryan thought it more likely the King would seek retribution in subtler ways.

So why not arrange for this man to be quietly executed or exiled? If he was such a threat that he instilled fear into the most powerful man on Gritt, why not get rid of him? Yet, the Seeker seemed . . . loyal, for some reason. And the King, despite his reservations, seemed to place value on his presence.

There's more here than what I'm seeing, Ryan thought with discomfort. She had known the King for the early years of her life and remembered his expressions well. Never had she seen him act this way. Had something changed in the last seven years?

"Check on the prisoners," the King said suddenly.

"My Lord . . . ?"

"See if there is a small girl among them, seven years of age. She might have blonde or brown hair. If there is one like that, bring her to me. I think I know who might be causing this."

Ryan closed her eyes as a pit opened in her stomach. The King was no fool. He knew she was here, somewhere, and had to be here for a reason. The only reason she would return was to rescue someone.

Right then, right there, she wanted to drop down and strangle him. She wanted vengeance for the suffering he had caused. Her fingers loosed, if only for a moment, as she leaned forward.

She calmed herself, gripping tighter into the wall. Killing them now would be a death sentence upon Eva, and any chance of escape would vanish in the wind. If the choice was vengeance or Eva, it was no choice at all.

Her sister would always come first.

The Seeker bowed and stalked from the room. The King left moments later, and Ryan climbed down from her perch, back onto the ground floor. As quietly as she could, she followed the Seeker, huddling close to the ground as though it would keep her from being seen. Every once in a while, he would hastily glance back, as if suspecting he was being followed, but the glances were so quick Ryan doubted he saw anything.

He took her on a route she was unfamiliar with. In her childhood, she had grown up in the northern section of the palace, on the fourth floor. There she had been sequestered away, hidden away from the world by her mother. Locked in those small rooms, she had dreamed of adventure and faraway lands where water was plentiful, and the land was as green as the eye could see. She had begged to be let out of her rooms to get just a taste of what was out there.

How naïve she had been. She would have thought she was foolish, had she not seen the childlike innocence of Eva. A child's imagination and their ability to see the good in the world was not foolishness, but rather a virtue, and should have been cherished. Instead, Ryan's had been squashed, and she had learned the hard way what life was really like.

It was why she tried so hard to protect Eva. Whatever happened to Ryan herself, she wanted Eva to still believe in the good—to retain that innocence as long as possible.

After a while, they came to a small door sequestered in a dismal section of the palace. The Seeker threw it open to reveal a spiral staircase before he descended. Ryan followed behind, anxiety thudding louder in her chest with every passing moment. They were already so far into the palace, and the further they went, the less likely escape became. Already she had doubts about her capacity to save Eva. What about Poppertrot, or the others that had been captured? Was she just going to leave them?

The way down the stairs was dimly lit. Ryan could barely see as she crept down the stones, squinting in the darkness. She wondered how the Seeker could move so swiftly in the dim lighting, with no hesitation. Thankfully, the spiral staircase wasn't long, and at the end, it deposited into a long hallway, with cell doors on either side.

"I'm seeking a young girl. Seven, with brown hair."

Shivers ran up Ryan's spine. Up ahead, she could see the Seeker, peering past iron bars into different cells. His hands were clasped behind his back as he walked back and forth, head tilted slightly as he examined the prisoners. Ryan's blood ran cold. It was said that, if the Seeker was near an Imperial, he could sense them even if they weren't using their abilities. If he laid his eyes on Eva . . .

"You'll get nothing from us, monster," a familiar voice said. Ryan recognized it as belonging to one of the council members, Kinroia. She was an older woman in charge of medicine in the Post. If anyone had the fight in them to still talk back, it would be her.

"Quiet yourself. I am not here to harm most of you," the Seeker said, unperturbed by Kinroia's comments. He continued walking past the cells until he came to an abrupt stop near the end. "You. You are the one I'm looking for."

A murmur ran through the prison. Ryan crept forward, hugging the wall, trying to remain out of the Seeker's vision.

"What do you want with her?" another voice asked. Ryan's breath caught in her throat. It was Poppertrot.

"The King has business with her," the Seeker said. "She is an Imperial. A powerful one. Her soul blazes like a dark green sun at noonday."

Gasps went through the crowd. Ryan cursed silently. No doubt, it was Eva. And the rumors were true as well. The Seeker could sense when people were Imperials, without them using their powers.

"You can tell the King he can lick the sand off my boots before he has her."

Gratitude for Poppertrot welled within Ryan's heart. He was a criver at the best of times, but underneath his snarky exterior, there was a soft underbelly. Yet she worried—would the Seeker kill him if he tried to fight back?

She reached for her messenger bag, intending to draw forth the dagger. There would never be a better opportunity than now to strike, while the Seeker was distracted.

She had just slipped her hand past the open flap when something cold slapped against her arm. She jumped, heart leaping into her throat. She whirled around, raising a fist, and drawing Imperia to strike before she froze.

Dmitri stood behind her, his face a mask of iron. In his hand, he held a sword, laid across her arm, pointed straight at her heart.

"Dmitri . . ." she gaped, lost for words. "How . . . ?"

"Don't move," Dmitri commanded. His voice held a tone she had never heard from him before. Hardened. Bitter. "Or I'll run you through."

The words were like a slap in the face. No, worse. This was Dmitri. Her closest friend and confidant. The man who had been her support for the last seven years and the one she had hoped would be for many more.

"Dmitri, what are you doing?" Ryan hissed, glancing back at the Seeker. He had opened the cell door and was stepping inside. "We need to save Eva."

Dmitri didn't respond. Instead, his eyes flicked toward the Seeker. "Be quick about grabbing her. The King is waiting for us."

There were sounds of a struggle in the cell. Suddenly, the Seeker was pressed up against the bars, held there by Poppertrot. He pulled back and then rammed the Seeker against them again, and they bent from the force of the blow. The Seeker grimaced and pulled something from his belt. Members of the Post in other cells began shouting while the ones near Poppertrot and the Seeker cowered.

"No!" Ryan screamed, lurching forward to help, but Dmitri grabbed her arm and twisted, holding her back. The Seeker buried a dagger in Poppertrot's stomach. The Trompkin grunted, stumbling backward, clutching his abdomen. He doubled over, and blood leaked through his fingers.

The Seeker nonchalantly dropped the dagger on the ground as he stepped past Poppertrot. "You'll bleed out in a few hours. Use the dagger to end your suffering sooner."

"Throw yourself into white-fire, criver," Poppertrot responded, spitting at the Seeker. He reached for the Seeker, but the man deftly stepped away. In one smooth motion, he turned and slammed his foot into Poppertrot's face. The Trompkin flew upward, his head twisting to the side before he slammed back onto the cold cobblestone, unmoving.

Ryan gasped, grabbing her Imperia. With her added strength, she yanked herself free, but Dmitri slammed the pommel of his sword into her head. The world went dark, and she felt herself falling. Her vision returned a moment later and she found herself on the ground. Shouts echoed through the chambers as people begged Ryan to save them. The Seeker was leaving the cell, carrying a small girl in his arms. He glanced toward Ryan, a grim smile spreading beneath the fabric on his head.

"Eva . . ." she groaned. She tried to crawl forward, but Dmitri kicked her in the back, and she went sprawling.

"Don't make this more difficult than it has to be," Dmitri said. "You'll come with us and there will be no resistance. If there is, we will kill her. I don't want to, but we will. Do you understand?"

Ryan hesitated, then nodded mutely, her vision swimming. Dmitri dragged her to her feet, and the world spun while her head throbbed where she had been struck.

"The King is in the throne room," Dmitri said coldly. "Let's not keep him waiting."

Chapter Five

THE THRONE ROOM WAS DIFFERENT FROM HOW RYAN remembered it.

When she had been a girl, it had been a lavish place. Ornamented with all kinds of gold, paintings, and suits of armor. Now it was an empty room. The walls were a dull, opaque white, save for the ceiling, and there was no throne. Just a larger than ordinary chair with no ornaments or carvings to distinguish it from anything else.

The King sat there. An older man, though not too old. He was a decade Marle's senior but at forty-two, he looked young for his age. His hair was a vibrant black, but greying, and his face had yet to be marred by wrinkles.

Ryan had always been terrified of that face. Now she loathed it as well.

Her head still throbbed as they came to a stop before him. The Seeker kicked her legs out from behind her, forcing her into a kneeling position while he and Dmitri bowed. The King gave them each a brief nod and they rose. Ryan remained kneeling, until Dmitri dragged her to her feet once again.

She met the King's green eyes with a defiant gaze. The King returned her glare with a weary look. "How is Marle?"

Ryan could see the pain in his eyes. So—he had cared for his wife. It was surprising she had been the first thing he asked about. Marle would have been happy—and sad—to hear that. "She's leader of the Post now."

The King nodded, as if that made sense. "I had thought as much. The letters delivered sounded so much like her. I would have thought she would have picked a wittier name than 'Crow.' I'm not surprised she's become the leader of that vagrant community. She did find a way to help you and your sister evade the Seeker." He shook his head. "I've missed her since the day she left. I knew she would, as soon as I told her what happened to your mother. Still, she must have changed some. I can see it in her words, the way she speaks. More confident, less timid. People always change when you least expect it."

He paused and looked up at the ceiling before meeting Ryan's eyes. "It's been a long time since I've seen her. A long time since I've seen you."

"I wish it had been longer," Ryan said in response. The Seeker moved to kick her, but the King raised his hand.

"No. She has more reason than most to hate me, and I do not fault her for it," he said. He rose from his small chair and strode toward them. His eyes flicked toward Eva, who was trembling with fear in the Seeker's arms, before moving back to Ryan. "I hoped this day would never come."

Ryan barked a laugh. "You mean you hoped we had died on the streets?"

"Yes," the King said frankly. "I don't hate you. I don't hate your sister either. And I didn't hate your mother."

Bald, blatant lies! Ryan could still see it as if it were yesterday. The moment her life had changed.

Don't—don't think of it. . . .

"Then why did you kill her?" Ryan whispered, trying to force back tears. She could barely force the words out. It was the question that kept her awake at night, caused her to toss and turn. It was the reason she had fled, and she had wanted to have the answers for so long. Seconds away from hearing why, she wasn't sure she wanted to know anymore. She just wanted to take her sister and leave.

The memory played through her mind in a flash, unable to be suppressed any longer. Her mother, viciously attacking her uncle with long nails and a dinner knife hidden in her dress. Her father, wrenching the knife from her hands and tossing it aside. Her uncle, ramming the sword he always carried at his side through her chest as tears fell down his face.

"I didn't want to," the King said. "Gods know I tried to reason myself out of it. It was a sacrifice that was necessary for Everfont."

"Why? Because she was an Imperial?" Ryan spat. She was crying. Crives, she was crying in front of the man she hated most. She was so weak.

"No. Because she had Imperial children," the King said. "Do you even know why I've had all the Imperials killed?"

"Because they are a power you can't control."

"Correct," the King said. He motioned toward Dmitri. "You may let her go."

Dmitri frowned. "Is that wise?"

"She has no power here. If she attacks me, her sister's life is forfeit," the King said, nodding toward the Seeker. The man stood motionless, and Eva seemed to grow smaller in his clutches. She had said nothing the entire walk and Ryan suspected she was in shock. Seeing Poppertrot stabbed and her older sister beaten would have crushed her.

Dmitri hesitated, then let go of Ryan.

For a fraction of a second, Ryan considered attacking the King. This man, who had been the cause of so much pain in Everfont, was within her clutches. With him gone, someone else, someone from a different family, could liberate the city and end the tyranny and suffering. She had even told herself, if she had the opportunity to kill the King, she wouldn't hesitate.

All it would require was the sacrifice of her sister.

Ryan looked at Eva. Her younger sister's eyes were wide and pleading, and Ryan's shoulders slumped. She couldn't do it. Crive her, but she wouldn't trade Eva's life for anything. She wiped her eyes and stared at the King with all the defiance she could muster.

The King nodded. "See? Even someone that hates me as much as Ryan will do something against her natural inclinations with the right motivations." He extended a hand. "Walk with me."

Defeated, Ryan stepped forward, though she didn't take the King's hand. He lowered his arm and clasped his hands behind his back, walking around the small throne. There was a door at the back of the audience chamber, and he opened it for her. She stepped outside, onto a balcony, into the dark of night where the twin moons hung, surrounded by stars. The King walked right up to the railing and motioned for her to join him. Behind them, Dmitri and the Seeker followed, stopping just inside the doorway.

"Look out to the horizon," the King said. "Tell me what you see."

Ryan grimaced but did as instructed. There was nothing. Nothing but sand, spreading as far as the eye could see. "The desert."

"Good. And how far does the desert extend?"

"Forever," Ryan said.

The King nodded. "Almost true. I've sent scouts to see if there are other parts of the world besides Everfont where we can live. Other places that have water. Do you know what they found?"

"Nothing," Ryan said.

"Wrong. They found ruins, many of them, which tell a tale that there was at one point other cities besides Everfont. More importantly, they found water. Water that stretched out as far as you could see, just like the desert. But, as the first man unfortunately found out, it was full of salt and undrinkable. Therefore, uninhabitable." His eyes became vacant as he spoke. "And of no use to us."

He had often done this when she was younger. Visiting unannounced to talk to his sister and niece. During that time, he had been much kinder. He had told her stories, laughed with their mother, and even played dolls with them. Occasionally, there had been a lecture, which Ryan had found boring in her youth. As she had grown older, however, she had become more fascinated with the stories of history, and many rumors of Gritt and Everfont and their origin circulated around the Post.

Ryan found herself drawn into her uncle's monologue. The rumors in the Post were just that—rumors. Here was actual information, something she had developed an interest in and could learn about. At the same time, she seethed inside. She hated that something she had a desire to know more of came from the man she most despised.

"What does it matter then?" she asked, trying to be as obstinate as possible. Perhaps, there was still a way out of this. She glanced at the Seeker, who still held her sister. They had taken her cloak but had left her bag alone. Inside, the dagger and vial sat undisturbed. If she could somehow wrest Eva away . . .

She stole a glance. Eva's eyes were wide and terrified, flicking back and forth between Ryan and the King. Thankfully, she was keeping her Imperia under control, though how long that would last Ryan couldn't say. Her sister, although valiant in her efforts to learn to control her power, had not yet achieved mastery.

The Seeker, on the other hand, stood passive and immobile, his face a mystery behind the mask he continually wore. A chill ran down Ryan's spine and up her arms and neck, despite how warm the room was. He was so still, like a statue. It was like he wasn't even human.

Dmitri tensed, hand on his sword. He was watching Ryan closely, awaiting any sudden movement. He drew his lips into a thin line at Ryan's glance. She returned her attention to the King, a knot forming in her chest.

Why? she thought. The suddenness of it still sent her head spiraling. Had this been planned? Or had it been something recently decided?

With a crooked finger, the King motioned them back inside. Ryan followed, as did Dmitri and the Seeker. In the audience room, the King pointed to the ceiling, which had a mural painted over it. It depicted a vibrant scene—trees grew in various places, and there were lakes and rivers and grass. People were farming in fields and different animals were scattered throughout the countryside. As the mural wrapped around the ceiling, however, the grass and the people and the animals all disappeared, leaving only an arid wasteland in their stead.

"This is not a fanciful depiction of Gritt," the King said. "This palace was built thousands of years ago, before the desertification ever began. When the land still had energy and life and creatures. Before it was dying. The ruins my scouts found attest to this fact as well."

He reached under the throne and pulled out a small, silver cylinder. It was completely smooth, barely bigger than the palm of his hand, yet he held it with reverence. "Soon, the desert will overtake this place. The Wellspring will cease and the last of this world's water will dry up. And then we will all be dead."

"Then why don't we leave?" Ryan said through gritted teeth. "You're the King. Why not order everyone to the safety of another world? The funnel exists. I know people have left and come back."

The King clucked his tongue. "Because there is a greater threat than desertification."

"I think you're just afraid the people won't let you rule anymore," Ryan said.

"You could not be further from the truth," the King said. He held up the silver cylinder. "Do you know what this is?"

"Couldn't guess."

"Then let me explain. This is called a bomb—and if I arm it, it has the capacity to destroy all of Everfont, as well as the Post, and turn all the sand within a fifty-mile radius to glass."

Ryan's blood ran cold. That little tube? It was no larger than her forearm. "You're lying. Not even Imperials hold that kind of power."

"Correct. Which brings us to the root of the problem," the King explained. "Niall, Rim, Wulfenraast, and other worlds—they're all stuck in the past. They all rely on their Imperials for technology, for their armies, for advancement. They're stagnant. In a thousand years, not a single one has ever grown closer to developing new technology. Elementalists carry water and heat baths. Amplifiers do all the heavy lifting and work. Spacers transport goods. Etchers are used for a variety of everyday uses. Memorists retain perfect memories and invalidate the need for books and written communication. Society never becomes better."

He spoke the last word with bitterness and anger. There was a dark expression on his face, one filled with malice. Ryan had seen that look once before, when he had learned Eva was an Imperial.

"This bomb," the King hefted it in the air, "came from a planet called Evaamara. Most have never heard of it, even on other worlds, and it took me several years to find. But when I did, I found a world of wonders. Ships that flew through the air and traveled into the stars. Weapons that could kill a man from miles away. Levers that poured never-ending water, just like the Wellspring. Lights that lit a room with no oil or fire. Infigalians with no soul."

He turned and put the silver cylinder back in its place, beneath the throne. "I realized how behind we were. How primitive our civilization is and all the other worlds around us. When I returned from my journey, I found my father had died and my mother had taken ill. I was to inherit the throne. When I was crowned king, I knew the charge lay at my feet. I would take Gritt and make it the greatest world among the stars. It all started with getting rid of the Imperials."

"You're insane," Ryan whispered.

"Just . . . determined," he said, searching for the right word. "If we hung onto the old ways, always relying on Imperials and the magic they carried, we would never advance. We could never invent technology to rival the ancient places of the universe. I killed them to force our society forward. Since Imperia is passed down through genetics, or as you would say, blood, I had to have everyone with distant Imperial relations executed as well."

"You don't have enough time," Ryan fumbled, growing sicker with every word he said, trying to think of a way to dissuade him. "You said yourself the desert is growing. Even if you could make technology like that, it will be years before you discover it."

"Hundreds of years, actually," the King said with a smile, "but there are ways to cheat death. And there are ways to slow the desertification, too, with technology. We may not know of them yet, but we will discover them. My scholars are already looking into it as we speak, searching for ways to breathe new life into this land."

"The Water Gardens," Ryan said, struck with a realization. "You made them to stop the desertification."

"Yes. Very astute, Ryan. By tapping into the Wellspring, we found a method to transport large amounts of water to places that had long since dried up. The Wellspring never runs dry, so it's the perfect source. We've been able to plant trees that had gone extinct long ago and plant grass in the Water Gardens. We can even farm there. Right now, we're genetically altering plants, so they need less water to survive. The hope is to rejuvenate the desert one day." His eyes shone as he spoke. "We're still a long way away from being like the worlds of Evaamara. But we will breathe life back into this planet. I will save my people and defend them from any threat. That includes you."

His eyes dimmed and Ryan could see genuine pain on his face. "Ordering the execution of every Imperial in Everfont damaged my soul. It nearly ripped me apart, but I endured. A king must make hard choices. They must sacrifice the few for the good of the many. Even then, I thought I would never feel happiness again, that nothing could rival the pain I was feeling then, but I was wrong. Soon after, I learned my sister was giving birth to Imperial children. Children that could use magic." He shook his head. "I died that day."

"You could have let us leave," Ryan said. "You could have let us run away."

The King shook his head. "No. Letting my own family have mercy when I had already killed hundreds of others for the sake of progress? It would have been hypocrisy of the highest order, a lie that could have toppled all I've worked for. My only option was to treat you the same as everyone else, whether you were family or not." His eyes flashed dangerously. "But I was too slow. Your mother heard what I intended to do, and she attacked me. It was only the intervention of your father that saved me. He was one of my advisors, you see, in this grand scheme. I trusted him so much I gave him a room next to my own. We spent many long nights discussing how to save Gritt. Without him, your mother may very well have succeeded in ending my life."

Ryan closed her eyes. "You threw him out for saving your life."

"I spared him. He knew what you and your sister were," the King said, "but he saved me, and I repay my debts. How I agonized over the two of you escaping. I thought all had been lost.

But you've been returned to me now, and the pieces of the board are fixed."

He looked to the Seeker with tears in his eyes. "I ask you to make it quick."

The Seeker nodded. "It shall be done, my Lord."

The King turned to Dmitri. "As for you—you will be paid what you are owed."

Ryan's eyes snapped toward Dmitri. His face was cold as he nodded.

"Dmitri . . . ?" Ryan asked. She could hardly breathe.

He didn't face her as he spoke. "My father was an Imperial. A Psychomancer, but I'm not. I'm normal. The Seeker killed my father and I was taken by the King's Hand because I have Imperial blood. For years, I rotted in prison. Until the King offered me a deal. I find you, and your sister, and he pays for me to leave." He turned to her. "You were my ticket away from here."

Ryan's heart shattered as tears returned to her eyes. "But . . . our dreams . . . our new life together . . ."

"A sham," Dmitri said. His eyes flickered and for a moment, Ryan could see regret in his eyes, the guilt at his choice. "I need a clean slate. One where I can leave all this behind me."

He turned away. "Send my drops directly to Sul. There's something I need to grab from the Post first."

"It will be done," the King said. Dmitri left the audience hall without looking back. Ryan watched him go, stealing away a part of her with him.

A soft sob formed in her chest at the pain. She closed her eyes and breathed in sharply. She hurt—but now was not the time to deal with that. She could grieve later.

"Now," the King clasped his hands behind his back once Dmitri was gone. "The Seeker will take you both to the dungeons below."

"If I refuse?" Ryan said, though there was no heart in it. Beside her, the Seeker tightened his grip on Eva, digging his finger into her side, forcing her to let out a scream. "Stop, stop! I'll go."

"Good girl," the King said. He sat down on his throne and looked up at her. The bravado and the excitement from before had faded, leaving a tired old man before her. Suddenly, his black hair no longer seemed to shine, and he had more wrinkles than before. His voice was haggard as he whispered, "I'm sorry, Ryan. I wish it didn't have to be this way."

"It doesn't," Ryan said as she was led from the audience hall. "It's just the easiest option for you."

She didn't hear his response as they walked away. The Seeker held tightly onto her sister and made her walk in front as they headed back to the dungeons. She thought of pulling out the dagger and ramming it into his chest, but she couldn't do that while he held Eva. She would have to wait until he put her down.

There would be a moment. She just had to be patient and wait for it. She had to believe there would be. If she thought otherwise, she would lose the will to keep moving forward.

⤳

Marle was waiting for Dmitri when he returned.

She stood at the entrance that led to the Water Gardens—the one that let out as close to the palace as possible. That was where he would be coming from. Sure enough, his form appeared in the hallway after a small wait. He saw her instantly and gave her a frigid stare.

"Figured it out?" he asked. Gone was the friendliness from his voice. Gone was the man Marle had known. In his place was an imposter, a shell of someone she had once called friend.

She slapped him when he came close. Once. Then twice. He did nothing to stop her. The slaps didn't seem to faze him; instead, he seemed to embrace them.

"You were the spy," she said softly. "You were the one feeding the King information."

There had been a leak for a while. Marle had first noticed it when she had been going over the ledgers. Little inconsistencies in the numbers. Some of the funds the Post had accrued had gone missing. More couriers being caught than normal. Little things most people wouldn't think to look for.

But Marle, despite being a terrible Crow, was an unparalleled statistician.

"A little late on that, Marle," Dmitri said. "I expected you to figure it out sooner."

"I didn't expect it to be one of the couriers," Marle said. "Then again, you are the ones with the least supervision. We handpick each of you, and you worked so close with Ryan . . ."

"She didn't know," Dmitri said. "She wasn't supposed to know. That's the whole point of being a spy." He sucked in a breath. "It's too late now. The King has her."

Marle slapped him again. She went for a fourth, but he grabbed her wrist and anger flashed across his face. "Out of respect for our friendship, I'll pretend you haven't been doing that."

"Our friendship built on lies?" Marle said. She wanted to cry but refrained. She had learned long ago how to hide her emotions, to keep herself safe and protected. The more someone knew what you were feeling, the more vulnerable you were. Of course, that hardly mattered now. Dmitri knew she was hurt and angry and she would have no advantage over him—but it gave Marle confidence to know she still had a little bit of control over herself.

"I did what I had to do to survive," Dmitri hissed. "Just like Ryan. Just like you. Willing to sell out the Post to save your skin."

"I did it to save the people here," Marle hissed. "I expected the King to strike once I proposed the treaty. He would think we were weak and would try to take us prisoner. The runes should have been able to repel an attack—we have a few years yet before they run out of power—and I would have been able to determine who the spy was." She pulled back, gazing at Dmitri with more hate than she had ever felt before, even for her previous husband. "I thought it was Ryan. Everything I told her, the King found out. I should have realized she was telling you everything."

Her ploy hadn't worked. She had been expecting the traitor to turn tail and run as soon as he heard about the treaty. Instead, Dmitri had brought the guard down—a preemptive strike. Something she should have foreseen. He had let them in.

Crive her. Always one step behind.

"The runes aren't failing?" Dmitri frowned.

"They are—but they'll hold for a few more years. Long enough for us to get the treaty signed. It's not the outcome I would have liked, but it will give us more autonomy than the rest of Everfont." She shook her head. "Do you know how many deaths are on your head, Dmitri? How many couriers have died? How many people are going to die now that they've been captured?"

It was all her fault. She had been too arrogant, too distrusting. She had been a fool to suspect Ryan—the girl hated the King. Then again, Marle knew she would have done anything to save her sister. Betraying the Post wasn't out of the realm of possibility.

"Dozens, I suspect," Dmitri said, "but I'm used to it by now."

Marle ripped her hand out of Dmitri's grip. The Post may be done for, but she would have vengeance. She pulled a sword from its sheath at her side and leveled it at Dmitri. He stared down the blade, unimpressed.

"Do you think you can beat me in a fight?" he asked softly.

"You're not welcome in the Post anymore," Marle said, leveling her sword at him. "If you take one step further, we'll stop you with force."

Behind Marle, Walton stepped from the shadows with several other of his guards. They had been waiting just around the corner for this moment. Walton held a large axe and stared daggers at Dmitri with one, squinty eye. Dmitri's eyes narrowed and he reached for his own sword at his waist.

"I'd like to see you try," Dmitri said quietly.

⤚

The stairs seemed to go on forever.

Ryan walked in front, continually glancing back to make sure the Seeker hadn't killed Eva. He hadn't—she was still in his arms, looking fearfully at Ryan. She hadn't said anything the entire time. She didn't want to draw attention to herself.

Good girl. They had discussed many times what to do if Eva was ever captured. It had always been a pain and Eva had never seen much value in those discussions but at long last, Ryan could see she hadn't just been pounding sand the entire time. She only wished they were lessons Eva had never needed to use.

They continued to descend into the darkness. Further and further they went. The Seeker had led them back to the dungeons, past the cells where members of the Post were, to a secret entrance embedded in the wall. It was similar to the entrances used to get into the Post. The Seeker had opened it by pushing a small indent, then taken them inside and down a cramped, spiral staircase. By now, they would have already been further into the earth than the Post—beneath it, in fact. Ryan couldn't help but wonder if this place had been built by the same people who had built the Post.

She still hadn't come up with a way to escape. With the Seeker behind her, there was no way to turn and fight him without him hurting Eva. If he didn't kill them right away, as he promised he would, he would surely lock them in different cells, and Ryan wasn't sure she had enough acid to break Eva out *and* free the people locked in the dungeon above.

An opportunity would present itself, somehow. She had to believe that. She had to hold onto hope, to the belief she did not come this far only for it to end now. There was a way out of this.

At last, they arrived in a large space. There were no torches to light the area, yet the stone glowed with a dull green light—just enough to light her way and illustrate some of the stains on the walls. Ryan could only assume they were blood. The smell of iron and water, though faint, crept up her nose, threatening to choke her.

"Head toward the back," the Seeker ordered. "The far wall."

Ryan obeyed. Her eyes flicked from side to side, looking for anything she could use. She passed an alcove where a man sat on the ground with his head bowed. Manacles bound his wrists and hands, but he didn't seem any worse for wear. A newcomer, perhaps?

"A Healer," the Seeker said, as if reading her thoughts. "A strong one. Any time I cut, his wounds reseal. The only way to kill him will be to let him starve."

He spoke with resignation, as if it was a tragedy the man would get to live a bit longer. As if he had wanted to kill him. With a sickening feeling, Ryan realized it was possible the Seeker wouldn't do as the King instructed. He would take his time carving into them.

They reached the end of the room. A set of manacles, a pair for her feet and a pair for her wrists, were attached to the wall. She turned back to the Seeker and he gestured toward them.

"Put them on," he ordered.

"Didn't you tell the King you would make it quick?" Ryan asked.

"I will—compared to my other prisoners," the Seeker said. "You will suffer far less, I promise. Please, put the manacles on."

Ryan looked at her sister, whose face was still stricken with fear. "If I don't?"

"I don't think I need to remind you what will happen," the Seeker said. His grip on her sister tightened, and Eva let out a whimper.

"All right, all right," Ryan said, holding up her hands. "I'll do it."

She stepped closer to the wall and began clasping the manacles around her ankles. She had no doubt the Seeker would kill them both the moment she pushed too far. Once the chains were clamped shut, the Seeker set her sister down and put the second set of manacles onto her wrists.

"Why not just get it over with?" Ryan asked.

"I will. But not now," the Seeker said. Once she was securely chained, he picked Eva back up, who hadn't moved, and walked down the hall. He turned into one of the alcoves and Ryan heard the clinking of metal as he shackled her. A few moments later, a scraping sound echoed throughout the chamber, and the Seeker reappeared, dragging a table and a chair, small knives and other instruments rattling atop it as he pulled it closer.

He set them in front of Ryan. He worked without speaking, dragging the chair out and sitting down so that he was facing her. Off the table, he picked up a quill and dipped it in a container of ink.

"What's this for?" Ryan asked suspiciously.

The Seeker looked up passively. Through his mask, it was impossible to tell what he was thinking, though she doubted if he didn't wear one it would be much different. A man like him would be unreadable, cold as iron.

"This is to be a memoir for you," the Seeker said.

"A memoir?" Ryan asked, puzzled. "For me?"

"Yes." The Seeker's hand was still in the air. "Unless you've already written one."

Ryan snorted. "Do you do this for all of the people you kill?"

"Yes," the Seeker responded. "Everyone has a story to tell, no matter how small. This way, you can be remembered."

It was so absurd Ryan almost laughed. "Remembered? Why?"

"You could not help the way you were born. None of us can," the Seeker said. He seemed almost . . . sad. Morose. He enjoyed the killing of people, that was easy to tell, but there was something else there. He was conflicted. But why?

"Why do we get to be remembered?" Ryan pointed out. "Why not the people of the slums, starving in the streets? No one is going to remember them."

"They were not born as Imperials," the Seeker said blankly.

Ryan hesitated. "We get to be remembered because we're Imperials?"

"Yes."

Ryan stared. She had known the Seeker was quite possibly mad—but the depths of that madness were unexplored. The more he spoke, the more she realized he wasn't completely there. Unfortunately, that hadn't stopped him from being such an effective killer. "Why not just stop hunting us? You wouldn't have to remember us that way."

"I can't," the Seeker said. He offered no other explanation and continued to stare at her.

"You always have a choice," Ryan said. "You don't have to kill me, or my sister. You can choose to let us go."

"No. I can't," the Seeker repeated.

Ryan bristled. "Writing about my life won't change what you've done."

"I know," the Seeker said solemnly, "but this way, you can live forever. Someone will read this in the future, and they will know about you. You will die, but you will live on."

"I won't tell you. Not now, not ever. You don't deserve to hear about my life."

The Seeker seemed to have been expecting this. He nodded and put the quill back in the inkwell. "You are not the first to say such things to me. I have ways of teasing secrets from your soul, no matter how deeply buried they are." He stood from his place at the table. "You will remain here until you decide to tell me your story. Once you have finished—then I will end your suffering."

"Criving sand-licker," Ryan spat as he began dragging the table away, toward the alcove he had placed Eva in. "Eva! Don't say anything! He'll—"

Instantly, the Seeker was back. He rammed his fist into her stomach, cutting her off. The wind flew out of her, and she lurched forward, unable to breathe. She would have folded in half, had the chains not kept her restrained.

"Please, do not talk to the other prisoners," the Seeker murmured. "It will interrupt their thoughts. It is best if people are calm when they are rehearsing their stories to me."

"Kill . . . kill . . . you," Ryan managed to sputter out. White-fire, she couldn't breathe! She leaned back up against the wall, opening her airway as much as she possibly could, sucking large gulps of air. "I'll . . . kill you."

The Seeker nodded, as if this, too, was expected. "There are many others who say that as well," he said. "You will not be the last either."

Once again, he disappeared into the darkness, down the alcove where Eva was. His voice gently trailed through the small dungeon, like a dull hum, too low for Ryan to make out.

He was distracted. For the moment, at least. Good. Ryan twisted her hands to her side, reaching into her bag. There was just enough slack in the chains to let her reach inside. At the very bottom, she grasped a vial of black liquid and pulled it up. Let's hope this works, she thought as she uncorked the lid.

⌒

The King watched the sun rise from his balcony.

He watched it every morning. No matter how tired he was, no matter how late he had finally fallen asleep, no matter how little sleep he got, he always forced himself up before dawn. Some of his closest confidants called him crazy behind his back. Others gave him pitying looks as though they understood what he was going through.

None of them understood. He doubted any of them ever would.

His hands shook slightly in the chill morning air. It was colder than most other mornings, something the King found extraordinarily strange. How could it be so warm during the day and yet so frigid at night? He knew there was a logical answer, one not bound in superstition and folklore—he had only yet to find it.

There was a whole world of possibilities before him. An eternity of learning and discovery. A lifetime of nursing this world back to health. All that, within reach. All he needed to do was have the strength for this last task. To endure for one more day.

Why then, did he want to weep?

He still remembered when his sister had been discovered. She was not an Imperial herself, but all her children would be. Genetics, as the people in Evaamara had called it. Here, the term was blood. Some people had tainted blood—some didn't. Not only had his sister possessed the gene, but the King did as well. He had forsworn then to never have children. He could not risk them being born Imperials as well.

But he couldn't simply forswear and leave it alone. In a cruel twist of fate, the people he had needed to rid himself of had infiltrated his own family. A test from the gods, perhaps. An examination of his resolve. He had faltered then, and it had resulted in the escape of his nieces and the death of his only sibling.

He had almost hoped, after all these years, that his nieces had been dead. If that were the case, he would have never needed to look upon Ryan's face—see the betrayal in her eyes. Hear the hurt in her voice. There was no way he could convince her of his cause, no way she would understand. So, he had wished for an easy out. An abdication of responsibility.

It hadn't been granted to him. Despite the odds being stacked against her, she had returned. To his surprise, the King had felt joy at the news. But it faded quickly when he had remembered what he would have to do to her.

He couldn't make exceptions. Not even for his own family. Not barring the fact he couldn't treat his own differently than he treated the commoner, Ryan had royal blood in her. Even if she left this world, there was a chance her descendants could come back and make a bid for the throne, something that could not be allowed to occur. It was easy to weather or repel an outside force. It was much more difficult to stymie an internal conflict.

The death of his last living relatives was necessary. For the good of Everfont, he would spill their blood upon the stones. They would be part of the foundation of corpses that would let Gritt live to see tomorrow.

That was why he woke with the sun every morning. To watch it rise, bathing the desert in a wash of red. A reminder of all the blood he had spilled. A promise of all the blood he would continue to spill. One day, when Gritt had been returned to its former glory, it would all end and he would be able to rest.

"Can't sleep again?"

The King sighed and turned. Cackler, the infamous beggar of Everfont, had climbed up the balcony and was staring at him. He was missing several teeth, and the hair had fled from his head. His appearance was a far cry from those that normally walked the palace walls, and an even further cry from when he had lived in the palace.

The King had never figured out how he maneuvered about. The disgusting, yet clever man had ways of moving about the city even the Post's couriers didn't have. There must have been some secret passageway to get past the palace walls. From there it would be simple enough to access the balcony. For all Cackler's trespassing, however, he had never revealed there was a secret way to access the palace. For that, the King supposed he owed him once again.

The King stifled his instinct to recoil and call for the guards. Even the smell was bad. This man had saved his life and he had once been a trusted advisor in the attempt to restore Gritt to its former glory. When Cackler discovered his former lover's children were Imperials, he had told the King. When she had gone insane and attacked the King, Cackler had held her back. For his loyalty, he had been spared.

"I could ask you the same," the King responded, leaning on the banister of the balcony. "You're up awfully early."

"I'm always awake when it matters most," Cackler responded. He hopped over the banister flashing a smile and leaned against it. He had a strange stick protruding from his mouth, one that had smoke coming out of it. The King looked at it, confused.

"Where did that come from?"

"Fogvir," Cackler said, pulling it from his mouth and holding it up to the light. Over the desert, the sun had just begun to rise. "He invented it. Or he brought it from somewhere else. I don't know. It's called a pipe."

"What does it do?" the King asked. Was it a weapon of some kind?

"You smoke it," Cackler said, putting the pipe to his lips and breathing in. He blew a stream of smoke that came out of his mouth and nose, then wheezed as he laughed, "It's great fun."

The King couldn't help but feel disappointed. "So, its worthless then."

"Not worthless," Cackler said. "Fun is never worthless. It lights the soul like a candle in the dark, and it can be shared with others. Then, they light candles of their own that fill the void. Soon, there's nothing but light and laughter left to look at."

"I'd rather light a bonfire with hard work," the King said with a sigh. "One that doesn't need to light others to be seen. One that others can see and be guided by."

"That's where you and I always had our differences," Cackler said, giving the pipe another puff. "You never slow down. You never stop making sacrifices. Work, work, work."

"Work is the lifeblood of the mortal creature," the King said. "Those who don't work, don't really live."

"Those who don't have fun don't really live either."

"I disagree with that," the King said. He felt alive. More alive than he ever had in his youth, wasting time chasing after frivolous things, traveling through the stars. What a fool he had been. He had also been young, and young men were allowed to be fools. That didn't change the regret he felt thinking of all the time he had wasted.

Cackler blinked one eye rapidly as he puffed on the pipe and looked at the King. "My daughter come to see you?"

The King stiffened, and eyed Cackler. "You knew she was coming? You've spoken to her?"

"Yes."

"And you didn't think to bring her to me?" Anger welled within the King. How dare Cackler betray him like this!

"Girl's an Imperial. I'm just an old man. There was never going to be a chance of me getting her to you."

"You could have told me. I could have sent the Seeker after her."

Cackler shook his head. "She uses her power in small bursts. She's smart that way. Seeker can't see 'em if they don't use enough Imperia."

The King bristled. "I wonder who taught her that."

Cackler fell quiet, a characteristic unusual for him. He continued to puff on his pipe until finally, he responded. "We made a lot of sacrifices when we were young, chasing this dream. Intending to make Everfont better for everyone. We thought we could change the world. When I told you what she was, I thought I was doing the right thing." He shook his head. "I was wrong. I've regretted her mother's death every day since it happened, and I regret leaving her alone all those years. Who would have thought being a father of all things would change me? But it has and I would watch Gritt die to save her."

The King stiffened. "She's one person, Cackler. One, against the millions that will live here. When we were younger and plotting all this, you spoke all the time about how it was necessary that some had to die for the greater good. You would go back on all that and sacrifice everyone for just one person?"

"She's my daughter," Cackler said. As if that was enough of a justification for turning on all they had built.

"Well, you needn't worry about that any longer," the King said. "The Seeker has her in the dungeon, right now."

The King expected an outburst or an exclamation of anger. Instead, Cackler laughed and gave the King a sympathetic look. "The Seeker's talented, but he won't be able to hold Ryan for long."

"No one has ever escaped him before," the King said confidently, any pity he had for the girl slowly draining away. "Your daughter is no different. She'll be dead by this evening."

"I doubt that," Cackler said, an insufferable grin spreading across his face. "Would you like to make a wager?"

"That your daughter escapes?" the King said. "The deed is done."

"Then, you have nothing to worry about," Cackler said.

The King eyed Cackler. The man was crafty, wiser than any other the King had known. But, he was also erratic and dangerous. Plus, by his own admission, he had been talking with Ryan. There was a chance he knew something about Ryan that would aid in her escape.

But she was also in the captivity of the Seeker. A man who had hunted targets halfway across the desert and back. A man that had become a myth and a legend and a horror story to tell children in Everfont.

"All right," the King said stiffly. "What do you want?"

Chapter Six

RYAN TILTED THE VIAL. BREATHLESS, SHE WATCHED as a drop spilled over the edge, falling onto her metal manacles. She recorked the vial before any could spill out, careful not to let any fall on her skin or clothes, and watched the acid do its work.

She could have used her Imperia, she supposed, to give herself enough strength to free herself. However, the Seeker would sense her doing that and would be on her in an instant. This way, at least she could give herself a little bit of a head start.

Fogvir had been right. The acid worked quickly and efficiently, eating through the metal in a matter of seconds. Smoke ascended from where it burned, and Ryan was careful not to inhale it. She pulled at her manacles, breaking her arm free as the metal corroded. She tossed them aside before it could touch her skin and they landed a few feet away with a clatter.

The speaking down the hall abruptly stopped.

Ryan uncorked the vial again and poured it on the manacles on her feet. The acid burned quickly—but not quickly enough. There was a scraping of a chair on the floor and footsteps followed. Ryan closed the vial, shoving it back into her bag and grabbing the dagger at the bottom. The Seeker rounded the corner, striding toward Ryan with a calm, but purposeful gait.

The acid ate through her foot manacles, and she kicked them off and rose, brandishing the dagger. The Seeker stared at it dully, unbothered by the blade. It was no threat—and why would it be? He was a Healer and could shrug off any damage she inflicted.

"This is foolishness," he said, spreading his arms. "Where will you go? You cannot outrun me. No one can."

Ryan lunged, plunging the dagger toward his heart. The Seeker didn't react. He stood there, waiting for Ryan to finish.

The dagger sank into his skin. He winced—he could still feel pain—but continued to stare dully ahead. He looked at Ryan and sighed.

Then he stiffened. His gaze shot downward and he let out a gasp. He stumbled backward, clawing at the dagger protruding from his chest.

"What—what is this!" he screamed, his voice filled with terror. He began to weep, and he ran into the alcove where Eva was. Ryan let out a yell and followed him, expecting him to attack her sister, but when she turned the corner, she found the Seeker at the desk, throwing aside papers. He had grabbed his inkwell and furiously wrote on a paper, mumbling to himself as he did so.

Ryan froze, unexpected pity welling in her stomach for the man. She didn't need to read the words to know what he was doing. He was writing his own story. But it was too late. His hand movements slowed, his body drooped, and he fell on the table, motionless.

Move. He won't be like that for long.

"Ryan?" Eva's voice whispered in the darkness. "Is he okay?"

Ryan rushed forward and knelt by Eva's side. She drew on her Imperia, her muscles growing larger and stronger, and she snapped the manacles off Eva's arms, before doing the same for her ankles. She scooped her sister up and ran out the alcove and down the hall, toward the stairs. She cast a glance backward at the table, hesitating as she stared at the Seeker.

The dagger had cost her fifty thousand drops and now she was just leaving it. Maybe she could chain the Seeker up and take the dagger out? No, that wouldn't work. He would find a way to escape, somehow. Every moment she wasted debating was another he grew closer to waking up. The only option was to leave now and figure out a way to evade him until they could escape Everfont.

They had done it for the past seven years. They could do it again.

"Please . . . help . . ."

Ryan glanced to the side, into the dark alcove where a bloodied mess had pressed itself up. The man who was being tortured. She set Eva down and ran back to him. His face was a bloody mess, and he stank of urine—but he was alive.

"Please," he begged. "Set me free."

Ryan didn't pause to consider. She snapped his manacles and helped him to his feet. Any Imperial trapped in the dungeon was a friend of hers, though that wasn't the only reason she was rescuing him. She towed him out of the alcove and picked up Eva and together, they ran up the stairs.

"Thanks," the man said as they ran.

"Don't mention it," Ryan said, clutching Eva in her arms. She still couldn't believe the dagger had worked.

They were *actually* escaping. "What's your name?"

"Samuel."

"Samuel. The Seeker said you were a Healer?"

"Yeah," the man said.

"Good. There's someone I need you to heal."

They reached the regular dungeons a few minutes later, much quicker than it had taken to descend. Ryan took the stairs two at a time, afraid any moment she would turn around and see the Seeker on their heels. Fogvir had been very clear—the dagger would incapacitate the Seeker, but it would not kill him.

She didn't know how long he would be out, but she doubted it would be long. Every minute counted now. She burst onto the dungeon floor, with Samuel close behind. In the cells, members of the Post rose to their feet to stare at her with wonder. She ran to Poppertrot's cell, setting Eva down and fumbling in her bag for the acid. She held it up to see there was still a fraction left.

"Stand back," she ordered to the people in the cell, pouring some on the hinges. The acid hissed and burned, eating away at it quickly. There wasn't enough for it to burn completely through—but there was enough to weaken it. Drawing on her Imperia, Ryan's arms grew, and she grabbed the cell doors and yanked. They came free, the hinges snapping off as she tossed the door to the side. She rushed in as people rushed out, like a swarm of locusts, clambering for the exit.

Poppertrot was inside, curled up on the ground. His eyes were closed, but his chest was moving. Barely.

"In there," Ryan ordered, pointing to Poppertrot. "Save him."

Samuel did as directed. He walked into the cell and put his hands on Poppertrot, a light green glow emanating from his palms. While he healed Poppertrot, Ryan drew on more of her Imperia and moved to the other cells. She pulled on the iron bars and they groaned as they were ripped from the wall, bits of rock flying from where the hinges had been embedded. People from the Post poured into the hallway, scrambling for the steps. Ryan let them pass as she caught her breath and moved to the next cell.

She had been planning on getting in and out quietly—but getting caught had necessitated a change of plans. Freeing the citizens of the Post would give Ryan and Eva a chance to escape—they could blend into the chaos. She ripped off another door and another swarm of people surged past her.

I just hope they all make it back to the Post safely.

◡

Poppertrot dreamed. He knew he was dreaming because it was the same one he always had. Every night, without fail, it passed across his eyes, reminding him of what he had done. Fitting, that he should dream of this before he died. The dagger the Seeker had slashed him with had been poisoned. He had less than an hour to live, at most.

He drifted, letting himself fall completely into the dream. At long last, he could be free. He only needed to live it one more time before the gods sentenced him to his punishment. Or he faded to nothing. He wasn't sure what awaited him after the bridge of death. Whatever it was, it wouldn't be good.

He was a young Trompkin, barely of age, hiding in the fireplace. He had crawled up the chimney and was halfway up the chute, listening to the struggle. Outside, his family was being arrested. The King's Hand had found them and had come to take them away to the mines. Trompkins, after all, were hardly of any use in the city. The King had revoked their rights as citizens and demanded all of them be taken to the north, where they would slave for the rest of their days mining precious gems.

His sister screamed and tried to fight her way out. She was older than Poppertrot, and stronger, too. She killed two guards by the time they got her under control. Then they beat her until she stopped crying.

His mother and father didn't resist. They slumped to the ground and let themselves be chained. His two younger brothers did likewise, though they were crying just like his sister. Poppertrot heard the smacks as the guards slapped them until they stopped making noise. He did his best not to move, not to utter a peep, as their captain strutted in.

"I must say, you did a good job of hiding yourselves. I had thought we cleaned out the last of the Trompkins nearly two years ago," Fault said. Poppertrot could hear the grin in his voice.

Poppertrot's family said nothing. He couldn't see them, but he imagined his parents staring down at the floor, shamed, and his sister too bloodied to speak. His brothers would follow his parents' lead.

Fault continued. "If not for the tip from your neighbors, we never would have found you."

"You lie," Poppertrot's father said. "No one here is weasel enough to sell us out."

There was a loud slap, followed by a grunt. "You don't seem to know your neighbors well enough. One did. He told us exactly when to be here so we could get all of you."

Poppertrot bit his lip, his muscles straining as he pressed himself up against the fireplace walls, trying his best not to knock down any soot.

"All of us?" Poppertrot's father said slowly.

"Yes. All five of you," Fault said. "Quite a big family for vermin. I would have expected you to be more careful. Then again, your wife is quite . . . lovely, as far as Trompkins go."

There was another scuffle. A scream rang out, followed by whimpering and two thuds. Fault's raggedy voice ripped through the air. "You'll pay for that. I have friends up at the mines, and I'll see to it they know you're a troublemaker."

"Don't . . . touch . . . my . . . wife . . . again," Poppertrot's father wheezed. He sounded like he could barely get the words out.

"I'll do whatever I please, Trompkin," Fault spat. "And you remember it."

There was a shuffling of feet. A lot of feet. Poppertrot's family was marched outside, and the door was slammed shut. He heard Fault screaming at them to walk faster, followed by a few more screams.

Poppertrot let himself fall out of the chimney, sending up a plume of smoke as he landed. Tears fell down his cheeks as he curled inward, wishing he could disappear.

His father had been right. It hadn't been any of the neighbors that had told.

It had been him.

He jerked awake to see a strange face kneeling over him. A young man, dirty and bloodied, with a concerned expression. His hands were pressed on Poppertrot's stomach, and there was a faint green glow emanating from them and the pain from his wound was receding. Behind him, he thought he saw Ryan, tearing metal bars out of the walls.

I knew she was an Imperial, he thought with grim satisfaction. Somehow, she had found someone to heal him.

He let his head drop back down, and a soft groan escaped his lips. Once more, he fell back into his memories, though this time they were jumbled by a mess of real dreams—things so fantastical they couldn't possibly be real.

Death hadn't come for him after all.

෨

It took more effort than Ryan had been expecting, and by the time she finished, she was exhausted to the point of collapse—but it was worth it. Dozens of people fled. People from the slums, Post members, even some people who lived in the Water Gardens. At one point, a young sergeant in King's Hand clothes saluted her as he passed—she assumed it was the same one who Captain Fault had been planning to execute earlier.

"Pick a better job next time," Ryan muttered under her breath as he passed.

"What is this?" Storin, one of the escapees, lingered behind. He was a council member, in charge of trade. Ryan had never had any issues with him, but he had always been a little . . . slow.

"Prison break," Ryan said, pulling off the last of the cell doors. "Run. Get back to the Post."

They hurriedly shuffled out of the dungeons, trying to be as quiet as possible. Ryan returned to Poppertrot's cell to find Samuel rising, dusting off his hands.

"He'll be fine," Samuel said. "He just needs some rest."

Ryan nodded. Stooping down, and flexing what was left of her Imperia, she lifted Poppertrot from the ground, grimacing. He weighed a lot more than she had expected and her Imperia was almost gone. She had used nearly all of it to rip open the cells. It had been more difficult without the acid to weaken them, but she had managed, somehow. She looked at Samuel, who stared at her with hollow eyes. She could only imagine what he had experienced in that room.

"Thank you," she said, stepping out of the cell. Eva ran to her side and with her free arm, Ryan picked her up as well. "Your debt is repaid."

"Where will you go now?" the man asked, following behind them as they left the dungeons, heading up the stairs.

Ryan pushed herself, trying to catch up with those who had fled. She wouldn't be able to climb back over the wall with Poppertrot and Eva. Her best bet was to get lost in the crowd of people fleeing and hopefully sneak through whatever guard would be posted outside.

"We're leaving Gritt," Ryan said. The crowd weaved through the various halls and a knot formed in her stomach as the crowd ran. Were they going the right way? Soon, however, they passed through a large doorway and entered the main entrance to the palace. To the left, the entrance doors lay wide open. The shouting had already begun as guards were raising the alarm.

"You have the money for that?" Samuel asked. She had expected him to have already made a run for it, yet he was still following her.

"Enough for me and my sister," Ryan said. She left out how she had enough for one other person. She still wasn't sure whether she was going to take Walton or Poppertrot. Could she find a way to take them both?

"Can . . . can you take me with you?" Samuel asked. His voice was strangled, as if it were difficult for him to ask for help. Ryan kicked open a nearby door and the three of them walked through. It was a different exit from the palace, one that would keep them out of sight of the guards. They stepped out into daylight, the sun just beginning to rise and illuminate Everfont.

The gate leading to the Water Gardens was overrun. Guards swarmed the area, while the prisoners fought with their bare fists. Thankfully, there were more people fleeing than there were guards—a few would be captured, a few skewered—but most would escape.

It's the best I can hope for, Ryan thought. She wasn't responsible for these people and she had done all she could for them. It still pained her to know some would die trying to flee.

She glanced at Samuel and saw the insignia on his clothes. She hadn't noticed in the dim light of the dungeon, but now the emblem of the King's Hand was unmistakable. Her blood ran cold and she stepped away, baring her teeth. His gaze followed hers and his face whitened as he saw what she was looking at.

He raised his hands. "I can explain."

"Explain?" Ryan hissed. "Explain that you've been working for the King? That you butcher innocents?"

"Please! I . . . I'm lost. I have no one left to go to. I can't go back to the King's Hand. They do things to your mind, twist your thoughts . . . make you something you're not. I just want to be a good man again," Samuel protested as tears fell down his face. "I just did what I needed to survive!"

"Do it again, then," Ryan snapped, moving away from the palace. Disgust welled within her. If he hadn't saved Poppertrot's life . . . "I've no intention of helping you."

Slinging Poppertrot over her shoulder, she took Eva's hand

and together they ran toward the gate, leaving Samuel staring after them. In an instant, they were surrounded by chaos. People shouted all around, and blood sprayed through the air. People screamed as they fought for their lives, clawing their way through the guards. Several times, a falling sword or spear just barely missed them as they pushed their way through.

A nearby guard took notice of her and charged with a sword held high. Ryan gritted her teeth. She had no hands to fight with. The guard grew closer, swinging the sword wildly. Beneath his helm, she could see the fear in his eyes, the panic of being in the middle of such chaos.

With more agility than Ryan thought she had, she swung her leg upward, stretching it as far as she could. Her foot met the man's breastplate. The steel of his chest guard crunched beneath her foot, and he crumpled to the ground. The light left his eyes instantly.

Ryan staggered from the force of the blow, barely keeping her balance. In her arms, Poppertrot began to feel heavier. She was almost out of Imperia. The well of power within her was drained to its last vestiges.

She was almost through. Water splashed around her feet as she entered the Water Gardens, leaving the battle behind her. The guards chased everyone around her, hacking away with swords and spears. Apparently they were no longer worried about capturing anyone. Hurrying to the hidden entrance, Ryan pushed it open and was about to slip inside when something slammed into her.

She lurched forward, staggering against the palace wall. Eva screamed in terror. Whirling around, she saw Fault with a greedy glint in his eye. He had no weapon, but his fists were raised.

"Where do you think you're going?" he hissed. "Back to the Post?"

He struck again. Ryan stumbled backward, narrowly avoiding his strike. On her shoulder, Poppertrot began to stir.

"Where . . . ?"

Ryan let him drop. His eyes widened and he hit the ground with a grunt. He hopped to his feet, mouth opened wide to protest, when his eyes widened at the pandemonium around him. Ryan shoved him into the hidden entrance and threw Eva into his arms.

"Take her back to the Post!" Ryan ordered.

Poppertrot stumbled away, still out of sorts. "What's going on?"

"Just go!" Ryan yelled. The message got through this time, and Poppertrot ran into the secret tunnel to escape. Spittle flew from Fault's mouth as he moved in for another grapple, but Ryan danced out of his way.

I can't beat him, Ryan thought. *Not without my Imperia.*

She was completely drained. She didn't use it enough to have a large store of power and what little remained would be inconsequential in a fight against the captain. He was twice her size, and twice as strong, too. He wore thick, steel-plated armor impossible to punch through.

He went in for another lunge. This time, Ryan was too slow, and he caught her arm. With a triumphant whoop, he yanked her back. There was a loud pop and she cried out as fire raced up and down her arm. She pushed at Fault, trying to wiggle out of his grip, but he pulled her in closer and wrapped a hand around her neck.

She gasped as his grip tightened. She slapped at him, reaching up and trying to claw his face, but he swung her around, laughing as he did so. Before her, the rest of the guard was faring badly, having been overrun by the fleeing prisoners. Fault didn't seem to care. His attention was completely fixed on Ryan.

He pulled harder on her arm, and she felt a ripping in her shoulder. The pain coupled with the exhaustion was too much and her vision began to grow dark. Her strength left her, and she began to loll forward.

Suddenly, Fault let her go. Air rushed into her lungs as she toppled forward, freed from his grip. She hit the ground with a splash, choking in as much air as possible, her vision clearing. She rolled for a moment, disoriented, before stumbling to her feet, putting distance between her and the captain. Behind her, Fault's mouth moved wordlessly as he stared at the tip of a sword protruding from his chest.

What? Ryan thought.

His eyes lulled back in his head, and he toppled to reveal Samuel standing behind him. The former King's Hand looked at Ryan, a confused expression on his face, before he turned and ran. Bewildered, she stared after him.

He saved me. A member of the King's Hand.

The whole world had gone crazy.

Stumbling into the secret passage, she shut it behind her and descended into the underground of Everfont.

⌒

The Seeker woke with a start.

Where was he? He rolled over and suddenly he was no longer on a solid surface, but in the air. He hit the ground with a thud, and his vision went black before coming back into focus. Dazed, he rolled over and tried to breathe before realizing something was stopping him. Feebly, his hands felt at his chest before feeling the dagger there. It pulsed, like a heart, as if it had become a part of him. With a grunt, he yanked it free, and tossed it aside, sending a spatter of blood across the ground.

Instantly, he felt better. His healing, which had somehow been subdued, returned to him, mending his heart. He coughed as his lungs emptied and he forced himself to his feet, steadying himself against the wall. Amazed, he held the dagger up for inspection. It was made of a material he had never seen before, yet he could feel something strange as he held it. It was a power he had never encountered before. Where the dagger should have been, vibrant with color, there was nothing but an empty space.

"Fogvir," he said aloud. The inventor had recently returned from a trip to the funnel. He had said he found a way to suppress Imperials' powers temporarily. The Seeker had dismissed the claims as childish nonsense, but perhaps—perhaps there had been some truth to his words.

That meant he had given the dagger to that girl. Ryan. The King's niece. Anger welled inside the Seeker at the revelation. Fogvir didn't understand their progress wasn't because of the little trinkets he made, or the technology he brought here.

It was because of the work *he* had done. The Seeker. Everfont would survive because of the Imperials he had killed and the blood that was on his hands. It was distasteful work. Awful at times, but necessary. Without the death of the Imperials, the world would never be forced into progress.

The King would hear of this. The Seeker would come for Fogvir. He rarely held personal vendettas, but for the small man, he would make an exception. He would take his time slicing into him in repayment for giving the girl the dagger and he would savor every moment of Fogvir's screams.

His pleasure would have to wait, however. There were still Imperials at large. The girl, her sister, and the man he had chained. They had all escaped. Even now, he could sense them, using their Imperia throughout the city. Strength returned to his limbs, and he sucked in a deep breath before leaving the chamber.

Three more people. He only needed to kill three more people. Then, Everfont would be safe at last, and he could have his reward.

꩜

Samuel fled.

He didn't know where he was going—only that he needed to get away. His mind fought against him, ordering him to go back, but he ignored it. Water splashed around his feet as he ducked into one of the nearby buildings. It was a lavish manor—every building was in the Water Gardens—and he slammed the door shut behind him. Tears of confusion ran down his face, a mix of joy and sorrow.

Why had he killed Fault? Why had he saved that girl? He wasn't sure. It had just felt . . . right. It had felt like he was doing something good. Like . . . like . . .

Like he was protecting someone.

He leaned against a wall and fell to his haunches, weeping bitterly as he finally accepted the truth. All his time in the King's Hand had been a sham. He hadn't been protecting people, not really. The King's Hand had tortured him, warping his mind until he believed what he was doing was a service when it was nothing more than petty bullying.

Strange, the torture in the Seeker's chamber had been the thing to help him see clearly. He had joined the King's Hand to protect people. In turn, they had turned him into a monster. Now, he could be free of them. He could become a better man.

He rose, wiping the tears from his eyes. Guilt lingered about killing Fault, but the man had deserved it. Everyone in the King's Hand knew he was the worst of them all. Had anyone but a captain committed half his atrocities, they would have been buried headfirst in the desert for their crimes. His death was no great loss.

Samuel, however, had no idea what to do next. He had just watched as members of the Post had overrun the King's Hand, routing them. Though they were a twisted lot, they still maintained some semblance of order in the city. Without their presence, the street gangs would overrun the slums and the Water Gardens would no longer be a safe haven.

The only logical thing to do was to leave Everfont forever. Samuel wouldn't be able to pay for a sand sailor, though. He had heard whispers of their fees, how much they charged for a trip. It would have cost him ten years' wages to pay for one.

Then, an idea struck him. He was in the Water Gardens, where the rich of Everfont lived. He was already inside one of their manors and there was no King's Hand to stop any robbers.

Immediately, he moved further in, looking for anything valuable. He would start a new life, a life he could be proud of. The life he had always wanted to live. But first, he had to steal a few things.

⌒

When Ryan arrived in the Post, she found the cistern was much as she had left it. The buildings were still burned and charred, though the bodies had been dragged away and disposed of. What was normally a bustling and energetic atmosphere was now silent and somber. As she cast her eyes about, she saw a large group of people clustered together near the center pillar. Her pace quickened and as she grew closer, she saw Marle, Walton, Poppertrot, and Eva among them.

They spotted her a moment later. The four of them broke away from the group and ran to her, with Marle in the lead. Much to Ryan's surprise, Marle slowed and wrapped her arms around Ryan. Ryan's anger melted away and she hugged Marle back. Her aunt had made many mistakes over the past year—so many, a hate had begun to fester in Ryan's stomach. A brush with death, however, had given her a broader perspective. Some things were more important than personal grudges.

Marle pulled away, tears glistening in her eyes. "I thought you would be captured for sure."

"I was," Ryan said. "I escaped. I freed the others. They'll be coming soon, and the guards will be chasing them. You'll want to retreat into the deeper caverns for safety."

Marle shook her head. "That won't be necessary. The Post will protect us until the treaty goes into effect."

Ryan blinked. "But they'll come for us before its time. There's still two days—"

"It was a lie," Marle said softly. "The runes will hold for a while longer. A few years or so. It was important we get the treaty in place to make the King think we were weak. He would try to attack, and when he couldn't, it would be the day of the signing. His twisted sense of honor would force him to go through with it." She looked away. "There was a traitor in the Post that brought the guards in. I let you think the runes were failing because . . . well, I thought it was you."

Suddenly, Marle's coldness and distance toward Ryan made sense and why she had forced the treaty vote while Ryan wasn't there. "It wasn't," Ryan whispered. "It was Dmitri."

Marle nodded. "I thought the spy would flee when they heard of the treaty. Instead, he let the guards in to capture us all." She looked down. "I'm sorry. I should have told you."

Ryan understood why she hadn't. For so long, it had been the five of them—Walton, Dmitri, Marle, Eva, and her. Ryan could only imagine how hard it must have been, wondering if you could trust your closest friends. Wondering if Ryan had betrayed them.

Well, one of the five had betrayed the rest. It just hadn't been Ryan.

"How much money do you have?" Marle asked.

Ryan shook her head. "Not enough. I had to pay Fogvir fifty thousand for the equipment to save Poppertrot and Eva. I made the delivery to the palace and that's worth a hundred thousand drops. That puts me at four hundred thirty thousand."

Seventy thousand short. Not enough for the five of them. They had nowhere left to go, and no time left to go anywhere. Ryan could have left with just her and Eva—but that wouldn't be right. She wouldn't leave Poppertrot and Walton to die. Nor would she leave Marle, for that matter.

They would have to run. Somehow make enough money to pay the sand sailors. Perhaps they could even make it across themselves. But no, that was foolishness. No one that left to walk in the desert ever made it out alive. Besides, only the sand sailors knew how to get to the funnel. Without one of them, they could wander the desert for years and never find it.

Marle put her hand on Ryan's shoulder. "Thank the gods. That should be enough for all of us."

Ryan blinked and looked up at Marle. "What?"

"I've been doing some saving of my own. I thought, if you were the spy, you wouldn't be saving your money. I've saved nearly a hundred thousand myself."

One hundred thousand . . . together, that put them thirty thousand over what they needed.

She hesitated. "What . . . what about the Post?"

"Flint's in charge. Most of our people that you've freed should come trickling down here in a bit and the runes will protect them until the treaty."

Tears welled in Ryan's eyes, falling freely down her face. She couldn't contain them, nor did she want to. She wrapped her arm around Marle once more, sobbing. Behind Marle, Walton and Poppertrot stepped forward and joined in the hug, while Eva squeezed in underneath them. Ryan's arm—the one Fault had grabbed—groaned with pain, but she hardly noticed it in the moment.

They were a small, patchwork family, but they were real. As real a family as if they had all been born to the same mother.

Finally, they could leave this place.

Marle broke the hug first, wiping tears of her own from her cheeks. "Walton found a sand sailor while you were gone. He's still doing preparations, but we're to meet him at the west entrance in an hour's time."

An hour. It felt so surreal. In only an hour, Ryan and the others would be on their way out of this place. Forever.

⤻

Guilt pricked at Dmitri as he walked through Everfont. Cuts, underneath his arm and on his cheek, stung in the hot dry air, but they didn't sting nearly as much as his emotions, broiling beneath the surface. He had just wanted to be free. That was all.

It was something Flint said all the time. *Men will do a lot to be free.* Well, this was what he was willing to do to be free.

He unconsciously felt at his abdomen as he remembered his fist sinking into Ryan's stomach. It had hurt him like he had been punching himself. And that look, the tears in her eyes . . . he could never escape that. The memory would haunt him forever. Unless he had it wiped away by a Memorist, though he wasn't sure he wanted to. He wasn't sure what he wanted anymore.

That wasn't completely true. He did want to get away. Away from the Seeker. Away from this city. Away from this world.

He cast a quick look over his shoulder, fearing the Seeker would be behind him. He wasn't. For all the King's faults, all his worthless goals, he was an honorable man. At least, he tried to be. If he had said Dmitri was free, Dmitri was free, though years of fear and terror could not be wiped away with a mere word.

He had grown up in the palace, the son of one of the butlers, who had also been a Psychomancer. An Imperial with the ability to change their own soul. He had known Ryan at the time, though she hadn't known him. He supposed that was part of the reason the King had chosen him to try and capture her. Perhaps there had been a part of her that recognized him unconsciously and made him more trustworthy.

His father had been found when Dmitri was nine. The Seeker had barged into their rooms and dragged him away. A short time later, he had come back for Dmitri. It hadn't taken long to find him. Dmitri had been hiding under the bed, crying to himself, hoping it was a bad dream.

In that deep, dark room beneath the palace he had listened to the Seeker torture his father. He had this twisted obsession with hearing people's life stories before they died. His father had confessed to every sin under the sun. Everything he had ever done, good or bad, beneath the Seeker's hand and even to things he hadn't. At the end of it all, the Seeker had killed him. A quick snap of the neck and it was all over.

Then it had been Dmitri's turn. Except Dmitri's torture had been different. As the son of an Imperial who had no Imperia, Dmitri had been taken because there was a chance his children could have Imperia. That alone was enough to warrant execution—but the Seeker had spared him and kept him alive for his own twisted fun. Over and over he had released Dmitri into the city, giving him a head start. He had promised if Dmitri could make it to the outer wall, he would let him go free.

Dmitri never did. Time and again, he had been released and then found seconds before touching the cracked and crumbling outer wall. When he had been caught, the Seeker would beat him, right there in the streets, before taking him back to the palace. When they returned to the dungeons, the Seeker would beat him some more.

For nearly five years, Dmitri had languished beneath the Seeker's hand, wishing he could die. Several times he had tried to take his own life, but in a cruel twist of fate, the Seeker was a Healer. Which meant that Dmitri's imprisonment would last for as long as the Seeker was alive.

A young boy whimpered nearby. Dmitri stopped, casting a glance over his shoulder, before looking for the source of the crying. The boy was young, probably about nine or ten. He clutched a leg to his chest and on his knee was a bright red scrape. Bits of blood trickled from the wound, and there were clumps of dirt pressed into the wound.

Dmitri winced. All around, people passed by, oblivious to his plight, either uncaring or willfully ignorant of the pain before them. Casting another glance over his shoulder, Dmitri pulled a few drop pouches from his pocket and kneeled in front of the boy.

The boy stared at him with wide-eyed terror. Dmitri tried to smile disarmingly and proffered the small water pouches to the boy. "Here. Take these. Get yourself some medicine and a meal."

The boy's terror melted away, though his eyes widened with wonder. Gingerly, he took the pouch from Dmitri's hand and stared at it as though it was sacred. He didn't say anything for a moment, then swallowed hard. "What do you want?"

Dmitri stifled a chuckle. Kindness was so far removed from the day-to-day life of Everfontans, that when they finally experienced some, it was judged for something else. "Nothing. I saw you needed some help, so I wanted to help."

The boy shook his head. "You must want something, mister. Everyone wants something."

Dmitri shook his head. "All I want is for you to get that scrape looked at." He stood up, gave the boy a nod, and continued on his way without waiting for thanks.

He cast another glance behind him, still afraid the Seeker was chasing him. He wasn't, of course. The King had given his word.

That was the ultimate reason he had betrayed Ryan. At first, he had deluded himself into believing they could escape. If they saved enough money, they could flee to Rim or Niall—crives, even Wulfenraast would have been better than here. Those mystical lands where no one need fear the Seeker, and they could be whatever they wanted to be. The fantasy of being free had been bliss.

It hadn't lasted. While on a courier route, Dmitri had been captured and brought before the King. Like a fool, he had defiantly told the King of Ryan's plan—how she was going to escape and she would be out of his reach forever. At that, the King had smiled sadly, and told Dmitri that, no matter how far she ran, he would catch her. She would never escape the Seeker. And that, by extension, Dmitri never would either.

That was when Dmitri's hope had come crashing down. For a few short years, he had dreamed of leaving his nightmares and fear of the Seeker behind. He would go with Ryan, and Eva, and Poppertrot, and Walton to a better place. He would finally be able to let the past die and move on with his life.

The revelation had crushed his soul more efficiently than the years of torture ever could. As long as he stayed with Ryan, he would never be able to escape his past. He would constantly live in fear of the Seeker. He would never, ever, truly, be free.

So, he had offered the King a deal. Give him a year to capture Ryan and he would leave Everfont forever. The King had agreed, though Dmitri had most of his freedom stripped away. He had been required to check in with the King at the end of every week, to update him on his progress. It had always been a strange meeting. While the King had been glad to hear of Dmitri growing closer to Ryan and gaining her trust, he had also been saddened. After all, the girl was family, and the closer Dmitri grew to capturing her, the closer her death came.

Dmitri had also gained a reputation for being a slow courier. The meetings sometimes took hours, and Dmitri almost never made any deliveries that day. He had been required to make them at night, while everyone else was asleep, or the next day to avoid arousing suspicion. In truth, he was one of the faster couriers, nearly as fast as Ryan. He just had other things to occupy his time.

He may have been just as fast, but he wasn't as strong. Ryan was an Amplifier and any attempt to overpower her would have been futile. That's why he had needed to capture Eva first. Having leverage against Ryan would leave her powerless. It had taken some finagling to get permission to use the guards for his little trap, but after Ryan had failed to show at either Morgia's or the Ardor's two days ago, he had been forced to bring them to the Post instead. It had been simple enough to bribe one of the guards to let him in early, along with the lie that he was bringing home a nightsheet. He wouldn't have been able to pull Eva out of the Post on his own otherwise. After that, it had been easy enough to bait Ryan into coming to the palace.

The thought of how much planning had gone into it all made him sick.

He arrived at the outer wall. Sul was there, waiting for him. The sand sailor had never really been captured—Dmitri had told him to go into hiding as soon as he had formulated the plan to let the King's Hand into the Post. The man was unscrupulous, as long as he got paid, which was why he and Ryan had hired him in the first place. He wouldn't have any reservations about transporting Imperials.

Dmitri winced again as he realized he would be making the trip without her. Not only her, but also without Walton, Poppertrot, Eva, and Marle. He wasn't as close to the other three as he was with Ryan and Eva, but they were still his friends. Or, they had been.

He didn't have friends anymore.

That was okay. He could make new ones. He could make as many as he wanted once he was gone from here. He could start anew, where no one knew him, and no one would question his past. Best of all, he would no longer have nightmares of the Seeker.

He was free.

He drew closer to the sand sailor, who greeted him with a grunt. There was a common misconception in Everfont, that sand sailors all belonged to the same cloth. The term was used interchangeably between two separate entities. The first were men or women that were Imperials, Elementalists like Eva, and had the capacity to control the wind. The second was an entire race, and that was what Sul was.

He stood taller than a man. He had a triangular-shaped head that looked more like marble than skin, and large thick arms ending in wide, stubby fingers. Coming out of his back were two tubelike appendages that snaked up and outward like an S, and in the center of each of his palms, there was a large hole.

Elementalists had it easy. They could control the air and blow it into a sail, propelling their small craft forward. Sand sailors, the actual species, on the other hand, had to use their own body to traverse the desert. They sucked air through the tubes on their back and expelled it through the holes in their hands. Sand sailors were slower than Elementalists but they got the job done and Dmitri didn't much care how slowly they made the journey. Only that it was made.

Most had been captured, like Trompkins, and used as slaves, though no one knew what for. Dmitri assumed they were sent to the mines. What ones were left lived in the Post, like Sul.

There was another man, one Dmitri didn't recognize, standing beside him. He wore the clothes of a noble yet was slumped over like he belonged to the streets. Dmitri gestured toward him. "Who's this?"

"Another customer, like yourself," Sul said, spitting off to the side, showing dark brown teeth. "Had the money to pay, so I figured we'd let him ride along."

"That wasn't part of the deal," Dmitri said crossly.

Sul shrugged. "He can pay. It's more efficient to take you both at once."

Dmitri sighed. It didn't matter. He had come this far, and he wasn't about to spoil his chances now. He stalked past Sul and the sand sailor spit onto the sand. The other man followed close behind them. They hauled themselves up onto the large sand sled, and Dmitri had to be careful not to damage the painting on his back.

It was his only possession, and the only reason he had gone back to the Post. He couldn't explain why but he felt attached to it for some reason. When he looked at it, it gave him hope. The title, *Safe in the Storm*, reminded him of what he was searching for. Not a life free of conflict or challenge, but one where he could be safe despite it all.

If you had really wanted that life, you would have left with Ryan.

"All ready to go?" Sul asked. He didn't wait for Dmitri or the other man to respond. There was a loud whine as air rushed through the waning tubes on his back, only to be expelled a moment later. The air caught in the sail, and the craft jolted forward, sliding across the sand.

Dmitri closed his eyes and clutched the painting close to his chest.

His new life, his life free of the Seeker, began now.

Chapter Seven

RYAN USED THE HOUR REPRIEVE TO TAKE A NAP. By white-fire, she needed it. She had been going full blast since Eva had been taken. Walton had set her arm—it had been dislocated by Fault—and they had wrapped it in a sling before she had fallen asleep on a small blanket that had been miraculously saved from the fire. She was so tired that sleeping on the cold ground of the Post hardly bothered her.

Her dreams were pleasant, if not rushed. She dreamed of flying over a green paradise, filled with grass and trees and water. She dreamed of resting by a lakeside with her sister beside her. Walton was fishing on the lake—she thought that's what it was called—while Poppertrot was swimming. Marle sat near a fire and was smoking some meat while Eva giggled at strange animals nearby. Dmitri was there as well, hand intertwined with hers as they looked over the scenery.

When she woke, tears were again on her face. It was one of her more common dreams. Normally, she woke with tears for the future she thought might never be. This time, she woke knowing that future was just within her grasp. Overwhelmed, she held herself for a moment, letting herself bask in the realization that she was almost there.

No. Not almost there. That dream would never be complete—not now that Dmitri was gone. She wasn't sure how she felt about him. There was pain and anger when she thought of how he had betrayed her—but there was numbness too. Beneath all that, a faint flicker of love still lingered.

She clutched her stomach, nauseous at the thought she still loved him. They had spent years of their lives together, and a single moment couldn't erase all that she had felt. It would take time for her to heal and even then, there would be scars left over.

She let herself rest for a moment to compose herself before rising from her makeshift bed and stepping out of her tent. There was a collection of them set up near the center pillar. None of the houses were safe to sleep in anymore. The beams were weak from the fires, and they could collapse at any moment. What a tragedy it would have been, had Ryan finally been ready and prepared to escape this place, only to be crushed by a burned building.

She found the Post bustling again. Nearly everyone had returned, and it seemed they'd even picked up a few stragglers as well. The entire cistern was filled with bodies all pushing against one another. In the middle, she saw Kinroia, tending various people with her apprentices. Most of the people that had found their way back were injured in some way—some had bruises, most had cuts—and there were even a few people with broken bones.

Despite their injuries, almost as one, they turned to look at her as she stepped outside her tent. Conversations died and movement came to a halt as they stared at her with almost reverent silence. Only the soft trickling of the center pillar fountain could be heard as Ryan shifted from foot to foot uncomfortably.

Then, they cheered and surged forward, hands outstretched. Ryan panicked as they grabbed her and hoisted her above them, careful not to disturb her arm in the sling. They cheered again and the noise rose like a cacophony to the ceiling before crashing back down. Bewildered, she clutched at the hands that held her for dear life as the crowd carried her to a small space near the center pillar where Walton, Marle, Poppertrot, and Eva were waiting for her. They set her down beside her friends.

"Get enough rest, Princess?" Poppertrot said. His normal, contemptuous sneer was gone, instead replaced with a tender smile.

"Did I miss something while I was asleep?" Ryan asked, still a bit befuddled.

In response to her question, a man stepped out of the crowd—Flint, the new Crow. He gave her a flourish and a grin as he bowed before her.

"They wanted to express their gratitude," he said as he rose. "For saving them."

Ryan blushed, turning nearly the red shade of an unripe poppo plant. "I didn't . . . it was nothing. They were the ones who got themselves out."

"Perhaps," Flint said. "But if not for you, they would have never had the opportunity. They're wounded, nearly all of them—but they'll live to see another day. And they'll do it as free men and women." He looked her in the eyes. "Though I don't suspect they'll have as much freedom as you."

Ryan looked at the faces around her. There was gratitude there, as well as admiration and perhaps a bit of sorrow. Yet they all gave her nods of approval and understanding. They knew what she had been saving for, what came next.

"We're leaving," Ryan said quietly and in response, the crowd cheered. Tears threatened to come to Ryan's eyes at the outburst and she turned away to hide them.

Flint smiled. The crowd behind him quieted as he took a step back. "I speak for all of us, then, in giving thanks. Without you, the Post would have crumbled for it is nothing without its people. You've freed us from prison, and in so doing, we live to fight another day against the oppression of the King. Under the conditions of the treaty of course."

The crowd gave one final roar of gratitude and bulged in places as people strained to get a look at her. She wanted to shy away—she wasn't used to all the attention—but she stood and bore it. The people continued to cheer for her until, at last, Flint drove them off and they returned to tending their wounds. Several of the other council members came to say their farewells, as well as a few other people she had become friends with over the years.

A pit opened in her stomach. Not a painful pit, or a sickening one, but one of discomfort. This . . . this was the last time she would see all these people. This was the last time she would see the Post. Was she really ready to leave it all behind? To leave them to the whims of the King?

They were Post members. They were strong. Looking at them, watching them tend to each other, Ryan's doubts vanished. They would be fine without her.

"Are you ready?" Poppertrot put a hand on her shoulder. He was uncharacteristically gentle as he spoke. Ryan fought back tears as she nodded, and he led her away from the large group of people. She cast a look behind her to etch one last memory of the Post in her mind. One she would never forget.

They walked to the western exit, where a man dressed in a large, brown cloak stood. Marle gestured toward him. "This is our sand sailor, Hansen Talmage."

Strange. Ryan knew all the sand sailors, yet she had never met him. Yet as he turned to face them, she recognized him from the other day. He had been the one to grab her arm and spout off nonsense terms like "God-Spoken," and "Twice-Blessed." She gave him a good look up and down, now she had the time and the attention to do so. Not that it helped much. Like the Seeker, sand sailors were covered head to toe in their garb. Yet unlike the Seeker, his eyes were uncovered, and Ryan could see his pupils were a vivid blue. They met hers and suddenly, she felt naked. As if he were disrobing her, probing at the secrets of her soul.

She turned to Marle. "Is there anyone else we can take?"

"Whoa there, miss. A bit quick to judge, aren't ya?" the sand sailor said, stepping forward before Marle could speak. His words had a strange accent to them, one Ryan had never heard before. That is, Ryan hadn't heard any accents before now. There was nowhere else in the world to have an accent from.

Which meant he was an off-worlder. Someone from beyond the funnel.

"I'm not judging you at all," Ryan said sternly. "I'd just rather sail with someone I trust. Are there any others left? Tava? Sul?"

Ryan had been planning on using Sul, after their last sand sailor had been captured, and beyond him, Tava. They were a few of the last sand sailors on Gritt. It occurred to Ryan perhaps Dmitri had lied about Sul being captured—she hadn't seen him in the prison—but she brushed off the thought. It was too painful to think about.

Marle shook her head, dismayed. "They all fled when the Post was raided. Sul has been missing for a few days now, and Tava never made it back. We think she was killed in the prison escape. Hansen is the only sand sailor left in all of Everfont." From the look Marle was giving him, she was just as unsatisfied with this as Ryan.

If he was really the only sand sailor left, they didn't really have a choice. With a sigh, she stuck out her hand. Hansen cocked his head, looking at it curiously.

"Well? Are we going to shake or not?"

"Oh. That's what you wanted. Sorry, you just have such beautiful hands. Didn't want to soil them with my dirty ones."

Walton snorted and Poppertrot laughed. Even Marle cracked a smile. Eva, however, grinned from ear to ear, looking from the sand sailor to Ryan. It wasn't hard to tell what thoughts she was having. She had always been fond of any new boy Ryan met and thought all of them would make good husbands, despite Dmitri's continued presence.

The thought of entering another relationship made Ryan wince. She thought she had found someone to spend her life with already. She had been wrong.

Her ears grew hot, and she took her hand back, holding it against her side. "Well, we have your word. No need to shake. Let's get a move on."

Hansen chuckled and shook his head as Ryan moved past him. Together, the group moved out of the cistern and into the tunnels. Before they left, Ryan took one last look at the Post. It had been her home for the last seven years, and Walton and Poppertrot had both been here longer. It felt . . . improper, maybe even disrespectful, to leave without saying a few words.

The Post was silent, as if waiting for more to be said. The words wouldn't come however, and Ryan could think of nothing poetic or dramatic, as would have been fitting for the moment. After a few seconds of thought, she finally decided on, "Thank you for protecting me and my family."

With that, she turned and left. The others were further down the tunnel, already heading up the stairs. They would be deposited near the western gate, and from there, Hansen would take them on his sand ship to the funnel. It would be a weeklong journey across the sand. A miserable, blistering weeklong journey—but Ryan could hardly wait.

She caught up with the others. "You said Dmitri was taking a sand sailor. Did he come back to the Post?"

Walton glanced toward her. He was nursing a wound on his shoulder, a deep cut that had been bandaged. He reached for it at her question and tapped it slowly. "Yes."

She got his meaning. "He did that?"

"He was the traitor feeding information to the King's Hand," Marle said up ahead. She was trailing just behind Hansen, and she looked back at the rest of them. "He was telling them where the couriers would be taking deliveries. He made a lot of money off those betting boards."

Ah. "Was he the one that bet against me?"

"Yes," Marle said. "I should have suspected him then. But I was too focused on you as the traitor." She looked down. "I thought you might be using him to make money off the boards."

Ryan felt a chill run up her spine. There wasn't a single secret she hadn't shared with Dmitri. They had promised each other, long ago, that there would be nothing but truth between them. Dmitri had suggested it as a way of growing closer. In hindsight, it was foolish of her to have agreed. At the time, she had just barely become a council member. He wouldn't have wanted to be close to her so much as he wanted information.

Crives. If she ever got her hands on him, she would make sure he burned in white-fire.

"Did Dmitri do something bad?" Eva asked. She slipped her hand into Ryan's and Ryan gripped it tightly.

"Yes," Ryan said softly.

"Will he come back?"

"I don't think so, sweetheart," Ryan said. "I think he's gone for good."

Eva fell silent at this. It was a lot to take in for a seven-year-old. To her, Dmitri had been like an older brother, or a father. It would take her a long time to understand what had happened, and longer still to heal from it.

Criving Dmitri, Ryan thought, a phrase she never thought she would think.

"So, how did it happen?" Ryan asked, turning her attention back to Marle and the others.

"One of our spies saw him entering the palace yesterday, after the raid. They reported it to me, and I knew then what he was. We confronted him in the tunnel, and it was like he was an entirely different person." Marle shuddered. "He admitted to all of it."

Ryan nodded. She knew what Marle meant. "What happened then?"

"Fight," Walton grunted.

Beside him, Poppertrot raised a hand to touch Walton's wound. Walton slapped his hand away and let out a low growl. "Don't."

"I'm in shock, Walt," Poppertrot said. "I thought you were immortal. Couldn't be hurt and all that."

"I thought the same," Ryan said, smiling faintly. "I've never seen you get hurt or lose a fight before."

The guards often had practice duels in the cistern. Walton was the best of all of them and would duel upward of five at a time—and win. Watching him wield that spear was similar to watching a ballerina dance without touching the floor. He was graceful, elegant, and deadly.

Walton grunted, and he seemed to grow embarrassed, another thing Ryan had never seen from him. The last two days had been a time for firsts.

"Fast," Walton grumbled, touching the wound.

"I'll say," Marle said. "He was like lightning. Before I could move, he had killed three others and wounded Walton. Once he broke through, he bolted. Grabbed his painting from the storage room, a few drops, and left."

"Smart man," Hansen said from up in front. "He was able to down a few of you but realized he wouldn't be able to fight everyone. It's what I would have done if I was him."

They arrived at the end of the tunnel. Hansen opened the end of the passage and bright light filtered into the dim hallway. They shuffled out one by one, with Walton bringing up the rear and closing the entrance. They were in the west side of town, in the slums, right next to the western gate.

To call it a gate was an overstatement. It was a simple archway, made of brick, that led to the outer desert. As far as the eye could see, there was nothing out there. Nothing but heat, and scavenger animals.

Hansen walked fearlessly outside the walls. He raised his hand in an exaggerated motion and the sand beneath him began to swirl. Suddenly, it shot out in front of him, like a giant wave, to reveal a wooden sand sled, hidden beneath the sand.

It was a wooden platform that stood on two, long curved legs, made for cutting through sand. Two posts stood high into the air on the deck, with a large tarp spread between them. A strange-looking vessel. It looked nothing like what Ryan had imagined.

Ryan gaped, and she saw that Walton, Marle, and Poppertrot had a similar reaction. They all looked to each other, then back to Hansen.

"You're an Imperial? An Elementalist?"

"No," Hansen said, and Ryan could tell he was grinning under his face mask. "But I will be using the same magic if that's what you're asking. Dangerous, especially with the Seeker around. But what's life without a bit of risk, hmmm?"

Ryan was impressed. So, it seemed, were Marle and Walton. Poppertrot, however, bristled with anger. "You fool! You will bring the Seeker down on us!"

Hansen seemed unbothered. "By the time he gets here, we will be long gone. There are no other sand sailors left, remember?

He'll have no way to chase us." He dusted some sand off the sled. "Besides, I doubt he'll be coming after us anytime soon after what you did to him. Isn't that right, Ryan?"

He looked directly at her. Again, Ryan felt a chill run up her spine, as if he could see straight through her. The others looked to her with questioning stares. She looked away, ears beginning to burn once more. "It's . . . a long story."

"Well, we've got nearly a week before we reach the funnel," Hansen said, climbing aboard the sand sled. "You can tell it to us on the way."

⌒

Fogvir was expecting him.

The Seeker burst into the tinker's shop, slamming the door hard on its hinges. All the metal gadgets Fogvir had on the wall clinked and tinkled, and dust fell from the ceiling. The Seeker strode in, a sword in one hand and the strange dagger in the other. His gaze swept over the establishment, searching for the glow that indicated a soul.

The Seeker didn't see like other men. He had been born without eyes and had never seen like normal men. However, he had been born an Imperial. Not only was he a Healer, he was a Soulseer as well—a man who could see into the spiritual plane and look at the souls of those around him.

It was much like regular sight, in that everything possessed a soul. Walls, the ground, bits of sand—each gave off their own colors. Things that weren't alive emitted dull colors. Buildings and objects were a dim grey, and the ground was a dingy red bordering on brown. Living souls, however, were always bright. He had seen bright white, bright blue, bright green, deep pink— it all varied, depending on the person.

Fogvir gave off a predominantly bright orange glow, tinged with yellow. It was faint, but the Seeker could see it. It was the color of fear.

He was sitting at his counter, staring directly at the Seeker. His arms were outstretched, and he held something in his hands, though the Seeker couldn't tell what—it held no color and seemed to be nothing more than empty space to his eyes. The Seeker narrowed his eyes and looked down at the dagger he held in his hand. It, too, was devoid of color, and hard to see with his Imperia, save for a few fuzzy lines delineating its shape.

"You tried to kill me," the Seeker said, raising his head back up.

"I did not," Fogvir replied. "You were never in any danger. That knife was only designed to incapacitate an Imperial Healer, not kill them. This, however," he hefted the invisible object—the Seeker couldn't tell what it was—into the air, "will certainly kill you."

The Seeker's eyes narrowed. "Why?"

"She paid me for the gear. I wasn't going to turn away a paying customer."

"Why did you tell her how to stop me?" the Seeker whispered. "The King will know they escaped. He'll kill me."

Fogvir was silent for a moment, and the yellow in his soul faded, replaced by a light green. The color of pity. "He'll kill you anyway. You know that, don't you? Once all the Imperials are gone, he'll find a way to dispose of you."

"No," the Seeker said. "No, he won't. I have served the kings of Everfont for generations. I'm too useful to him. He wouldn't get rid of me."

"He will. There will be a time when there are no more Imperials left on Gritt. No Imperials beside you. Once that happens, he may use you to kill political dissidents, but even those will dry up eventually. And when that time comes, the King will find a way to dispose of you. It could be exile, but I doubt it. He doesn't like loose ends. If I had my guess, he'll cart you out to the middle of the desert, dig a hole, and bury you in it. If you're ever found, it will be hundreds of years later, by men who dig to find relics of the past."

The Seeker balled his hands into a fist. Tears would have flowed from his eyeless sockets if he had the ability to cry. He wanted to scream, to tell Fogvir he was wrong, and to say the King would never betray him.

He knew that wasn't the case. He knew, deep down, the King would discard him just as easily as he had discarded his niece. He was a tool to be used, then abandoned once its purpose had been fulfilled.

It was a truth he didn't care to think about. One he tried to bury deep inside. Slowly, he stuffed his emotions away. He would deal with that when the time came.

He stiffened. "If you've thought of a way to kill me, then I presume you've also made something that can cross the desert."

Fogvir's soul flickered, a line of fuscia shooting between his chest and head. Surprise. The little man was surprised. He had expected the Seeker to come here seeking revenge. Well, he would have it eventually. When he came back from killing the King's niece, he would gut Fogvir like a sand flipper. But for now, he needed something to get him across the desert. To stop that girl and her friends before they reached the funnel. Fogvir was the only one who could provide him with something to catch them.

He stayed his hand, even though it twitched to be rid of the small man.

Even now, he could sense them, using their Imperia as they sailed across Gritt. Little ripples, like waves, coursing through the air. Pulses from Imperia that had been used. They came frequently, telling him the girl thought they had escaped. Why use her Imperia after all this time if she thought they hadn't? Fools. No one was safe from him.

He *was* death. He would collect what was owed him and bask in the blood that was rightfully his.

"You're still going after them?" Fogvir asked. "Even after what I just told you?"

"Do you have something to take me across the desert?" the Seeker asked again.

"The King is using you. Don't you see that? You don't have to obey him. Those are innocent people out there and you—"

The Seeker slammed his hand against the wall, causing several metal items to clatter to the ground. "I will pay you. Double what the girl paid you for this dagger." Drops were the only language Fogvir understood.

Fogvir stared at him, a bit of yellow glow returning. Then, he let out a sigh and scratched the back of his neck. "In the back. It's a large metal tube that will propel you through the sand. It's designed after a mix of scorch wyrms and sand gators. I'll have to show you how to use it."

"Then show me quickly. They grow further every moment," the Seeker said, sliding across the counter. Fogvir nodded and left for the back room. The Seeker followed, ready to chase after his quarry.

꒦

"You fought the Seeker?"

Marle's voice filled with wonder as she spoke. It was their fifth day on the sands. The four had gone surprisingly quickly. Each of them had taken time to themselves, thinking about what it meant to be leaving. Ryan had played with Eva and her dolls to keep her entertained.

Each night, they stopped to set up camp with some tents Hansen owned, as well as fur blankets. He instructed everyone to stay wrapped up tight—during the night, temperatures dropped low enough for people to freeze to death outside of Everfont, something Ryan wouldn't have believed had she not experienced the cold. When dawn broke, they would clean up camp and continue onward.

Her arm still hurt from where Fault had twisted it, and the best medicine she could give it was sleep. The cut on Walton's face had scabbed over and the bruising on Marle had begun to fade.

They sat at the back of the sand sled, behind a triangular wind shield. It prevented dust from flying into their faces and they all had to sit behind it lest they be blown off. Ryan had peeked out once and had been blasted by a mixture of sand and wind that nearly ripped her face off.

Ryan looked away, embarrassed. "It wasn't really me. The dagger Fogvir gave me did all the work."

"Even still," Marle said, eyes shining. "You fought death himself and escaped! No one else in Everfont can say that."

"Once we get off Gritt, we should have you fight Walton," Poppertrot chuckled. "See if you'll be able to land a blow on him like Dmitri."

"Shut up," Walton grumbled.

"It wasn't anything, really," Ryan said. "I caught him by surprise, is all. I don't think he was expecting it. He's been immortal so long, I guess he thought nothing could be a threat."

"Did you bring it with you?" Marle asked.

Ryan shook her head. "I left it in his chest. Fogvir said it would only work if it remained in his body." She still felt guilty about that. Fifty thousand drops, all for three items she no longer had. Even though it had been worth it, it felt wasteful spending so much money.

Poppertrot clucked his tongue. "Shame. We could have used it. Where we're going, there's bound to be other Imperials and I hear Healers are the most common kind. If we run into one that meant us harm, it would be useful to stop them."

Ryan's thoughts flickered to Samuel. He was the only other Healer she knew, and it was doubtful she would ever run into him again. He would be stuck in Everfont for the rest of his life, and she would be on one of the other worlds. She did have to admit, the dagger would have come in handy if they ever crossed paths again. Especially after she had abandoned him.

"What world are we going to?" Ryan asked, changing the subject. It still didn't feel real to her. Not yet. She doubted it would feel real until they reached the funnel and maybe not even until they had passed through.

Poppertrot scratched his head. He opened his mouth to speak, but Eva cut him off, eyes gleaming. "I want to go to Wsulfenraast!"

Ryan winced, and Walton shook his head with disapproval. Of the three worlds they could go to—Niall, Rim, and Wulfenraast—Wulfenraast was the worst. It had many gorgeous sights, with towering mountains, deep and colorful oceans and even lava fields adorning its landscape. The problem, however, was no one but Elementalists were allowed to be citizens. They would be just as poor there as they were here.

Ryan touched Eva gently on the arm. "How about we go somewhere else? Somewhere where we can be happy?"

Eva frowned. "We . . . wouldn't be happy on Wulfenraast?"

Poppertrot snorted. "Not unless you like being a slave. If we're going there, I might as well stay here on Gritt."

"Too late for that," Marle grunted, shifting her legs. "Unless you want us to push you off and you can walk back."

"Might be worth it. You lot are already getting on my nerves," Poppertrot yawned, then winked at Eva. She giggled.

Still, the question persisted in their minds. Where would they go now that they could go anywhere? There were only three choices, yet it felt like an infinity of possibilities. Would they go to Rim? Ryan had heard from Fogvir they had an entire continent made of metal there, built thousands of years ago. What about Niall? The center of the world there was ravaged by a never-ceasing storm, but the lands where people lived were far enough away, they only experienced a light rain, something none of them had ever seen. Wulfenraast was even a possibility, though it was her least favorite of the bunch.

"I'd like to go to Niall," Marle said softly. "They say the rains never end there."

"Wouldn't you get tired of it?" Poppertrot asked. "It'd be fascinating to see once—but water falling from the skies isn't natural. It's something best left in fairy tales."

"It used to rain on Gritt," Walton said. Everyone turned to him, amazed he had spoken so many words at a time. They waited for more, but he said nothing.

"Well, I still say it's not natural," Poppertrot muttered. "Water comes from the ground. It always has."

"What does rain feel like?" Eva asked, tugging at Ryan's arm. "Is it nice?"

"I . . ." Ryan faltered, trying to think of the right words. "I don't know what it feels like, sweetie. But I'm sure it will be wonderful."

Eva smiled, her eyes brightening. "Well, I'd like to go to Niall then."

The idea of never-ending rain did seem appealing. Their water had come from the center pillar, and though it was clean, Ryan had to imagine water from the air would be cleaner. She did like the sensation of water on her feet in the Water Gardens, and she assumed the ground on Niall would be similar. "And you, Walton? Where would you like to go?"

"Niall," he grunted. Like always, he offered no explanation.

"Looks like you're outnumbered, Pop," Ryan said with a grin. Poppertrot rolled his eyes and stuck out his tongue. Eva giggled and Marle chuckled.

"There," Walton suddenly said. He pointed outward, into the sand flying past their faces. Ryan followed his finger, trying to see what he was pointing at.

"There's nothing there, you old fool," Poppertrot said, squinting. Ryan didn't see anything either. Marle, however, held up a hand.

"A wreck," Marle whispered.

Ryan saw it as soon as she said it. Through the dust, she could faintly see a white sail sticking out of the ground. They had turned around and were circling it while slowing. It seemed Hansen had spotted it also and intended to investigate.

Slowly, they came to a stop, the cloud of dust settling behind them. From the wreckage, a large plume of smoke was billowing into the air. Ryan was just about to rise from her seat when Hansen appeared.

"Sorry for the stop, ladies and gents. And Trompkins," he added after a moment. "Someone's sent up a signal fire, meaning they're in distress."

"We know what a signal fire is," Poppertrot said.

"Well then. As part of the sand sailor code, we stop to help all shipwrecked and wayward travelers upon the dunes. For a small fee," he smiled faintly as he said the last part. "So don't worry your little heads. We'll offer some assistance and then we'll be right back on our way to the funnel. Oh, and, while I'm gone, don't get off the ship."

He hopped off the sand sled, trudging through the desert to the wreckage. He had stopped a long way from the wreck, far enough away Ryan couldn't make out the details of the wreck. She thought she saw three people, scrounging about, but the heat obscured her vision, making it impossible to tell.

"I can't believe this," Poppertrot muttered. "Now, of all times?"

"Hush," Marle said. "We've waited years to make it to the funnel. We can wait a little bit longer."

"That's the problem," Poppertrot growled. "I don't want to wait any longer!"

Eva scooted over and rested her head on Ryan. In return, Ryan wrapped her arms around her little sister to comfort her. Sweat began to glisten on her skin and she wiped a bit away from her forehead. Now they weren't moving, it was easy to feel just how hot the desert was.

It wasn't just hot. It was sweltering. Within minutes, they were all drenched, fanning themselves with their hands as they clamored for shade underneath the sail. Ryan continually wiped her forehead on her sleeve, only to find there was more sweat than before.

"Crives," she muttered. "Why is it so hot?"

"No runes to protect us," Marle said, faring worse than Ryan. "Everfont is cooler than the rest of the desert."

Ryan frowned. Something about that didn't make sense, but she couldn't put her finger on what. Regardless, it was blistering. It was like she was going to melt right out of her skin. Fortunately, it didn't take Hansen long to return, with the three figures in tow. Unfortunately, however, Ryan recognized them.

Hatred welled within her. It was an emotion she had only felt once before in her life, for the King, and now it filled her to the brim, though it was mixed with longing and hurt. Beside her, Marle and Walton also rose with spiteful looks on their faces. When Hansen drew into earshot, Eva was the first to speak.

"Dmitri!" she squealed. Despite the heat and how flushed her face was, she jumped up and down with excitement. Dmitri heard her and looked up with surprise. Shame flickered across his face, and he looked down, refusing to meet her eyes.

Much to her surprise, Ryan also recognized Samuel, though he had found a different wardrobe since she had last seen him. His clothes had changed from dirty and dingy to the fine silks of those who lived in the Water Gardens. Their color was darker than intended, for he had already sweat through them. They were built for style and not practicality. He constantly pulled at his collar and wiped sweat from his brow, trying to beat the heat. Serves him right, Ryan thought. *Serving in the King's Hand.* The third figure was Sul, the sand sailor, and Ryan's suspicions were confirmed. He hadn't been captured—he had merely been hidden until he could take Dmitri across the desert. He briefly glanced at Ryan though it was hard to read his expression. The triangle face and the awkward placing of his eyes and mouth made it hard for her to understand what he was thinking.

"I hope you're not bringing them with us," Marle said. Her voice was even and controlled, but there was a dangerous edge there. Beside her, Walton nodded and balled his hands into fists.

Hansen held up his hands. "They've paid me already. I've no choice but to take them. And we don't have time to talk about it. We're in sand gator territory."

"Sand gators are real?" Eva asked, looking up at Ryan.

Ryan shook her head. "He's just trying to get a rise out of us."

"I'm not," Hansen said, close enough now he could speak in a normal voice. "You've never seen them because the ground isn't soft enough near Everfont. But out here, they breed like rabbits."

"What are rabbits?" Eva asked, confused.

Ryan opened her mouth to object, but she didn't have time to get the words out. As if to prove Hansen's point, the ground erupted beneath Sul. Two, giant, gaping jaws burst from the sand, lined with wickedly sharp teeth. He didn't even have time to look terrified before they snapped shut, swallowing him whole and disappearing back underneath the sand.

"By white-fire," Poppertrot breathed. Walton paled and Marle turned green. Hansen began shouting orders at Dmitri and Samuel, who dashed toward the boat. The sand bubbled beneath Samuel's feet, but he dove to the side as a second gator burst from the sands, narrowly missing him. In the distance, just at the cusp of the horizon, the desert rumbled, clouds of sand shooting up into the air like little sandstorms.

"Crives! What are those?" Ryan gaped, stumbling backward.

Hansen was the first to reach the sand sled. He leapt up with ease, dashing past Ryan. Already, the wind was whipping around them as he pushed into the sail. They jerked forward. Ryan wobbled. She grabbed Eva to keep her little sister from falling.

"The backs of the gators," Hansen said. "We're near a nest."

"A nest?" Marle said, horrified. Down on the sand, Dmitri had reached the sand sled and was pulling himself up. Samuel followed soon after. The two of them glanced at Ryan, but she ignored them as Hansen worked to channel the wind.

"Can you get us out of here?" she asked.

"If we can get up to speed," Hansen grunted. His face was twisted in concentration, and he made strange hand movements in the air, as if trying to push the wind harder. It began to whip up faster and faster around them, but the sand sled was hardly moving. In the distance, the gators grew closer.

Ryan looked back. There wasn't enough time. With the extra weight, it would take too long to get up to speed—by which time the gators would have arrived and they would be lunch.

She looked down at her hands. The well of power within her had refilled during her sleep. It was a foreign feeling to her, the use of her Imperia without fear of being hunted. But they were free of Everfont and the Seeker now. It was time she started acting like it.

"I'm going to give you a shove!" she shouted to Hansen.

"What?"

She was already moving to the back. "Don't stop for me. I'll catch up."

At least, I hope I can.

She leapt off the sand sled as Marle and Poppertrot cried in protest. They moved to the edge, begging her to come back on, but she ignored their cries.

She leapt a good distance away, rolling onto the sand. It burned her skin wherever it touched and she winced from the pain. Beneath her, the sand began to boil, and she threw herself to the side as a sand gator rose from the ground. She caught a glimpse of its eyes underneath the sand, hollow slits with sand spilling out of them.

Whatever gods made this place need to be thrown in white-fire.

She rose to her feet. Power welled within her as she grabbed hold of her Imperia. The muscles in her arms grew, as did the muscles in her legs as she ran back to the sand sled, tearing off her sling and grabbing the wood. Her feet dug into the sand, the grains scorching her feet as she sunk a few inches as she pushed.

The sand sled hardly moved at first. Then, blessedly, it picked up speed, moving with ease beneath her touch. She winced as the arm Fault had grabbed cried out in pain, but it functioned well enough. The sled picked up speed, sliding easier and easier across the sand. Sweat cascaded down her arms, her face, her legs as she pushed with all her might, the heat bearing down on her, yet it was working. Soon, the sand sled would be faster than the sand gators.

The sand boiled beneath her.

"Get on!" Poppertrot yelled.

She gave the sand sled a final shove, pushing it away from her as the sand gator erupted from the sand. The others looked at her with fear and despair, and the last face she saw was Dmitri's, his expression riddled with horror as the jaws snapped shut around her.

The gator caught her in its mouth, its rancid breath prickling her skin. Its mouth clamped down on her, darkness covering her like the night sky covered the world. Ryan could feel them turning in the air as the gator twisted its body to drag her to the depths of the sand.

But it had never faced anything like her before. She was an Imperial.

An Amplifier.

Imperia still coursed through her body, and she focused it all into her one arm, her muscles bulging and veins popping out of her skin as she slammed a fist into the bottom of the sand gator's mouth. There was a loud crunching sound and light flooded around her as the sun burst through the sand gator's mouth, its bottom jaw forcefully ripped open. The snapping of bones reverberated in the air as the sand gator was flung to the side from the sudden force. Ryan tumbled out of its mouth, slamming into the ground, scattering sand around her.

The giant reptile twisted and writhed in the sand, its jaw whipping about limply. It let out a low whine and its tongue flapped about awkwardly as it slapped at its face with its short stubby flippers. The sand boiled beneath its body and a second sand gator leapt from the desert, clamping the broken one in its jaws. The whines turned to screams as it thrashed to free itself, but the second gator had a firm grip. The two giant beasts slowly wiggled back into the sand, the screams muffling before fading altogether, leaving Ryan alone in the desert.

Ryan stared at the spot where the sand gators had disappeared. The creatures had been massive, the size of buildings, and it was eerie the way they had been able to just disappear. She stood hesitantly, legs shaking, ignoring the burning of her feet. She raised her eyes and, in the distance, she could see sand clouds rushing toward her, growing closer every moment.

She turned. Behind her, the sand sled was becoming a distant speck, kicking up a sandstorm in its wake. She grasped the Imperia that was still in her arm and moved it to her legs, breaking into a sprint. She kicked up sand as she flew, gaining on the sand sled. The sand licked at her heels, as if trying to burn her, but she was moving so fast she could hardly feel it.

As she ran, she couldn't help but smile to herself. Now, the fact they were leaving felt real.

∽

The Seeker felt a wave of Imperia wash over him.

It was stronger than he had ever felt before. He could sense it in his bones. It was like someone had shot a bonfire into the sky for all to see.

But no one could see it.

No one besides him.

He pressed the thruster on the sand torpedo, propelling himself forward through the ground. For the first time in his life, he felt challenged. Here was a worthy hunt for him—nothing like stalking the streets of Everfont, towering over the townspeople as they whispered prayers of warning. Out here, authority meant nothing.

The knowledge sent a soft shiver down his spine. Beyond the walls of Everfont was a true test of his skill. Beneath the desert sun, after he finally ended the last three Imperials, he could return to his king with pride.

Chapter Eight

THE OTHERS GAPED AS RYAN TOOK ONE FINAL BOUND onto the sand sled. It took her only a few minutes to catch up to the sand sled, moving as quickly as she did across the desert. She flew, wind tearing at her clothes and skin, before landing on the wooden deck with a roll.

A sandstorm whipped around them, kicked up by the sand sled. Ryan had covered her eyes with her arm as she had run, only peeking when absolutely necessary. Poppertrot's eyes were red, and he turned away, trying to hide the fact he'd been crying. Eva's face was also red, with streaks of water running down her cheeks. Marle and Walton were much the same.

"Crives, Ryan," Marle croaked. "You scared me half to death."

Sweat glistened along Ryan's skin and she gave Marle an exhausted smile as she collapsed beside the small wind covering. Both Dmitri and Samuel stared at her with mixtures of wonder and fear, but they said nothing. For that, she was grateful. She didn't want to talk to either of them right now.

"Yeah. Me, too," Ryan breathed, laying down and letting her feet hang off the side. The unfortunate part of being an Amplifier, she had just learned, was that it had limits. Her endurance, her speed, her strength all increased—but just like a regular person, she tired.

But . . . white-fire, it felt good to use her Imperia to its fullest. It was like a part of her had been unchained. Something she had always seen as a curse or a hindrance had been brought into light and she now saw it was a blessing instead. Anxiety still pricked at her, as it always did when she used her Imperia, but she assumed that would disappear with time. Without the threat of the Seeker looming over her, a lot of things would change.

"Breaking people out of prison, escaping sand gators, running across deserts. It makes me wish I was an Imperial," Poppertrot said.

Ryan draped a hand over her eyes, chest heaving up and down. "I'll trade you the last seven years for it." She took in quick gasps of air. Her Imperia made her quicker and stronger, but it did not spare her from the effects of fatigue. She felt something push into the crook of her arm and peeked down to see Eva snuggling in close. Her sister looked up with eyes still filled with tears but a smile on her face.

Ryan smiled back and ruffled her little sister's hair before laying back down.

Poppertrot laughed. "Well. Looks like we won't have to worry about anyone robbing us. Ryan will just break their legs for us."

"I wouldn't rely on me," Ryan said defensively. "I didn't have much of an opportunity to practice in Everfont. Fogvir said it's like a muscle, and I haven't worked it very much."

"No doubt, no doubt," Poppertrot said, still grinning from ear to ear. "But now we're gone, you'll have plenty of opportunity."

The thought was foreign to Ryan. True, she could use her Imperia without being chased or hunted—but becoming skilled with it? Practicing it, like she had practiced the different routes in Everfont? It was a discomforting notion. After all, because of the King, she had grown up hiding her power. To be able to use it so brazenly was something that had never crossed her mind. All she had thought about was escape.

"We'll see," she said after a moment. She draped a hand over her eyes to blot out the sun, exhaustion pressing in on her. The conversation died down as they continued forward, and Ryan drifted off to sleep.

It was a few hours later when she woke. She sat up, alarmed at the unfamiliar settings, before remembering where she was and what was happening. The panic ebbed in her chest and she relaxed, looking around.

The sun had begun to dip in the sky and everyone else had fallen asleep. Eva was nestled up beside her, and Marle was on the other side. Walton and Poppertrot had curled up at the edges of the wind shield in what looked like an uncomfortable position, both snoring loudly, while Samuel was on the opposite end. He was so quiet Ryan would have thought he was dead if not for the soft rising and falling of his chest.

Only Dmitri was awake. Ryan jumped, some of her alarm returning, as she saw him staring at her with a cold, dispassionate gaze. Her first instinct was to ask what was wrong and why he was so gloomy. It took a moment for her to remember—he wasn't gloomy and nothing was wrong. This was his true face.

The others were asleep. She would never get a better chance to ask.

She steeled herself and swallowed as she whispered a single word. "Why?"

She supposed there were a dozen other questions she could have asked. Like how he could have done it, or how long he had been planning on betraying them. If he had captured any of the other couriers. None of those seemed of consequence at the moment. Nothing mattered more than the reason behind his actions.

"I wanted to survive," Dmitri said at last. He didn't bother to look at her, and there was a faraway look in his eye. "Giving you to the King was the only way to do that."

Ryan bristled. "No, it wasn't. We were almost there! You could have left with us!"

"You don't understand," Dmitri whispered hoarsely. "They would have found me. They would have found us, eventually. We would have always been running away."

Ryan shook her head. "Once we're off world, we don't have to worry anymore. The King won't be able to find us. We'll be free!"

"No, we won't," Dmitri said miserably. He looked outward, across the desert, a hollow look in his eye. "The King will never stop hunting you."

Ryan blinked. "He has no reason to find me anymore. We're not a threat to his authority."

"If you were anyone else besides his niece, that would be true, but you're related to him by blood. That gives you a claim to the throne. If there were ever a revolution, if the people were to ever turn against him, they would merely need to prop you up as a figurehead, or someone that looks like you. Until he knows you're dead, he can't rest."

Ryan blinked, bewildered. She hadn't thought of that. Never had she had a desire to rule the Everfont, or to overthrow her uncle. She had just wanted to survive, and to provide a good life for Eva.

Dmitri continued. "He needs to know you're dead. Both you and Eva. It's the only way to be sure, if there ever is a revolution, neither you nor your descendants are leading it. He will send assassins after you until the job is done."

"That's . . ." Ryan couldn't find the right word. Crazy? Insane? Neither of them came close to describing the situation. She had thought she was finally free, now that she had escaped the Seeker. Eva could finally live a normal life.

How wrong she was.

"Why didn't you just kill me?" Ryan asked. "You could have left years ago."

"Because I . . ." Dmitri's voice rose, his body shaking with anger. Some of his demeanor fell, and she saw him battling inside himself. The moment passed, and his wall of emotion returned. He closed his eyes before opening them and calmly stating, "Because I fell in love with you."

Ryan's heart twisted, and she forced back tears. She shook her head. "No. No, you didn't. You would have never done anything like this if you really loved me."

"It's the truth," Dmitri said. He looked away, misery flashing across his face. "I was going to do it when I first came to the Post. Your life for my freedom. It would have been so easy. Instead, I saw how you cared for your sister, and the other couriers. I wanted to be part of that." He shook his head. "I thought I could escape with you. But my nightmares stayed. I don't think they'll ever go away until I know I'm free. Every night, he's coming for me. I . . . I couldn't take it anymore." Tears fell down Dmitri's cheeks and he struggled to keep his breathing even, "Ryan. I'm . . . I'm truly sorry."

Tears began to leak out of Ryan's eyes, too. Her anger at Dmitri was still there, but it had simmered. She understood why he had done what he did. It was no different than what other members of the Post, or some of the members of the King's Hand, or the people in the slums had done to survive. Even though she understood, that didn't lessen the pain of betrayal. If anything, it made it worse.

They sat without words for a while, until they stopped crying. It was a few minutes before Ryan trusted herself to speak without her voice cracking, and when she did, she asked, "Where will you go?"

Dmitri shrugged. "I don't know. Rim, maybe. It's bigger than Niall and easier to hide in."

Ryan nodded. That would be for the best, since the rest of them were going to Niall. A part of her wanted to offer him a place with them—her feelings were still raw, and she was used to the comfort his presence provided—but she knew she couldn't. Not after what had happened. If he did come with them, she would never be able to trust him again.

"Well, I wish you the best then," Ryan said. Part of her meant it. Another part felt like the words were acid on her tongue.

Dmitri smiled sadly at her. Ryan opened her mouth to ask him why he had brought the painting when his eyes narrowed. Ryan followed his gaze and through the sandstorm, she caught a glint of something speeding toward them. Something fast.

She got to her feet. "Another sand gator?" she asked Dmitri. He didn't say anything and continued to peer out into the desert.

She called out to Hansen. "Hey! Sailor! Is that a sand gator following us?"

She was surprised he heard her over the wind. He cast a glance backward, frowning. "Couldn't be! It's moving too fast!"

Then what in white-fire was it? Ryan began waking the others, nudging them one by one. Poppertrot cursed at her, and Walton grumbled. Marle sat up straight away with a dull look on her face. Ryan didn't touch Samuel, but he woke up on his own from all the noise and so did Eva.

"What's going on?" she asked.

"Something's following us," she said, pointing out into the desert. It had grown closer now, and she could see it had a silver glint to it. Something metal?

"Whatever it is, it means trouble," Dmitri said. He drew his sword.

"What good do you think that will do?" Samuel asked. "You won't be able to swipe at it from up here."

Dmitri ignored him. "Marle, take Eva up next to Hansen. Walton, Poppertrot, Ryan, by me."

"What makes you think we're taking orders from you?" Poppertrot said. "You tried to kill all of us."

"We don't know what this thing is. We all want to live," Dmitri countered. "Even if it's harmless, we should be prepared to fight it together."

"Maybe it's just hunting fresh meat," Marle said. "Maybe we should toss you overboard to stop it."

Walton nodded. "Good idea."

"No," Ryan said. The others turned to her, astonished. She shook her head. "We left Everfont behind us. We're about to start new lives. Do we want our first decision as free people to be to murder someone else?"

"He tried to kill us first," Poppertrot protested.

"And if we kill him now, we're no better than him," Ryan argued. She looked at Dmitri, who stared at her passively. "We're not in Everfont anymore. Any grievances we have are now in the past."

The others muttered their disagreement. Walton shook his head, and Poppertrot seemed ready to explode. Marle, however, just sighed. She leaned down beside Eva, who had a terrified look on her face, and held out her hand. Eva took it and Marle led the two of them to the front of the ship, walking backward so they didn't get sand in their eyes.

Ryan looked at Poppertrot and Walton. They met her gaze with defiance. Walton was the first to break. He mumbled something beneath his breath and hefted his spear, walking past Ryan to stand beside Dmitri. Poppertrot was next, shooting Ryan a distasteful look as he took up his position.

Ryan gulped, grateful they had listened and completed the formation. The silver thing was getting closer.

"What do I do?" Samuel asked. He stood warily behind them, giving each one of them a distrustful look-over. Something about him seemed . . . off. Ryan couldn't put her hand on why.

"You're a Healer, right?" Dmitri said.

"Yes."

"Heal us if one of us gets hurt," Dmitri ordered. Samuel seemed dissatisfied with his answer, but he didn't get a chance to argue. The silver thing suddenly leapt from the sand, jumping high into the air. It looked like a tube, with a pointed end. A glass window at the front burst off the machine, and a figure leapt out. He flew above them before landing on the center of the sand sled, between Ryan and the others and Marle and Eva.

The figure in black turned around, raising a dagger, and leveling it at Ryan.

Ryan's blood ran cold, and Samuel let out a shrill shriek. Dmitri cursed, as did Poppertrot and Walton. Marle shouted something Ryan couldn't hear, and Eva began to cry.

It was the Seeker.

He had chased them across the desert when Ryan thought they would be safe.

And now there was nowhere to run.

Chapter Nine

THE SEEKER STRUCK.

He attacked Ryan first. Before she could react, he was upon her, ramming the dagger into her chest. She tensed up as the blade sunk into her heart. He pushed her backward, yanking the dagger out, and she fell onto the sand sled, blood pouring out of the wound. Within seconds, Walton and Dmitri were upon him, swinging their spears and swords. Ryan was faintly aware of Poppertrot leaning over her and the world dimming. . . .

Then it flooded back to life. She gasped as Samuel grasped her arm, healing her body. He gave her a quick nod as his Imperia worked its way through her body, patching up the hole the Seeker had left. Within moments, it was finished, and Samuel moved toward the fight. At the front of the sand sled, Marle brandished a small sword, with Eva cowering behind her.

"You all right, lass?" Poppertrot asked, helping Ryan to her feet.

Ryan nodded, turning to the side and spitting. The spit was red as it left her lips, and she wiped her mouth with the back of her hand. "Yeah. A little woozy."

"Getting stabbed will do that to you," Poppertrot grimaced. With a roar, he too, moved to attack the Seeker. He had no weapon, but he didn't need it. Trompkins were stronger than humans, and his fists were like clubs.

The Seeker was a blur as they fought. Dmitri and Walton were barely keeping up with him, knocking away the dagger and avoiding getting stabbed. Behind them, Samuel continually healed each one as they were cut, healing their wounds as quickly as they appeared. The Seeker did the same, however. Dmitri swung his sword, nearly taking the Seeker's head off. Blood poured out, and the Seeker's head hung by a thread of skin. He simply snapped his head back into place; his neck sewed back together while he continued forward as if the wound were nothing more than a nuisance.

Ryan growled and reached for her Imperia—to find her reserves were gone.

Panicked, she searched inside herself. She could still feel her Imperia—but the well was empty, most of it taken by the dagger. It would take time to refill, but time was something she didn't have.

Crives.

She dashed around the fight and the Seeker's gaze followed her. He tried to swipe at her with the dagger, but was blocked by Poppertrot, who ran a fist into his face. There was a loud crunch and the Seeker fell, his face caved in. Crackling filled the air as his bones realigned themselves, and his skin stitched itself back together and he forced himself to his feet. Dmitri ran him through, to which the Seeker stabbed him in the neck. Samuel pulled Dmitri away and healed him while Walton stepped in front of the Seeker and shoved him back with his spear.

Ryan arrived at the front. "Can't you help us?" she screamed at Hansen.

He shook his head. "We're still in sand gator land! If I stop, we're all dead!"

Crives. Ryan looked to Marle and Eva. They were so close. It was just this last obstacle. Once the Seeker was gone, they were home free. But how was she supposed to kill the unkillable?

The Seeker rammed his dagger into Poppertrot's side. The Trompkin grunted as Samuel reached out to heal him, and the wound began to seal. There was a moment, a break in the formation between them, that left Ryan exposed. The Seeker seized the opportunity, lunging for Ryan with the dagger raised high. Ryan froze as it plunged downward, heading straight for her heart. A shadow moved in front of her.

The dagger slammed into Samuel. He let out a groan as he stumbled backward. Fear filled his eyes as he fumbled for the blade, now embedded in his chest. Behind them, Dmitri ran his sword through the Seeker, and Walton stabbed him, but the Seeker remained unperturbed. Casually, unbothered by the blades sticking out of his body, he shoved Samuel off the side.

⌐

Samuel hit the sand hard and then bounced. He bounced like the stones he used to skip in the Water Gardens when he was off-duty. Smooth rocks were the best to throw. He had discovered that after his third time skipping them on the water. It had something to do with the angle, and one of the other guards had said surface tension was a big part of it.

He wasn't smooth, like those rocks, but that didn't stop him from bouncing. He hit, then he hit again, then again until finally, he skidded to a stop. The heat hit him instantly, as did the pain.

He reached for his healing, but there was none. The dagger . . . somehow, the dagger had taken it all. He reached down to his stomach to see it there, as well as his hand, bloodied from sliding across the sand.

A groan, mixed with a gurgle, emanated from his throat and fear knotted in his chest. He couldn't heal. He couldn't heal! There had never been a time when he couldn't heal before! He reached for his Imperia as he watched the blood pour from his body and the heat seared his wounds; he tried to heal, but nothing happened.

He pulled the dagger from his body. At once he felt a trickle of Imperia flow back into him—enough to mend the wound and for his anxiety to abate. It didn't matter, though. The sand sled was already a speck in the distance, leaving him alone in the desert. The heat bore down like fire in the air, further drenching his already sopping clothes.

He knelt on the sand. Strangely, he felt at peace. Throughout his life, he had wanted to be a good person. To help others, to protect them and be a shining example of hard work and dedication. His time in the King's Hand had muddied that goal and changed him into something else—but, here, at the end, he had done what was right. He had finally protected someone else.

Was protecting one person, at the very end of his life, enough to give him redemption? Probably not. Still, his soul felt lighter. As if . . . as if he had been forgiven.

Maybe he had been saved after all. Just not in the way he expected.

The sand beneath him began to rumble and Samuel closed his eyes.

ꝏ

The Seeker turned from the edge of the sand sled as Samuel disappeared. He drew a second dagger from his belt. Ryan's blood ran cold as, for a second time, he pointed it at her.

Dmitri and Walton backed away, raising their weapons warily. Poppertrot nursed his side—Samuel had been able to heal most of it before he had been flung over, but not all. Blood still seeped from the wound, and Poppertrot winced as they stepped backward. They formed a triangle, with Ryan behind them while Marle and Eva looked on with fear. Hansen cast occasional glances backward, looking at each of them with concern.

"You, uh, want to hurry this up?" he called, casting a backward glance at Ryan. "I don't like passengers who haven't paid."

"We could use some help," Ryan growled.

"Can't. Gotta keep the sailor moving. Sand gators," he said.

The Seeker advanced, unwarily now. He could afford to be loose with his actions, and to get cut. The others could not. He dashed toward Ryan, only to be met by Walton, who shoved him back with his spear. The Seeker stabbed down, catching Walton's spear and flinging it aside. It disappeared as it flew into the wind. The Seeker lunged, arm extended, but Walton sidestepped him and caught his arm.

There was a loud snap as Walton broke the Seeker's arm across his knee. The Seeker didn't flinch, and there was a loud popping as his arm fixed itself. Dmitri plunged his sword into the Seeker's stomach, and Poppertrot punched him in the face. The Seeker went limp, and for a moment, Ryan thought they might have won. The Seeker was pushed toward the edge of the sled as Dmitri, Walton, and Poppertrot prepared to throw him off.

The Seeker jerked awake right as they reached the edge. He twisted out of their grip and darted to the side. Walton yelped as his forward momentum carried him off the side. Ryan gasped, but Poppertrot dove forward and snatched Walton's leg while gripping the wooden boards of the sand sled. He grunted and his muscles strained as he worked to pull Walton back onto the craft.

Which left only Dmitri standing between Ryan and the Seeker. He faced the man clad in black with grim determination.

The Seeker stared at him before lunging forward. Dmitri swung, but the Seeker ducked beneath it and rammed his dagger into Dmitri's stomach. The Seeker pushed him forward before slamming Dmitri down on the wooden boards.

"No!" Eva wailed from behind Ryan. "Dmitri!"

The Seeker turned to face them. Ryan stood between them, setting her face resolutely against him as he approached. If Dmitri, Poppertrot, and Walton couldn't stop him, she had no chance.

That didn't matter. She would fight to the last for her sister.

"No one left to protect you. Nowhere left to run," the Seeker hissed, approaching with dagger in hand. Behind her, Eva's wailing grew louder. A gust of wind whipped over her shoulder, chilling her skin.

Ryan fought for her life. As the Seeker lunged toward her, she fell to her knees and dashed forward, ramming her shoulder into his stomach. He swiped down, but she rolled to the side, kicking his feet out from under him. He hit the wood with a thud, grunting angrily. Before he could push himself up, Ryan kicked him in the face, sending his head spinning. She pulled her leg back and kicked again, this time aiming for his groin, and he doubled over from the blow.

She didn't think. She couldn't afford to think. There was no way to beat the Seeker and right now, she was only buying seconds. Precious seconds that she hoped would give the others time to think of something, *anything*, to bring this monster down.

She raised her leg again, aiming for his neck. As she swung, his arm shot out, gripping her ankle. He yanked her to her knees. Eva cried out as he sliced forward with the dagger. Ryan rolled backward, the blade narrowly scraping against her cheek. She came up on her feet to see the Seeker advancing, dagger held splayed to the side.

She couldn't win. Behind her, she heard Eva wailing, her voice carrying over the sound of the wind and sand rushing past. *Crives. Once he's done with me, he's going to kill Eva. The others, too.*

She looked to the side of the sand sled. There was only one way . . .

She dashed forward with all her might. The Seeker thrust the dagger in her direction, slamming it into her wounded shoulder. She screamed in pain, using it to drive her forward as she slammed her body into him. He stumbled backward, surprised at the sudden onslaught. Off balance, he stumbled backward as Ryan pushed him toward the edge.

Keep going! Keep going! They were almost to the edge. She would push them both over and—

The Seeker slammed a palm into the side of her skull. Her vision went white for a moment, her legs and arms turning to jelly. She gasped as the Seeker yanked the dagger from her shoulder, and pulled her up by her wounded arm. She whimpered at the pain as he raised the dagger to her throat. She feebly tried to pull away, but his grip was too strong. Through his mask, she could see his lips pulled into a grim line.

She had failed.

Then he stumbled back, pulling the dagger away as if something had struck him in the chest, and he dropped Ryan. Ryan gaped, then glanced back, expecting to see Hansen had pulled away from steering for a brief moment. Instead, she saw Eva. Tears still streamed down her sister's face as Marle held her back, but her arms were raised, and her face was twisted in concentration.

The Seeker regained his posture and frowned. He raised the dagger again, this time plunging it toward Ryan's head. There wasn't enough time to evade. It seemed Eva had only bought Ryan a single moment.

But a moment was all it took.

Dmitri slammed into the Seeker from the side, his face a bloody mess. The Seeker grunted and flipped the dagger around, slamming it into Dmitri's back, but Dmitri didn't stop. He pushed the Seeker right up to the edge as the Seeker continued to drive his blade into him. He looked back, his eyes meeting Ryan's, wincing as the dagger was shoved into him over and over and over again.

Time froze and a dozen thoughts ran through Ryan's mind. The Seeker screamed but Ryan didn't hear. Walton and Poppertrot yelled and leapt forward, but they wouldn't make it in time. Dmitri and the Seeker were already falling.

All she could hear was the sound of a heartbeat, her own, as she watched them both plummet over the side.

Then they were gone.

Everything grew quiet. The wind still whipped around them and Eva was still crying, but Ryan couldn't hear any of it. The only sound to her ears was the thumping in her chest, repeatedly, as she waited for Dmitri to appear. Seconds passed. Then minutes, and she was still rooted to the spot.

A part of her expected him to leap back up at any moment. To reveal that he, too, had been an Imperial this entire time—he had just been hiding it. The rational part of her knew otherwise. He was dead. Or, if he wasn't dead from the fall and dagger wounds, he would be shortly.

The sting of his betrayal lessened. Or grew worse, she couldn't tell. It was all too much to process. Yet in her mind's eye, Ryan thought she saw a glimpse of him. Of who he truly was, beneath all the murk and muck. A tortured soul, lost in the chaos of life, trying to find his way. In the end, despite his coldness and the pain he had suffered, he had sacrificed himself.

For her.

She felt a hand on her shoulder, the one that wasn't injured. She looked up to see Marle and realized tears were streaming down her face. Behind Marle, Walton and Poppertrot wore sorrowful expressions, staring off into the desert sand kicked up behind the sand sled. Eva was sobbing as well and ran to put her arms around Ryan's neck.

"It's over. For real this time," Ryan said, voice hoarse. The words had been joyful the first time she had spoken them but now they were bittersweet.

No one else said anything. What could they say? Dmitri had betrayed them, but at the end, he had sacrificed himself for them. In his last moments, he had shown who he truly was.

Ryan stood, wiping away her tears, clutching Eva in her arms. She looked at the others and cleared her throat, trying to sound confident. "We'll live a little extra for him. So his sacrifice isn't wasted."

It wasn't much by way of a memorial. There were so many things Ryan wanted to say or could have said. By Dmitri's standards, he would have appreciated it.

She glanced at the painting he had left behind. It had meant something to Dmitri. It was his only possession. In that sense, it was the only part of him left.

She would take it with her. That way, at least a part of Dmitri would escape Everfont to a better world.

᠊ᢏ

The Seeker screamed as they fell.

They thudded against the ground, bouncing several times before sliding to a stop. The Seeker's wounds sealed as he stood, channeling his Imperia. He strode over to the boy, who was barely conscious from the loss of blood. The Seeker grabbed him by the hair and pulled his head up, channeling a little bit of healing into him. Just enough to keep him alive and conscious.

"Why?" the Seeker asked. "You served the King, now you betray him. Why did you not let me kill her?"

The boy coughed, blood spewing from his lips. The Seeker had never really liked him. He had been too unstable, too fickle, to serve the King. He should have killed him the moment the girl was captured. If he had, she would still be in his grasp.

"Won't . . . won't be . . . scared of you . . . anymore," the boy coughed. There was a peaceful expression on his face. His body was broken and he was dying—but despite that, he seemed stronger than ever. "Won't . . . live . . . in fear. . . ."

"You've committed an act of treason," the Seeker said. In the distance, he could see the sand gators slinking beneath the sand, coming toward them. "Everfont will fall because they escaped. Their descendants will have claim on the throne! Gritt will fall!"

"Lies," the boy said weakly. "All lies . . . she . . . won't . . . won't come back."

The Seeker had heard enough. He placed the dagger against the boy's throat and unceremoniously cut. The boy went rigid for a moment, his face growing pale, before he stopped moving altogether. The Seeker stood back and stared at the body. Still, the boy's face was peaceful, a small smile gracing his face.

How dare he.

The Seeker kicked the boy's face. Then his chest, next his stomach, until his foot was mangled. He sent a wave of healing energy through his body and turned away.

A wave of exhaustion swept over him, and he fell to his haunches. There was no joy in this kill. No pleasure. He had let his emotions get the best of him. He should have at least listened to the boy's story or asked about it. He knew most of it, but there were bits and pieces missing. Instead, he had killed him in a fit of rage.

He always needed to hear the story. Everyone had one to tell. The Seeker's dislike for the boy didn't change how he had things to say, things he had experienced, that no one else had.

"You've gone crazy," he told himself, shaking his head. What would he have written on? The sand at his feet? More than that, why bother to listen? He had moments left to live before the sand gators found him. There would be no outrunning them, and even if he could, he wouldn't survive the heat of the desert.

He was a dead man. His body just hadn't caught up yet.

He stood and looked into the distance. The sand gators weren't far now. He had a few minutes, at best, before they arrived. A few minutes to . . . to . . .

To do what? Contemplate how he had failed his king? How all was lost now?

No. There was only one honorable thing left to do. Drawing deep inside of himself, he filled his body with as much Imperia as he could, drawing all of it out. In a single burst, he forced all of his stored power into his veins.

He was always using his Imperia. Like a muscle, it had grown the more he used it—and he never turned it off. A burst of white filled his vision and his body quivered with the healing energy that poured into his skin. With so much Imperia pouring through him, his Soulsight and Healing couldn't be contained, and the power burst out of his body. Faint blue and white steam leaked from his pores, while light of the same color coursed through his veins and muscles, emerging from his pores and evaporating in the sun.

For a moment—for a fraction of a second—he thought he saw something beyond death. A place of pure white, full of peace and purity. It seared his skin and soul as though he were standing right next to the sun. He would have screamed had his voice not been stolen away by the light. He threw himself backward, onto the sand, desperate to get away.

His Imperia burned out and his vision went dark. The healing that kept him upright extinguished and his body sagged, shaking with effort. His skin had turned cold and despite the heat of the sun, the temperature around him felt as though he had fallen into a frozen lake.

He gripped his dagger with a feeble hand. He barely had enough strength to hold it. His hand shook as he raised it to his throat, placing the blade against his quivering skin.

He had lived by the sword. In his failure, he would die by it.

Chapter Ten

THEY ARRIVED AT THE FUNNEL LATER THAT EVENING. The sun had set, and the moons had risen and with them, the temperature had fallen. In contrast to the heat they had felt during the day, the night was cold and unwelcoming. Somberly, the group embarked from the sled, with nothing but the sound of the water slamming the shore filling the air.

The air was frigid, though Ryan felt cold for different reasons than the temperature. Dmitri kept flashing through her mind, again and again, his last moments etched into her thoughts. She saw him mouthing the words "I'm sorry," right before he fell, though she didn't know if he had actually done that or if she had imagined it.

Several hours had passed since the incident and only now was the adrenaline beginning to wear off. Her head throbbed from where the Seeker had struck her, and she couldn't move the arm that had been stabbed. Hansen had taken a brief look while steering the sand sled and said it would heal, with time.

"They're called waves," Hansen called, breaking the silence. The group turned to face him. He was still on the sand sled, swinging his legs over the edge. "It happens to every planet that has a moon. The technical term is tidal force, but you really only explain that if you want to impress people or look pious."

His voice shook Ryan out of her stupor. Her eyes snapped to the ocean, watching as the white-tipped waves crashed against the shore. It was one of the most beautiful—and strange—things she had ever encountered. Never had she seen so much water in one place. It was hard to believe it was toxic. "How does the *moon* make water move?"

"You'll learn," Hansen said with a cheerful grin. "There are whole other worlds out there, unstifled and brimming with potential. When it's not suffocated by deserts or tyrants, you'll find that life flourishes."

"There aren't tyrants on other worlds?" Poppertrot asked.

"There are," Hansen said. He slipped off the sled, kicking up sand where he landed. He shoved his hands in his pockets and came to stand beside them, tilting back on the balls of his feet. "Other worlds have resources, though. Multiple cities, kingdoms, and continents. Gritt has the worst of everything."

"Comforting," Marle said dryly. "To know we were born in such a desolate place."

"Comforting to know we're leaving it," Poppertrot muttered. "Hard to believe, after all we've been through."

"Agreed," Walton added.

"Why is it so cold?" Eva asked, her teeth chattering, shifting the subject. It was only when she said something that Ryan realized her bare arms were exposed and being nipped at by the brisk wind. Walton, Marle and Eva all had their arms wrapped around themselves. Poppertrot, on the other hand, was unbothered. For once, his fur was a blessing rather than a curse.

"The runes around Everfont regulate the heat and the cold," Marle explained. "It's colder out here because there are no runes to warm up the air."

"What criver came up with the idea to only put runes around Everfont?" Poppertrot muttered. "They could have put runes elsewhere, too."

Normally, Ryan would have joined in and made some kind of comment or quip. However, her attention was captured by something else. She could see the funnel, hovering just at the edge of the waves. It was different than she had imagined. She hadn't known what she had expected, but in her mind's eye, she had seen some kind of door, standing in the middle of nowhere. This was much different. It was raised off the ground a few feet, maybe three or four, and was circular in shape. There was a ring around the outer edge that flickered like fire, spiraling and undulating. In the center, there was nothing but darkness.

It was both amazing and terrifying. That spiral, that circle, was their ticket out of here.

The others seemed to have noticed it as well.

"By the gods of heaven and devils in white-fire," Poppertrot breathed, uncharacteristically reverent. "That is something to see."

"It's beautiful," Walton said, which, for him, was like a declaration of true love.

Eva was disinterested in the funnel. With a whoop, she ran away from the group, heading for the waves. Ryan started after her, but Marle put out a hand to stop her. "Let her go. This is her first time to be free."

"It's too cold for her to play. She'll—"

"She'll be fine," Marle said and made a gesture to the air around them. Ryan started, realizing that it had become warmer for a brief moment. The heat faded the further away Eva went.

Of course. Her little sister was an Elementalist. If she wished, she could warm the air as well as herself. Some of the tension left Ryan's shoulders. Her sister instinctively knew how to warm things. The ocean and the cold wouldn't bother her. This was also her sister's first time to be free. Truly free, without anyone hounding her. Ryan wasn't going to take that away.

"If you're that worried, I'll go watch her," Marle said. The two watched as Eva reached the ocean, stooping down and slapping the waves with unbridled glee. A moment later, and the water was rising into the air, swirling around Eva like a tornado as she controlled it with her Imperia.

"Are you sure?" Ryan asked.

Marle nodded, already jogging toward the beach. "You deserve a rest."

She was gone before Ryan could offer protest. Poppertrot and Walton followed close behind. Soon, the four of them were in the waves, splashing in the ocean and dancing gleefully. Eva doused Poppertrot, who spluttered from the torrent but was soon warmed by a blast of wind from Eva. Walton picked Eva up, who squealed as he tossed her into an oncoming wave.

Ryan watched it all, arms folded, with a heavy melancholy in her chest. She wanted to join in with the rest of them, to splash and let go of her inhibitions. She had been so wound up for so long, it was time she let herself go, too.

But she couldn't. In her mind's eye, she saw one other person splashing in the waves. Someone who would never be in that picture, no matter how much she wished otherwise.

"You did some good work out there."

She started as Hansen appeared at the edge of her vision. He wore a devilish smile as he came to stand beside her. He had taken his hood off to reveal a scruffy face, and sandy blond, shaggy hair that extended to his eyes. "You've got good instincts."

Ryan shrugged. "I did what I needed to protect my family. Anyone would have done the same."

"Ah, but you did it so well," Hansen said. Together, they watched the others play in the ocean. By now, Walton, Poppertrot and Marle had encircled Eva. Each time one of them got close, she pushed them back with a wave of water, giggling all the while. "You and your sister are both very powerful. Are you God-Spoken?"

"God-Spoken?"

"Ah, that's right. I forgot. You don't know anything about Imperia besides the basics." He clicked his tongue. "A God-Spoken is someone born with only one Imperia. It's rare, but it happens. Twice-Blessed is anyone born with two, and Thrice-Gifted is anyone born with three. Four-Cursed is anyone born with four, but that's just as rare as being God-Spoken."

"Oh. I only have the one Imperia. Eva, too," Ryan said. It was useful information to know, especially now that they were going to live among Imperials. They would look foolish without knowing the terminology. She gave Hansen a long look up and down before asking. "And you?"

"And me what?"

"Are you God-Spoken?"

Hansen laughed. "I don't have any Imperia at all." He raised his hand and pulled back his sleeve to reveal several straps on his arm. There were six in total, each one a different color. "These bands give me the ability to use Imperia. I like it better than actually being one."

Ryan stared, both intrigued and baffled by the straps. "There are items that *give you Imperia?*"

Hansen smiled and let his sleeve fall back down. "Yes. They're hard to make, though, and fewer exist than actual Imperials. They have a lot more hindrances. They don't recharge as fast as regular Imperia, and they never grow stronger." He whistled softly as he shuddered. "There are items that nullify Imperia, too. Like that dagger you got from Fogvir."

"You know about that?"

"Of course. Fogvir and I are good friends."

Ryan stared. Until a few days ago, she had never even heard of Hansen. Yet in a matter of moments, he had proven his knowledge and connections. Not only that, he had the ability to use *six* types of Imperia. Whoever he was, he was dangerous, and Ryan was thankful he was on her side, at least for now.

"Still, it's rare for siblings to both be God-Spoken," Hansen said, interrupting her thoughts. He sounded truly impressed. "You two could do anything you wanted out there. Rim. Niall. People would follow you. Not only because you're God-Spoken, but because you're a natural leader."

"We just want to live a quiet life," Ryan said. And she meant it. Her whole time in the Post and in Everfont had been spent running messages at the whims of others. A constant influx of danger and stress. She would be grateful to have a life that was the opposite.

"I wouldn't blame you, after what you've been through," Hansen said. "I would be careful, though. A dull life can lead to a dulling of the senses. Spend long enough at rest and you'll find rest is a harsher mistress than work."

Ryan raised an eyebrow. "And you would know this?"

"All too well."

"Hmph," Ryan grunted. "I suppose you have a solution then?"

Hansen nodded. "I'm a man of some . . . repute, among the different worlds. I often find myself in need of assistants."

"You want me to be a secretary," Ryan said flatly.

"It's a bit more hands-on than being a secretary—but yes, the idea is the same."

"Thanks, but no thanks," Ryan said, moving away from him. "I'd rather stick with my family."

"I would pay you well," Hansen said, though the argument seemed half-hearted. He knew she had already made up her mind. "You would never worry about needing to be cared for. Eva would be taken care of as well."

Ryan laughed. "You already said Eva and I were God-Spoken. We can do anything we wanted, remember?"

What he said next was lost to the wind and waves as she dashed to the beach, a sudden burst of energy running through her veins.

No longer would she be bound by others. No longer would she be hunted for being born an Imperial. No longer would she fear for the life of her sister, or Walton, or Poppertrot, or Marle. No longer would she have to worry. Her uncle would send assassins after her, but she wouldn't let that knowledge temper the moment. She could deal with assassins and whatever else life threw at her.

After seven years, she had escaped.

They were finally free.

Epilogue

"PUT IT RIGHT THERE, PLEASE."

Cackler smiled to himself as the palace servants moved his bed. It had been several weeks since he had won his bet and he was back in his old room; the room that was his before he had been banished. He had finally taken a shower and his skin was soft as a child's. His hair was nicely combed over his head and his beard had been trimmed to an acceptable length and dyed brown. All in all, he looked better than he had in a long time.

The servants set the bed down in the center of the room, the last piece they had to move. Everything else was already in place—dressers, floor rug, table, and sink—and he shooed them off as he plopped himself down on the covers, eager to finally sleep in a real bed again. He sunk into it, like he was being swallowed by quicksand.

Ah, it was good to be home.

It was different than it had been before. Before, the decorations had been more ornamental but now they were all plain. Such was the price of progress. The King had sold everything worth more than half a drop, and most furniture and ornaments beyond the basic necessities had been removed. In some ways, living in the palace was no different now than living in a home in the Water Gardens.

Still, it was better than living in the streets and stealing from street vendors to stay alive.

"Already settled in?"

Cackler glanced lazily at the door. The King had stepped into his room and was looking around disapprovingly. Cackler doubted he had many other expressions these days. The cynic in the King had grown, and that once-youthful, hopeful man had been replaced. Now, everything was distasteful to his eyes.

Cackler flopped onto his side. "Didn't take too much time. I just had them move things in."

The King nodded. "I see. Don't get too comfortable. I'm having a meeting with my advisors in an hour and you're going to be there."

Cackler sat up and sighed. "I've just come back. Can't I get a moment to myself?"

The King's lips twitched. "You said you wanted to be returned to your former station. That means working as hard as you used to."

Cackler grumbled as he swung his feet out of bed. "Should have asked for more," he muttered. "What's this meeting about?"

"The King's Hand is decimated. We only have a few remaining members left," the King said. "Fogvir has an invention that may help with that, but it will require some funding be put into place and we're waiting on another shipment from the mines. In the meantime, we'll be conscripting some of the personal bodyguards of merchants in the Water Gardens to take care of security."

"A budget meeting then," Cackler said flatly.

"Yes. Among other things. We also have to deal with the matter of the Post."

"I thought you were going to sign a treaty with them?"

"Only to get at Eva and Ryan. Without its safeguards, they would have been mine. Now they're gone, the Post will continue to serve the same purpose it did before—one that I would leave unbothered."

Cackler nodded. "Controlled crime."

"Precisely," the King said. "Every civilization has it, even on Evaamara. Rim and Niall, of course, have dozens of sophisticated spy networks and assassins for hire and there are always organized street lords that prey on the weak. The Post is an easy way to let the common people rebel against me without them gaining too much power. It's why I make it legal for them to do business, but not legal for them to be in Everfont."

"You were going to throw that away to get Ryan?"

"The threat of Imperials to the foundation of this kingdom is greater than the loss of the Post. The royal blood that runs through their veins increases how much of a threat they are tenfold." The King tensed as he spoke of them. He was still unhappy they had escaped. "I'm sending an envoy to the new Crow informing them the treaty is invalid, because of the recent prison break. I've also sent one of my most trusted guards to Rim to see if we can find an Etcher who will repair the runes on the Post."

"That will be dangerous. If the residents there find you are working to strengthen them, they may rise up against you. You will have no excuse not to root them out."

"We will use discretion. We'll spread a rumor the Seeker has gone to chase after an escaped Imperial, which is why the Etcher will be willing to help them without fear of getting caught. When the guard returns, he will also come back with another Twice-Blessed to replace the Seeker. We will kill two birds with one stone." The King hesitated. He put a hand on Cackler's shoulder, lowering his voice. "There are two other things that must be addressed, before we continue our partnership together."

"Fire away, old friend. I've missed hearing your droning voice."

The King raised an eyebrow, annoyed, but didn't rise to the gibe. "I'm sure you are aware, but you are still not allowed to have children. You may take mistresses, but not foster any heirs. If you truly wish for someone to inherit your title, you may adopt."

Cackler nodded. It was another secret kept between the two of them. Cackler's lover had the Imperial gene, as did the King himself—but so did Cackler. Cackler was sure the King would have ordered his death, had he not already lost so much. His family. Thousands in Everfont. He couldn't afford to lose his closest friend, too.

Instead, Cackler had been banished and forced to make a vow to never have children. If he had, the Seeker would have killed both him and his descendants.

The King continued. "Second—you know I cannot allow your daughter to live."

"I do," Cackler said. He had known this conversation was coming and had prepared for it.

"I will be sending assassins. They may have killed the Seeker, but the next ones I send will be from off world, hired from Niall and Rim. They won't make the same mistakes as him." The King drew back. "You are not to interfere. That is a royal order. Do I make myself clear?"

"Perfectly," Cackler said.

"Good." The King extended a hand to the doorway. "Then let's be on our way."

"I thought you said it was in an hour?"

"It is. We need to help the servants prepare the meeting room."

Cackler grumbled under his breath as he followed the King out of his room and through the hallways. It was a nasty habit of the King's. Though he ruled all Everfont, he still deigned to perform menial tasks in an effort to connect with the common people. His efforts had been severely hampered by his culling of the Imperials, but he still insisted on doing chores that should be beneath him.

As Cackler followed his old friend through the palace, his thoughts trailed to his daughter and he said a silent prayer for her safety. He didn't know which god he should be praying to, so he directed it to all of them. Despite all he had done, he did love her, and he wanted her to be safe.

Which was why it was a good thing he was terrible at following royal orders.

Acknowledgments

THIS BOOK, AND THE FACT THAT IT IS BEING PUB-
lished, has been somewhat of a miracle for me. I have
dreamed of becoming a professional author since I was young.
I've never had a doubt about what I wanted to be—but how and
when I was going to get there has always been difficult to nail
down.

There have always been people to push me along the way, to
encourage me when I've doubted, and provide realistic guidance along my path. I have had great influences in my life that
I am grateful for, some of which I will make mention of here. I
won't list too many names but know that if you know me and
feel you deserve a place on this list—you do. I will make certain
to mention you in future acknowledgements. I hope to have the
opportunity to write many more of these in years to come.

First and foremost, thanks to my wife, Emily Holman. It
seems trite to say, but she has been my rock, anchor, and cheer-
leader for the years we have known each other. I quite like who
I am now, but she has refined me to make me better than I ever
thought I could be.

Thanks to my parents, Loraine and Rob Holman, and Bar-
bara and Doug Calchera. They instilled in me the work ethic to

make this possible and their examples have helped shape me. I could not ask for better support. To my siblings as well; there are too many to list, but as the oldest, the desire to be an example to them has always been at the forefront of my mind.

Thanks to John and Connie Porter, and Tim and Michelle Welch. The lessons and impact that these men and women have made on my life have changed me for the better more than any other single influence.

Thanks to the editors and publishers at WiDo Publishing. They have been instrumental in helping to refine *Everfont* and turning it from a decent, if flawed book, into something that I can truly be proud of. Special thanks to Jay Christopher for believing in this manuscript, to Stephanie Procopio for editing, and Karen Gowen for being patient with all my questions.

Thanks also go to God. There is so much I could say about how many miracles I have seen in my life, and how good he is— but suffice to say that I have a testimony he is real and that he cares about his children. This book would not have happened if not for his personal guidance and promptings, and I hope this is something he can be proud of me for.

Finally, thanks to you, the reader, for picking up this book. I hope you've enjoyed reading it as much as I enjoyed writing it. Words can't express how grateful I am to you, but I hope you can feel my sincerity.

About the Author

ALEXANDER ROB LOVES MOST THINGS NERD—MOVIES, books, video games, and trivia. His favorite pastime is teasing his wife and playing chase with his son, but when they're too annoyed or not available to spend time with him, he can be found working, writing, reading, or playing video games. He is currently working his way through the books of Lord of the Rings, and afterwards he has plans to re-read the Mistborn series. When he has time, he also loves to play League of Legends.